A whim needled at Roy as he stood gazing at the bell, until at last he grasped the lip with both hands and gave it a shove; the clapper struck a clear note that pierced the thickening air.

The crisp sound dispersed his anxiety like a dreamless sleep, and he awoke with a clear mind focusing again on the idea of life vectors. He had nearly forgotten about them in the confusion of the morning. It was odd how the thought had come to him, like a defiant voice speaking across a desert of time, from another dimension. Roy chuckled to himself at the thought of being able to travel through time and distance on someone else's life, imagining himself as a transient, a hobo on the train of life. If he could just take that step sideways into someone else's vector and soar through the cosmos to a world that treasured his gifts, if . . . But it was a ridiculous thought. He turned and pushed the bell again, savoring the bright metallic sound.

The rains lashed at him, stinging like a whip. He hunkered down closer to the bell, trying to escape the worst of the storm. As he ducked, pressing his temple against the blackened brass, the sky ignited with blue light. He could taste the ozone before he knew what was happening. The hair rose on his body, and then the muscle-tearing electricity surged through him as lightning struck the bell. He could hear its shrill complaint, and then could hear nothing. The force of the blow hurled him backward across the belfry floor, and he tumbled across the railing, spinning slowly, and fell like a diver, twisting toward the deadly gray stones of the square below. . . .

Other  Books

THE FALCON RISES

Michael C. Staudinger

Cover Art
John and Laura Lakey

THE FALCON RISES

First Printing: June, 1991
Printed in the United States of America.
Library of Congress Catalog Card Number: 90-71513

9 8 7 6 5 4 3 2 1

ISBN: 1-56076-075-3

TSR, Inc.
P.O. Box 756
Lake Geneva, WI 53147
U.S.A.

TSR Ltd.
120 Church End, Cherry Hinton
Cambridge CB1 3LB
United Kingdom

For Suzanne,
who knew I could even when I didn't.

—M.C.S.

I wish to express my thanks to my wife, Suzanne, and to Mike Lane and Bill Larson for taking the time to read the book; to the wonderful poets of the English language, who inspired it; and to Patricia Bockmeyer, one English teacher who helped cause poetry's light to thicken in my heart.

—M.C.S.

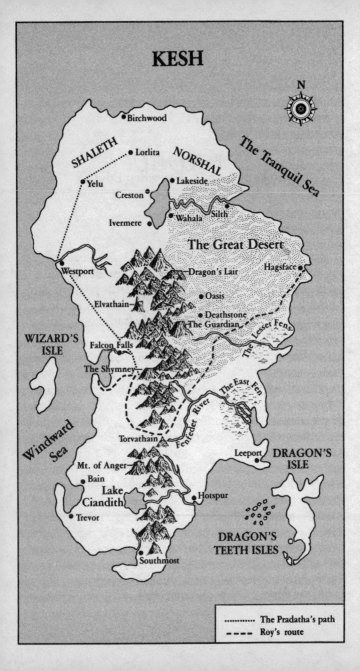

PROLOGUE

The two men stood alone and frozen in the shadow of Shymney, the great granite monolith that marked the center of all creation. Although it was not long past midday, a darkness hung about the stony finger of rock. On the northern edge of a small clearing, Ratha, the Archmage of Shaleth, leaned wearily upon his staff. On the southern side, Morlin the Usurper, the edges of his black cape brushing the scattered stones at his feet, looked on his enemy through narrowed eyes.

The Archmage's movement was quick and, Ratha hoped, unexpected.

"*Quintah!*" he shouted, light exploding from his Staff of Fire as he lifted it high above his head. His heart raced with sudden hope, until he saw the darkness once again swelling about him, darker than night, deeper than the coldest cavern. It crept toward him like a plague. Across the meadow, the Archmage could see the ebon lord raising his left hand. Darkness sprang forth and devoured the last of the weakening light.

"Die, Ratha! Feel the cold bite of death," Morlin

laughed as darkness enveloped the Archmage.

From the shadows, the Archmage's voice rang clear and ominous. "You may be able to send me to the Pit, but you will never destroy me. Even from Dethlidra, I will return to tear your throat out and banish your lies forever, Morelua." The Archmage's voice carried the power with the insult even now, at the edge of utter defeat.

But the dark wizard, staring down at his prey, only began to laugh. "Morelua? Lord of Nothing? You flatter me and know it not! But I accept your gift, little mage, O greatest of all our teachers! By your proclamation, I shall no longer be called Morlin, servant of our dead king! Henceforth I am Mordeth, Lord of Darkness. Darkness, Ratha . . . as thick and sweet as boiled keyth. Let Morlin die with you today, little mage. He can join you in the dark pit Dethlidra, where I am known as prince. And to Dethlidra you go indeed, little mage. There I am your master and you my slave. And from there, I guarantee, you will never return!"

Mordeth clenched his fist, and the darkness intensified around the Archmage. A small gasp escaped from the lightless shroud, and the earth shook violently, stones battering against the ground. A large boulder sailed past Mordeth's head, breaking the Dark One's concentration. For a brief moment, the darkness waned and a faint light shone through the veil of night, but Mordeth again raised his hand, and the night doubled about the dying Archmage. The air echoed with thunder, and then there was silence.

And when the darkness dispersed from around the stone pillar, Mordeth stood alone, unaware of the black dragon perched atop the granite monolith, or the movement among the *marelock* bush.

❖ CHAPTER ONE ❖

Vectors

Steam rose like a phantom from the mug of coffee on the corner of the desk. Crumpled papers, old folders, and dog-eared books crowded around it. In the center of the desk sprawled a worn copy of the *Oxford Anthology of English Literature*. Roy lifted the book, cradling it like a sickly child. He took a sip of coffee to calm his anger, gently setting the book back down on his desk.

For years, the English department at State had been small. To no one's surprise, the Board of Regents had just voted to reduce the staff by two, leaving Roy alone to teach all eight literature courses offered by the university. Three thousand incoming freshmen, seven thousand underclassmen, and only one lit teacher. He had seen it coming years ago when the Regents had decided that literature would no longer be a requirement for graduation. Enrollment had dropped almost instantly and declined steadily ever since. It was a miracle that the department had lasted as long as this.

Roy sipped his coffee, sloshing the fine grounds around the bottom, staring blankly at them as they clung to the creamy white sides of the mug. Vainly they clung, he thought, vainly trying to hang on to a perchless place. He swirled the last of the coffee, catching the dark brown flecks off the sides and casting them down into the depths of the cup. Roy combed his long black hair with his fingers, noticing the coarser texture of the graying strands. When had he gotten so gray?

A single computer-enhanced chime echoed through the building, signaling the end of the class period. Roy snorted in disgust, angered by the artificial sound. An ancient bell still hung motionless in the belfrey above the old commons building, unused for nearly a decade. Inefficient, the Regents had called it. Unimportant. They had been considering salvaging it for scrap metal. Roy pictured the leisurely swing of the bell, the clapper striking a note just slightly higher than a true C, the rhythm unpredictable and irregular. Anything unique disturbed the Regents. Thinking of the creativity and individuality of a bell infuriating the all-powerful Regents coaxed a rare smile from Roy. He stood abruptly and left his office, the empty mug a silent monument atop his desk.

Rene Delac sat in the tiny antechamber that passed for a reception room, a ten-foot-square cubical with a computer terminal on one side and a simulated-leather couch on the other. Rene was sitting on the couch reading a copy of *David Copperfield*. On the wall behind her hung a playbill, bold black letters with red borders on a startling white sheet of paper: "The Players Present *Of Mice and Men*."

"Read any good books lately, Rene?" Roy asked. It was an old joke and not such a good one, but it had become their ritual greeting. Rene looked up from the text, a half-scowl on her face. Fluorescent lighting shadowed her fine features. She seemed older, too, he thought.

"I figured you'd be over at the dean's office arguing the Regents' decision," she replied. "I can't believe it's just the two of us now."

"I know. The bastards even sent someone to pack their offices, books and all; didn't even wait for Sam or Gwen to come in and find out. I hear the dean called them last night and told them not to bother coming today. Their entry cards were deactivated during the night."

"Gwen called me last night after talking to the dean," Rene answered. "She was so stoical about it. She quoted Tennyson to me from memory for half an hour, then simply said good-bye. I tried calling back, but she wouldn't answer her com-link."

Roy's eyes gave way to a faraway look, Byzantine kingdoms rumbling through his imagination. He and Gwen had been good friends since she first arrived at the university. They had often discussed the Romantic poets over coffee. Gwen especially loved Tennyson and the poet's need for immortality; she would quote him at any opportunity. Unconsciously Roy intoned Tennyson like a priest chanting a liturgy:

". . . you and I are old;
Old age hath yet his honor and his toil;
Death closes all: but something ere the end,
Some work of noble note, may yet be done,
Not unbecoming men that strove with gods.
The lights begin to twinkle from the rocks:
The long day wanes: the slow moon climbs: the deep

*Moans round with many voices. Come, my friends,
'Tis not too late to seek a newer world."*

"Yes, that was part of it. Gwen sounded so detached, though. Roy, I'm worried."

"We'll stop by to see her this evening," he volunteered. Rene blinked sullenly, but Roy seemed to consider the matter settled. She stood and left the tiny room, leaving Roy alone, awash in the green light of the computer terminal.

The general computer belched a monotone warning, and Roy hastily grabbed his well-worn book of Romantic poetry and shuffled down the hall to his freshman literature class, entering the room a full minute late. Three of the more impatient students were shutting down their terminals already and preparing to leave. They gave Roy a disgusted look, disappointment ravishing their young faces, as he entered through the slate-gray door.

"Terminal recorders on, please," Roy ordered as he set his book down on the lectern, then turned and walked between the two aisles of students. In unison, the twelve students reached out their right hands and pushed identical green buttons. The symmetry struck Roy as funny, and he laughed out loud. The students scowled.

"Today we concern ourselves with the Enlightment and science's impact on literature," he said. "Three major names emerge in our studies, three men who should be credited with having thrust science into the forefront of our lives: Copernicus, Galileo, and Newton."

He continued, lecturing by rote, seven years of teaching the same introductory material having ingrained the lesson into his memory. Each step he took was precisely timed for impact, coinciding with his lecture; each movement a counterpoint for each of the lecture's main ideas.

He began his third trip down the center aisle as he started his background lecture on Galileo, just as he had begun the same talk last year, and the year before, and for each of the five years prior to that. Students will comprehend the lesson best if I say this at the precisely timed point, he thought to himself, even as he continued to lecture about science supplanting the church's authority. Roy's educational training had been extensive: Precision was the apex of performance; repetition, the foundation. The Regents were adamant that the correct, undeviating formula always be used in the instruction of the students.

"Galileo dared to confront the authority of the church in matters of science, rejecting the church's doctrine that taught that the earth was the center of the galaxy and universe." Roy exhaled the patter unconsciously, without emotion or concern. "In so doing," he continued, "Galileo opened the path for others to choose their own authority in matters of belief, nullifying the external pressure from the church toward uniformity."

The green lights of the twelve computer terminals blinked in unison. Roy paced up the aisle, inspecting each one in turn. Emblazoned on the screens in cold green fire were the exact same words, echoing his lecture: ". . . nullifying the external pressure from the church toward uniformity." An image of a large brass bell, blackened by time, swinging leisurely in the wind, swaying in the belfry of a stone cathedral, danced behind Roy's closed eyes. His breath caught the bell and pushed it, drew it back again. The clapper struck note after note. Roy sensed the sound of the bell, slightly higher than true C, the sound reverberating around him.

Roy opened his eyes and returned to the classroom. The late morning sun tumbled through the open windows of the second-floor classroom and sprawled across the floor. He blinked lazily at the twelve students who sat staring at him, puzzled expressions on their faces. Roy glanced down at a nearby computer monitor, expecting to find where he had left off in his lecture. Instead, the monitor glared reproachfully, the last three words Roy had uttered captured eternally in the computer's memory: "*ding, dong, ding.*"

He might have laughed. It wasn't the first time Roy had daydreamed while lecturing, letting the mechanical responses guide him through his carefully prepared lines like an actor playing a part or a child saying his prayers. But this was the first time the dreams had become visible to the scrutiny of the class. His hands began to tremble lightly, a knot flexing in his stomach. Fear tingled along his back and neck, a fear that he would have to explain the veering from his predetermined lecture to the Regents. Surely the computer would flag the discrepancy and automatically forward it to the Regents. His slip couldn't have come at a worse time, and his thoughts turned to Gwen— intelligent, spontaneous Gwen, who lived Tennyson and tales of noble individuals who strove against a hostile world.

"*Come, my friends, 'tis not too late to seek a newer world,*" he said aloud, and the words appeared dutifully upon the optic green screens.

Several of the students cast glances at each other, shoulders barely shrugging, eyebrows raised. It was clear to Roy that they were unaccustomed to professors discarding prearranged lessons in such an offhanded manner. It delighted Roy to see the faces of those bored and boring students flush with embarrassment, their bodies squirming on the padded seats as if some electric prod was being waved before their faces. Adrenaline coarsed through dilated blood vessels, heightening his awareness, stimulating his bravado. A sudden insight flashed, a predatory instinct that sought his disoriented prey.

"Yes," he continued, "science is responsible for a tremendous influx of literature: The Renaissance was the church's attempt to compensate for science; Romanticism was a reaction to the overshadowing of emotion by harsh human intellect. If nothing else, science became a base for writers to begin their work, the framework for authors such as Jules Verne, Isaac Asimov, Arthur C. Clarke, George Orwell, and others. It could be true for us, too. If one of us today, let's say, were to take a scientific principle, he could forge a story from it. We need to remember that science was never meant to be a substitute for imagination, only a tool to enhance it."

The students stared blankly at him, fear showing openly in their faces, fear of this madman who stood before them waving his arms wildly and treading so readily over hallowed ground. But for Roy, there was no turning back. The excitement of breaching the forbidden had grabbed hold of him firmly, hurtling him forward, threatening to strangle him if he resisted. He caught his breath and paced quickly to the large scriptboard at the front of the classroom, clutching a pen from the tray beneath it. An idea flashed into his head, as if placed there by some unseen force. In response, Roy whirled and threw the pen across the room, the spinning object arcing through the air and clattering against the wall and onto the floor. Students flinched as it flew by.

"Vectors!" he shouted, leaping onto the rostrum to gain full advantage of the bewildered students. "Vectors! Abrams, tell me what they are."

The startled student's jaw hung slack a moment, then the rigorous training he'd had since childhood overtook him. "Vectors are a way of describing movement of any body through a plane."

"Good," Roy snapped. "Now, Fielding, explain the movement of the scriptwriter as it flew across the room. Use vectors in your answer."

Brittany Fielding, a slender blond science student with a face once ravished by acne, blinked at Roy as a turtle in the sun might blink at an annoying fly. "Force can be described as a vector. You threw the scriptwriter, causing a force, or vector, to be at work on the object in an east-west direction. Gravity caused a downward vector to work upon the object. The wall caused a vector to work in an opposite direction to the one used to initiate its movement. Likewise, a multitude of vectors worked upon the object, primarily air molecules that provided resistance." Her drowsy eyes slid closed and opened again.

"Fine." Roy nodded, the idea burning bright within him. "Now think. Are vectors only a description of movement in a plane? What are the other possibilities?" He could feel the excitement inside himself, his lust for danger growing.

"Multiple planes," volunteered a voice from the back of the room. Roy looked hard at the lump of boy, greasy hair sliding sideways across an alabaster forehead. The mass squirmed, looking at the toes of his shoes. "And time," he added.

"And time," Roy echoed. His eyes lost focus for a moment as he caught a memory, much as a person might catch an aroma upon the air, articulating it as it took form.

"*Time is but a Stream we go a-fishin' in*, Thoreau once said." The green letters appeared dutifully on the twelve recording screens.

"Consider the possibilities," Roy said aloud, but even as he said it, he knew he was speaking more for himself than for the benefit of any student in the room. "Be creative. If the fourth dimension is time, then perhaps the line that describes the force of time upon any object, any person, is a life vector. We believe nothing is eternal. The conclusion could be drawn that, because we all live on a life vector, when we come to the end of the line, we die, much as the motion of the scriptwriter ceased when it hit the floor. And yet if someone could jump from one life vector, his own, to another, he could live forever. Or at least until his own life vector intersected with the new one. What would it take to transfer vectors?"

His question was rhetorical, but from the back of the room, the fat voice answered. "Energy."

Roy prepared to answer, but as he did, two gray-clad security officers suddenly appeared at the door, hands clasped behind their backs, heels precisely four inches apart. The students straightened themselves in their chairs, a subconscious reaction to the presence of the special Regency guards. It was not necessary for them to speak; Roy knew why they were there.

"Computer recorders off, please. Class dismissed." Roy immediately turned, leaving his precious books on the lectern, and followed the two men. They walked briskly down the hall in front of him, down to the eleva-

tor held open by a third guard, and entered it. Roy filed
in behind them, and the third guard stepped in front of
him. The elevator door gulped like a fish swallowing its
prey, the jerk of the moving lift tightening the knot in
Roy's stomach. The four men were spat out onto the
concrete of the campus square of ash-gray blocks sunk
into the earth.

Roy followed his escort across the great square. He
watched his feet as he stepped from stone to stone,
avoiding the cracks, an old childhood habit. The sun
was high in the spring sky, shadows short and crisp beneath the bulky university buildings. A few hundred
feet to his left was the commons building, its steeple
stabbing the pale blue sky in defiance. Somewhere in
that belfry, the old black bell was swinging idly in the
afternoon breeze. Roy smiled.

The three guards walked in front of him, their heels
clicking against the stone in muffled unison. Their faces
always looked straight ahead, their necks as unyielding
and pallid as the stones of the square, their eyes hidden
behind black glasses. Roy wondered why the guards
seemed assured he would naturally follow, never looking back in doubt. He fought back an urge to duck into
the shadows of Royer Hall, to hide in the smell of burning butane, the lightly sulfuric odor from the science
building hanging about his head, masking his spore
from the uncanny Regency guards. Instead, he bit his lip
and stepped through the shadows and into the sunlight,
the three guards shimmering five paces ahead.

The glass doors of the Regency building sprang apart
as the guards approached, exposing the polished marble
stairway that led the thirty-nine steps to the Regency
room. The guards turned aside to let him pass, and he

placed a tentative foot upon the first step. Flourescent lights beat down upon him, glaring like wounds upon the black marble. Gone were the thoughts of inventiveness and individuality. Vanished was the surprisingly clear vision of intraplanar travel. He tried to fill his mind with numbers . . . one, two, three, step and step, as he climbed the thirty-nine steps. His earlier bravado proved to be just that, and his knees felt weak with fear, making the climb more difficult, more desperate.

The door of the Regency room appeared. It was a door for titans, immense, much too tall for mortals; even after he stood firm upon the clerestory floor, the door seemed bloated, ponderous. Roy turned and looked through the windows behind him. There the campus wallowed, regular in shape, descending in size from east to west, like a pipe organ. He doubted any music would be issuing forth any time soon.

The great door behind him heaved open, the air disturbed by its movement. Roy felt the draft and turned; his hands began to tremble again, and he thought for a moment that he wouldn't find the strength to enter. The sunlight barely pierced the depths of the chamber, and although Roy knew that the temperature was set at a constant twenty degrees Celsius, the stone floor and empty space felt as cold as a tomb. He breathed deeply and entered the room.

Electric shimmering began on three sides, violet shades that pulsed like a heartbeat; despite the light given off by the flickering shapes, the room grew darker, more foreboding, until a voice crackled from within one of those heaving images, a somber, deliberate voice, lacking any lyrical inflection.

"Professor Arthre, it has come to the board's attention that you deviated from the approved lesson plan in your introductory literature course. Do you deny these allegations?"

Roy looked at the hologram and shook his head. "No, I do not deny them."

"You are aware of the penalties for deviant behavior." It was a statement, not a question. Every professor at State had been drilled repeatedly on the third basic premise of education: *With infinite information, only the most valuable need be taught.* Failure to teach in accordance with his contractual agreement was grounds for dismissal. Roy stared back at the hologram, waiting for what he knew must come.

"Professor Arthre, you are aware that we have recently found it necessary to discontinue two positions in the English department. We are considering eliminating the department altogether. This most recent action does not reflect well on you or your department. While we consider our decision, you will refrain from deviating from your approved lectures." The hologram crackled furiously and disappeared, followed closely by the others. Roy remained staring at the empty wall until a guard came in and led him by the arm down the thirty-nine steps and out onto the plaza below.

Roy considered what he should do. His next class, if indeed he ever had one, wasn't until tomorrow, and Rene would be busy teaching until five o'clock, another four hours. He considered going to talk with Gwen, but he wasn't ready to face her with more bad news. Roy idly walked across the great stone square, scuffing his feet against the rough bricks.

The sunshine had disappeared while he was in the Regency building, and the campus was devoid of the crisp shadows of the morning. A stillness poured into the vacuum left by the sunshine, black clouds simmering low in the sky. A fat raindrop slapped on the square in front of him, then another struck his shoulder. A rattling sound, like a dying man's last breath, grew louder as the rain began to quicken. Roy headed for the nearest shelter, ducking beneath the awning of a nearby building.

The rain boiled on the pavement, coming hard and fast now. Roy withdrew his security card and placed it in the door slot. He felt relieved when the doors slid open. He stepped in, shaking the rain from him like a dog. He looked around at the walls, empty and chalk-white, the same as every wall of every building on campus. He turned around and looked at the wall behind him, and knew at once he was in the student commons, the oldest building on campus. The university's lone painting hung unobtrusively above the door, a picture of a slave ship on a murky sea, a great fish devouring the body of a jettisoned slave. The painting had been a gift to the school, along with a substantial endowment and the stipulation that the painting had to hang in the commons for at least fifty years. That was forty-nine years ago, and it was rumored the Regents were considering the sale of the painting next year. In the meantime, they had hidden it away in the back area of the building, out of view from the students. Rarely did anyone enter through this door. Roy wondered where it led. He pressed the two buttons on the control panel, and a door slid open to reveal an empty closet. Across the room, a second door slipped open to a stairwell leading up a narrow corridor. Roy shrugged and started to climb.

The stairs were wooden, a novelty in any building. The edges were worn and rounded with ancient use; the dust lay in undisturbed sheets. The stairwell was narrow and steep, the walls a rough stucco painted gray, or perhaps they were painted white and age had grayed them. He ran his fingers through his hair, feeling the coarse gray hairs that seemed more numerous than they had even this morning.

The stairs spiraled upward, distorting the distance. It seemed to Roy that he had climbed impossibly high, higher than any building on the campus. At last he reached a door, not metal or glass like the other doors on campus but wooden, with metal straps holding the thick planks together. A ring hung midway to one side, black and pitted, and there seemed to be neither locking mechanism nor hinges. The antique simplicity of the door, an air of mystery about it, reminded Roy of stories he had read as a child, tales of swashbucklers and pirates. He pushed it, but it wouldn't budge. His hands caressed the jambs, vainly searching for a locking mechanism. Convinced there was none, he braced his shoulder against the rough wooden surface and heaved. The door sprang open with a sharp crack, sending Roy stumbling onto a small gazebo, perhaps three meters square. He had to stop quickly to avoid running into the large black bell that hung in the center of the belfry.

Roy examined the bell. He had never been this close to it before, and the sight of it now made him feel nostalgic. He swept a hand across its surface; the black sheen rubbed off onto his palm. The bell, too large for Roy to put his arms around, hung from an oak beam that extended out to two iron wheels bolted into opposite walls. The rain was falling through holes in the roof, running off the bell and splashing at Roy's feet. He looked up at the dark sky, framed by the irregular tear in the roof. In the distance, he could hear the savage voice of thunder; nearer, he could hear the now frenzied voice of the wind rushing through the narrow chamber. The clapper rattled lightly against the side of the bell, pushed by the increasing force of the wind. A bright flash illuminated the square below, and a tremendous explosion vibrated the floor.

Adrenaline coursed through Roy's body, stimulated by the thunderstorm. *"The wild winds weep and the night is a-cold, / Come hither, Sleep, and my griefs enfold,"* he quoted to the stormy sky. "Damn, I wish I had brought something to read." It seemed natural to stand there talking to the wind, to the bell swinging urgently in the blustering wind. A whim needled at him as he stood gazing at the bell, until at last he grasped the lip with both hands and gave it a shove; the clapper struck a clear note that pierced the thickening air.

The crisp sound dispersed his anxiety like a dreamless sleep, and he awoke with a clear mind focusing again on the idea of life vectors. He had nearly forgotten about them in the confusion of the morning. It was odd how the thought had come to him, like a defiant voice speaking across a desert of time, from another dimension. Roy chuckled to himself at the thought of being able to travel through time and distance on someone else's life, imagining himself as a transient, a hobo on the train of life. If he could just take that step sideways into someone else's vector and soar through the cosmos to a world that treasured his gifts, if . . . But it was a ridiculous thought. He turned and pushed the bell again, savoring the bright metallic sound.

The rains lashed at him, stinging like a whip. He hunkered down closer to the bell, trying to escape the worst of the storm. As he ducked, pressing his temple against the blackened brass, the sky ignited with blue light. He could taste the ozone before he knew what was happening. The hair rose on his body, and then the muscle-tearing electricity surged through him as lightning struck the bell. He could hear its shrill complaint, and then could hear nothing. The force of the blow hurled him backward across the belfry floor, and he tumbled across the railing, spinning slowly, and fell like a diver, twisting toward the deadly gray square below.

Images flooded past Roy as he tumbled toward the ground. He was aware of the sluggish movement of time, as if a force was pushing against it, trying to make it stop. He sensed the electricity still vibrating in his body. He took notice of the storm still raging about him, although the raindrops seemed lethargic now, as if moving through syrup. He had heard that a person's life passed before his eyes before he died, but he never expected it to be so true. The images rose before him: his cocker-spaniel, Runt, that he had when he was four; his room in the house in Dillingford; his sister's death when he was seven; the day he first met Gwen. The images twirled slowly, like a broken movie projector.

Suddenly another flash of blue light erupted beside him, sending a second surge of power through his aching body. Images returned, but now they were different. These images were not his own. He saw a woman, tall, lithe, with pale skin and white hair, her eyes the color of thick ice. He saw a man, dying, an arrow shaft lodged in his throat, blood spurting around the edges of the wound and oozing down to the dark brown earth. A falcon swept across the unknown sky, heading straight for Roy. He wanted to duck, to dodge the sharp talons as they stretched out toward him. Instead, he merely watched as the falcon landed on his shoulder.

He looked over at it. But it could not have been Roy's shoulder that the falcon rested upon. The clothing beneath the raptor's talons was unfamiliar, rough, well worn; it looked nothing like the synthetic fibers of the suit he had put on that morning. He wanted to reach down and let his fingers examine his clothing, but his arms refused to respond. Even as he thought these things, the falcon looked back into his eyes. Roy could count the black flecks that floated in the golden iris, the narrow pupils adjusting as the great bird stared back at him. A feeling of rightness flooded over him, and he sensed that he could hear a voice through his deafness.

Ratha, it said. *Ratha Keshia-ne.*

Then the darkness overtook him.

❖ CHAPTER TWO ❖

A Newer World

Through the dark veil that had dropped over him, Roy first became aware of the sound of water, a clean sound, as regular as breathing. He opened his eyes and saw gray and brown and white, granular and thick. He tried to swallow and choked on sand, the spasm pricking his senses even more. Stretching his muscles, he slid his arms and legs along the earth, the fine sand crumbling beneath his touch. He tried to stand, but vertigo overtook him, sending him retching to his knees, the heaves coming painful and dry.

Once his nausea was spent, Roy sat up and blinked at his surroundings. A beach sprawled before him, wet sands spreading thirty or forty feet down a gradual slope, the white teeth of ocean biting into its edge. Low tide, he thought mechanically, silently tallying essential information. The breakers came in long and low; he could see the curling whitecaps swelling in the dim light. Shallow area, he thought, and like the computers he hated, his mind recorded the information. Inland, Roy could see a hundred yards of beach rising to meet a deep green forest, the flat, pointed leaves of the trees, a type unfamiliar to him, quivering in the breeze. Trying to get his bearings, he looked upward toward the sky. Clouds rolled above him like cotton in the wind, big, billowy, and white. Behind them, the sky hung gray and blank.

Roy tried to stand again, this time with success. He staggered toward the trees, muscles aching, his body barely responding to the need to move. The aches were dull, at least, reassuring him that nothing was broken. The sand shifted as he stepped, making it difficult to walk, and he rested frequently upon the beach.

Reaching the first line of trees, Roy found a level space beneath one and sat, stretching his long legs before him. The leaves hung before his eyes, six-pointed and emerald green. No nuts, he thought. No fruit. Similar to oaks, but somehow different. His stomach growled a protest, his hunger honed by his labor, and he began to look more closely at the surrounding trees. Most were like the one above him, but a few seemed smaller, and he thought he could see color glinting behind their rustling leaves. He stood and walked to the closest one; yellow, oval fruit hung glistening and moist, in bunches of five and six, about the size of cherries. He broke one from a branch and sampled it. The fruit tasted of cloves and honey, the juice sweet and satisfying. He removed his shirt and laid it on the ground, tossing handful after handful of the fruit onto it. After he felt he had enough, Roy sat down and ate until he was satisfied, saving the rest and carrying it back to his resting tree.

Not until he had thrown his aching body onto the soft ground beneath the tree did he begin to shake uncontrollably, like a small child who's lost his mother. His eyes glazed on the rhythmic wave of ocean; his ears filled with the steady drum of tide. His mind raced with a jumbled recollection of the insane events that led to his being stranded on this foreign beach. He remembered the storm, the explosion in the bell tower, his fall. Perhaps he was dead after all. The shaking stopped suddenly, and a feeling of detachment swept over him, as if he were merely an observer of his situation rather than a participant in it.

It was his imagination, or a deep-rooted instinct for survival, that finally brought him round to the new world and its particular needs. Crazy or not, he felt keenly his own desire for survival, and even more sharply felt compelled toward action. With a tremendous effort, he pushed himself up off the ground and got to work, hoping the effort would help blank his mind of the insanity festering there.

Roy began by searching for a more permanent shelter than the boughs of the huge tree. He gathered driftwood and fallen branches and built a lean-to, covering the roof with the thick, wiry grass that lined the beach. Occasionally he would stop and eat some of the yellow fruit. The sky was still no lighter than it had been, but neither was it darker. Around him, the world was shadowless, making it impossible to gauge the time of day by the sun's position in the sky. He gave up trying to do so and redoubled his efforts on the lean-to.

Food and shelter taken care of, Roy began to look for a source of fresh water. Up the beach about two hundred yards, he found water cascading over a low precipice, splashing onto the sand below. He sampled the water and found it to be sweet, tasting slightly metallic but cold, so cold his teeth ached when he raised his cupped hands to his mouth and drank. He knelt down beside the stream and drank deeply, then fell back, exhausted, into the wiry grass that lined its edge.

His gaze fixed on an enormous black cloud that boiled overhead; its shape subtly altered until, through his fatigue, it became a gigantic winged creature, breathing fire into the sky. The thought sent a shudder through him, and he rolled over and rose to his feet. He looked both directions down the beach, hoping to satisfy himself that the water was nearby, yet far enough away that any predators it might attract would fail to notice him. He bent down and took a last drink before he began to comb the beach, looking for anything that might prove useful.

The discovery of fresh water had sparked a new concern: predators. He bent over and picked up a driftwood stick, testing it against a log. It splintered easily, and he heaved it as far as he could out toward the sea. He continued to search through the driftwood piles until he finally found a suitable club, a straight piece of wood, not waterlogged but heavy, smooth to the touch, sturdy enough to withstand a solid blow and long enough to be used as a staff. The upper tip of the staff was a weathered knot resembling the eye of the falcon in Roy's vision, and Roy smiled at the good omen, taking the staff with him.

At last darkness began to spread just as heavy clouds appeared in the sky, sagging near the shore. Roy turned back toward his makeshift shelter, quickening his pace as the rain began to fall. He was running hard by the time he reached his camp, his long legs churning sand and tossing it behind him. The rain was cold and thick, and Roy guessed that within the hour it would become sleet.

A half-remembered book set his next course as he gathered leaves to make a bed beneath the lean-to, then broke two twigs from a deadfall that leaned against a nearby tree. Nestling himself into the leaves for warmth, he found a stone and crushed one of the twigs to splinters. Roy gathered what relatively dry grass he could find and encircled the crushed twig with it, placing the tip of the other twig in the center. He rubbed his hands together vigorously, the stick between them, and shoved down against the dry tinder.

The sleet came, and still Roy was without fire. His arms were rubbery and his palms had begun to blister. He placed a tentative finger against the tinder. It was hot, but still it refused to produce a flame. He uttered an audible sigh and began again.

The sound of the surf seemed nearer as the fire ignited, puffs of smoke lazily finding their way up through the drizzle. The fire smoldered until Roy began blowing on it lightly, sending smoke along the ground. A small red ember glowed bravely and erupted into a flame. Roy fed the tiny fire with grass and small twigs, encouraging it to grow. By the time the fire was snapping cheerfully, the forest was dark.

Roy looked out toward the approaching tide. It sounded close, but the night was lightless except for the flame of his campfire. The sleet had ended, but moisture clung to the trees, occasionally dropping down onto the roof of the lean-to. Roy curled up among the leaves and fell asleep to the delicate, rhythmic sound.

The sharp crackle of the fire had disappeared, and its absence startled Roy awake. His firewood was a dwindling mass in the dying firelight, yet Roy didn't dare venture out into the enveloping darkness. He hugged his staff against his chest and shuddered. Fear pricked his senses, his swift eyes darting hawklike into the night. He listened and heard the pounding surf blotting out all other sound, then nervously reached out and shoved his final piece of dry wood onto the dying fire, praying for daylight. As if in response, a low howl rose into the night from deep within the surrounding forest.

Minutes passed, perhaps an hour, although Roy was having difficulty gauging time. The fire would soon dissolve into flameless coals if he didn't add more wood. The blisters on his hands ached, and he dreaded the thought of having to build another fire in this damp wilderness. He was worried about predators lurking in the dark, but he was still more afraid to stay and wait for them as darkness encroached upon the dying fire. Groping his way through the dark seemed preferable to staying still, and he decided he could keep the fire in sight as he walked so that he could find his way back to his camp. Grasping his staff firmly in his right hand, Roy felt his way blindly down to the beach, then turned toward the gnarled piles of driftwood a hundred yards away.

The surf pounded regularly, keeping a meter as he walked. Iambic pentameter, Roy thought, and he tried to remember a line from Shakespeare to match the meter.

"*Good things of Day begin to droop and drowse, / While Night's black agents to their preys do rouse,*" he quoted aloud, instantly regretting his morose choice. His feet slid clumsily across the uneven sand until an unexpected piece of driftwood thrust a bony finger up and snagged his foot, sending him sprawling facefirst into the packed earth. He lay there for several moments, breath coming in gulps and eyes closed, trying not to dissolve into tears.

He had avoided thinking about where he was or how he had gotten there, afraid of the answers he might find. Had he gone insane, a raving lunatic who at this very moment was really running half-naked through the campus, the Regency guards pursuing him, their dark glasses glaring angrily? Perhaps the Regents had drugged him and were torturing him for his morning's indiscretion. Or was he dead and deposited on some hellish shore, to spend eternity looking for firewood in the dark? He squeezed his eyes and let the tears slip down his dirty cheeks.

There was another possibility, but he hastily brushed it aside as the thought fluttered into his tired and tormented mind. It was an absurd notion, a fantasy his sick mind had created, a nightmare sucked up from his subconscious. The world around him was alien, the smells and sounds disfigured, and yet not unpleasant. In spite of all his fears, he had yet to see a living creature. The thought startled him as he realized that he hadn't heard even the cry of a gull, the irritating buzz of a mosquito. The world seemed empty of animal life. Why would his mind create such a loathsome world unless the world itself were real?

Roy picked himself off the sand and dusted the grains of sand from his clothing. The touch of his slick polyester tunic at first reassured him, then disturbed him. A foreign land would surely include foreign materials; a mind that could create the reality of the sweet yellow fruit could certainly create something more interesting than polyester. Roy shook the thought from his mind, his long hair lashing at the darkness.

He groped his way farther along the beach, poking his staff ahead of him, listening for the sound of solid wood, reminding himself of the necessity of the fire.

The darkness distorted distance. Roy glanced behind him and found the red glare of the fire, reassuring in the chasm of darkness in which he stood. He listened to the sounds around him and thought he could distinguish the sound of running water. The spring, he thought, and headed in that direction. He hadn't realized he had walked that far. The earth softened and became more pliant beneath his feet, the sound of his boots sucking into the mud rising to his ears. He reached out a cupped hand and let the water splash into his palm, slurping the water like an animal. The biting cold of the spring tensed his muscles, making him nervous, fidgety. The driftwood pile lay somewhere behind him, back toward his tiny camp. He looked again toward the fire smoldering two hundred yards away, the red coals a vigilant eye in the black abyss. Then the eye blinked.

Roy strained his eyes into the darkness, leaning forward against his staff. The fire reappeared, red and comforting. His mind was playing tricks again, he thought. He shook his head to dislodge the vision and the fear of being lost and adrift without the safety of light and fire. Picking his way carefully toward the surf, Roy tried to find some wood. Halfway down the streambed, he saw the vague silhouette of the driftwood mound, rising malignantly between him and his precious firelight. He walked toward the pile, making certain to keep his view of the fire unobstructed as he walked. His eyes focused on the red coals pulsing in the darkness, heat rippling the air above it. Suddenly the fire seemed to disappear again.

Roy's heart thumped wildly as the darkness enveloped him. He grasped his staff tightly to help keep himself oriented, never taking his eyes off the spot where his fire once had been. As if by force of will, the fire reappeared.

Roy ran wildly toward his fire, the fear of its disappearance tugging him forward. Once more he tripped over a driftwood log, his staff jabbing deep into the sand, keeping him from falling. He had begun to run again when the sound reached him: a low snarling sound that rose above the pounding surf. Blood drained from Roy's sweating face, and his knuckles turned white from the desperate grip he kept on his staff. The low animal rumbling came from the direction of the fire, a sound like sliding gravel, ominous, carnivorous. The sound repelled him like a blow, sending him staggering back toward the driftwood mound, knees fluid, heart racing, ears straining to locate the source of the sound, his eyes darting vacantly through the night. The fiery eye still glowed before him, smaller now, too small and too distant to bring relief.

A huge log pressed itself into Roy's back, signaling the presence of the driftwood pile. He ducked under the log and nestled into the deep, protected pocket, gathering chips and sticks to cover his shaking body. He tried not to breathe as he waited for the inevitable approach of the wild beast that stalked around his dying fire. Ocean mist pelted his face, and he realized that the tide was in, the rolling waves only a few feet away. He drove his frightened body deeper into the wooden nest.

Time moved slowly, measured only by the monoto-

nous pounding of the surf. The waves grew more determined and surrounded Roy's driftwood haven, now only
an island in the shallow sea. Occasionally Roy thought
he could hear the shuffling sounds of a great beast as it
rooted along the shore, no doubt trying to pick up the
scent of its hidden prey. Cold and wet, Roy tried not to
shiver, afraid the sound might give him away to whatever was out there. He tightened the grip on his staff
whenever the sounds approached, gaining what security
he could from his makeshift weapon.

And then it was over. Roy awakened to the distant
sound of waves rushing against an outgoing tide. He lay
curled beneath a slate-gray log, its roots extending out-
ward above him like a benevolent hand. The day was
full and bright, as bright as the night had been dark.
Roy carefully peered out from his protective shelter,
looking toward his deserted camp. The beach was silver
in the morning sun and empty, except for scattered flotsam along the high-water mark. He breathed a sigh of
relief and stood to gain a better view.

The high water had enveloped his tiny island, extending some twenty yards past it. Blue-green kelp was
strewn along the beach, and murky water still lay in the
many shallow recesses in the hardened sand. The leaves
of the trees scintillated at the touch of the soft breeze.
Low in the landward sky, he could see a bright orb
climbing above distant mountains, hanging on to a sky
of cobalt blue. The world appeared tranquil and safe.
Perhaps, he thought, the lurking creature had merely
been a dream.

Roy vaulted over the surrounding logs and headed toward his camp, stretching his legs in long strides, savoring the feeling returning to them after a night of

cramped sleep. Ahead he could see the lean-to nestled in the trees. He moved toward it, then stopped abruptly as he reached the high-water mark, as if an unexpected blow had risen from the sand and punched him in the stomach.

Before his feet was a giant track, sunk deep into the hardened sand, shaped like a deformed hand, thumb extended, little finger missing, the three remaining fingers long and incredibly thin. The track itself was about twenty inches in length and sunk deep into the sand. Roy pressed the heel of his boot into the sand, trying to make an indentation, shaking his head when he barely made a mark in the packed earth. Warily he looked around him at the surrounding area, half-expecting some giant lizard to come charging down upon him. The beach was covered with similar tracks, most following the trail he had used to find water and shelter. The thought sent nervous shudders through his body, and he hefted his staff, the symbol of his security, swinging it tentatively, as if testing its balance as a weapon.

Fear prickling his senses, Roy quickly moved toward a large tree, its branches thick and low enough for him to climb. Setting his precious staff against the trunk, he pulled himself up onto the lowest branch and stood. The tree's branches poked out from the trunk like rungs on a ladder, aiding him as he climbed upward. He was amazed at the strength of even the thinnest branch. Amazed and thankful.

The view from atop the tree surprised him. He had assumed that the forested area was flat, extending around him for miles. Instead, Roy discovered that the level forest was only a finger jutting between the shore and the mountains that guarded the eastern horizon, silent, jagged sentries quietly pressing up out of the rich green earth. The sun burned through the blue-quilt sky that draped across the snowy head of the mountains. In the foreground, protected by the mountains behind it, stood a giant granite monolith, rough-hewn, cold, and gray in the morning light. The air between him and the granite stone was clear. The tower's nearness was magnified by the lenselike quality of the air, yet distorted by the ponderous mountains that broke the sky behind it. The solemnity of the monolith reached out to Roy like an incantation; the morning breeze rattling through the leaves became a liturgy.

The sea was a green-gray carpet stretching out behind him; the fog, a white, blazing blanket in the morning sun, was being pushed farther from the shore by the outgoing breeze. To the north, the beach curled westward out to sea in a giant arch. Roy turned and looked southward, seeing that there, too, the beach bent toward the sea, creating a huge bay. A shallow one, too, Roy thought to himself, remembering the long, low breakers.

Below, the sands were pockmarked with the tracks of some heavy beast, but the imprints seemed to be located only in this immediate area, the sands beyond stretching out undefiled.

Roy climbed down the tree and took his staff in hand. There had been no sign of animal life, no human inhabitation visible from where he had climbed. Depression had again begun to gnaw at Roy's resolve, nagging questions surfacing like dead bodies floating in a stagnant pool. In the clear brilliance of the morning, Roy had become convinced that he was both sane and alive, but in some unknown land. Even realizing his psychological conditioning at the hands of the Regents, he could not bring himself to believe that they would deposit him, unarmed, without food or shelter, in some desolate land to meet his death. The only other interpretation remaining to him was that he had indeed been transported into some peripheral life vector by the sudden surge of energy from the lightning bolt and the shock of impending death.

Roy sat down with his back pressed against the trunk of the tree he'd just climbed. His eyes swept across the length of beach before him, watchful and alert. "Energy," he said aloud. "Power. How do I channel sufficient power to snap myself back to my own plane? And if I do, will I reappear just before I strike the ground? Is it my death to try, or my death to stay here?" The questions poured through his mind, through the sieve of answers, coming back empty. He closed his eyes, and the image of the great monolith appeared, a silent watcher over a foreign world. The image was almost mystical, frightening in its reality. Roy opened his eyes, trying to dispel the power of the stone.

A low rumbling growl brought Roy back to his present situation as hunger attempted to gnaw a hole in his belly. He stood and walked to a nearby tree, plucking the sweet yellow fruit and popping it into his mouth, the juice dribbling down his chin. He gathered as much as he could carry and walked back over to his vista, sitting in the spongy grass beneath the tree. Questions still turned in his mind as he looked out at the retreating fog. The obvious answer came: lightning. If lightning had gotten him there, then lightning could get him home.

The excitement of insight quickly faded as he realized

he had no metal to forge a lightning rod. He kicked at the nearby stones, noting their sedimentary nature. No metal, he thought, and spat a pit out onto the ground. Where can I get metal? His eyes closed, and the image of the monolith danced before him, seductive, aloof. The vision drew him closer, beckoning to him, offering him hope. Roy's heart raced with excitement and fear. The granite walls of the stone flew toward him, and he could see them as through the eyes of a bird. High upon the stone, he could see an opening. It appeared to be tall enough for a man to crawl through. Then he heard a voice, real and seemingly beside him, screaming a single word: *Ratha!*

Roy was on his feet instantly, staff clutched in both hands, ready to swing. The beach spread out before him, empty except for the pounding surf. The forest around him was silent, too, except for the sound of his racing heart. His hands, moist with perspiration, squeezed the solid wood of the staff as he stood poised for battle. It took several moments for Roy to convince himself that the voice was only within his head, although he continued to keep one eye open as he sat to rest beneath the tree.

Morning waned, and the day grew humid and warm, completely different from the day before. The breeze that caressed the morning turned lethargic, refusing to move in the stubborn heat of midday. Roy rested in the shade, silently listing his options. He could stay here, gathering wood, food, and materials to make a better shelter. Perhaps someone would be sent to find him. Absurd as the idea was, Roy clung to its offer of hope for his troubled mind. The other option was to leave the area, perhaps journeying inland to the monolith in hope of finding some sign of civilization, or at worst, some forgeable metal. The heat coaxed him into deciding to remain.

The afternoon was too hot for work, so Roy, barefoot and shirtless, wandered toward the stream. The brook laughed to see him, tickling his toes as he stepped into the cold water. He leaned over and splashed water onto his chest and face, the cold bracing him and tightening his muscles. He sat down on a nearby log, moss-covered and spongy from decay, letting the afternoon heat dry his body. To pass time, he began to quote aloud lines from various poems he remembered, poems he had been forbidden to read aloud to his students, words the Regents had felt too unimportant to quote. The words of Wordsworth seemed to come most easily:

> *"The sounding cataract haunted me like a passion:*
> *the tall rock, the mountain, and the*
> * deep and gloom wood,*
> *their colors and their forms*
> *were then to me an appetite,*
> *a feeling and a love."*

The poem reminded him of Gwen, distant Gwen, who at that very moment was probably crying in her room or reading poignant poems lamenting someone's untimely death, his own death prematurely in her ears. The thought disturbed him, and he closed his eyes, searching for a more upbeat verse. Instead, the vision of the granite monolith, rising like a citadel over the surrounding land, sprang upon him for the third time that day. He could see the fissures in the stone, the speckled granite walls, the needles of the mountain forests. He saw them below him, with the eyes of a bird, soaring past them as the wind moves past a stationary world. And again, the screeching voice erupted in the silence: *Ratha! Ratha!*

Roy was bolt upright before the echo had died, his muscles poised, his staff quivering in his hand. The stream burbled at his feet and the surf pounded in the distance, but there were no other sounds and no sign of movement along the beach. Roy shuddered as he recalled the sound, a predatory voice that he would have sworn spoke from right beside him. The voice was haunting, and yet somehow comforting. The paradox disturbed him almost as much as the nearness of the voice. It was nonsense that the voice, so alien in nature, should seem unfamiliar and trustworthy. Roy's subsconscious wrestled with his fear, assuaging it, dispersing it. He began to want to hear the screech reverberating in this empty land, like the voice of an old friend in a new place.

The image of the Citadel rose before him, and he let it form freely, his own imagination guiding him. The voice and the Citadel seemed linked, a bond that struck Roy as strong and familiar. Roy turned the puzzle over in his mind like an unusual stone, inspecting every aspect.

In spite of his subconscious desire to trust the crying voice, Roy had become more wary of his surroundings. He began to think it odd that he had allowed the makeshift staff he carried to be his only means of defense, and that he had been so careless with his firewood. He strode back to his camp, inspecting the pile of ashes.

He turned some of the larger coals over with the tip of his staff and breathed a relieved sigh when an orange spark pulsed beneath one piece. Quickly gathering dry grass and bits of broken twigs, he coaxed the fire into igniting, patiently watching the glowing ember as he touched the grass to it, blowing lightly until the kindling began to smoke. Soon flames licked the fuel, turning it black, then red and orange. Smoke bubbled into the sky and drifted toward the sea. The fire burning comfortably, Roy turned back to the beach to gather more wood. After an hour in the stifling humidity, he decided he had stored enough.

Hunger again came looking for him, and he in turn went and found more of the sweet yellow fruit. Whimsically he looked at the piece of fruit he had ·just picked.

"You need a name," he said. "Let's call you something exotic, something foreign, to match this land." A word flashed into his mind. "How about *qomrah*?" He paused, a feeling of rightness washing over him. "I thought you'd like it," he said, smiling down at the newly christened *qomrah*, then popping it into his mouth.

The fruit had an almost narcotic effect, and Roy visibly relaxed for the first time since his arrival. The sound of his own voice added to the reassurance, and he spoke openly to himself.

"I feel like Adam, giving everything its proper name." He continued to gather as much qomrah as he could carry in his folded shirt, then returned to his camp.

The day stretched into evening, and the clouds began to roll across the bay toward Roy's camp. The wind shifted, bringing the salt air briskly across the shore and chilling the air. Roy's fire snapped defiantly, sending out cheerful light and warmth. He snuggled into the dry bed of leaves he had gathered, laying his staff across his outstretched legs. He tossed a large log onto the fire and watched the golden tongues lick the smooth, gray wood. The fire was hypnotic and soon Roy was asleep.

But he awakened to a cold world, his fire having died to a few glowing embers. Lazily he reached over and groped for a log, tossing it onto the fire-bed. Flames began to dance with instant joy as the hot coals touched the dry moss on the wood. Roy watched the dancing fire and felt cheered by it. He got up and wandered a few paces away, relieving himself behind a tree, then returned to his camp and watched the fire until silver crept into the sky, chasing away the silent stars. Soon the sky turned blue, the sun casting shadows along the beach. Roy stood and walked out onto the sand, stretching his knotted body. The smoke from his fire spun slowly upward, untouched by any wind. He let the sunshine warm his body, savoring the delicious touch.

The sunlight sent long shadows out before him as Roy wandered down toward the surf. He was about fifty yards from his camp when a second shadow, huge and sinister, slid across his own. He turned and looked into the sky, spotting the black silhouette of a great creature speeding toward him three hundred yards away. Even at that distance, Roy could see the extended talons, huge, powerful claws that could easily rend him in two with a single crushing blow. Immense batlike wings, wings that beat slowly as the creature approached, spread out from the serpentine body. Roy ran toward his camp and his staff, lying useless beneath the lean-to, keeping his eyes on the circling beast. Its nostrils flared as it caught his scent, its obsidian teeth glistening with saliva. A strong reptilian tail lashed behind its powerful frame. The beast reminded Roy of pictures he had seen of flying dinosaurs.

Roy reached the camp and his staff just as the giant creature landed on the sand. Its back talons sunk deep into the hardened beach, its front claws resting effortlessly above the crust. Roy knew he could never run, could never hide from this creature. Its eyes sparkled as it looked at Roy, backlighted by the sun. Roy silently cursed the luck that had brought him to this deadly land.

And then the weight of two days of insanity finally toppled down upon him. Adrenaline raced to his muscles, tightening them, pricking his senses. There was no logic in what he intended to do, but the same dementia that had overridden his common sense in the classroom now forced his every move. He raised the puny staff above his head and marched directly at the beast. It seemed smaller on the shore, perhaps only fifteen feet from nose to tail. Smaller, he laughed to himself, is relative. Humor is where you find it, and right now, I must look ridiculous, a single man with a stick taking on such a beast.

Fear became hysteria, and soon Roy was laughing wildly, a maniac looking for death. He stepped out of the shadows toward the reptilian beast, his staff raised above him, poised for attack. The image of the Citadel again flashed before him, and with it the faint echo of the predator's call rumbled through his memory. With a sudden whim that he felt sure would be his last, Roy charged the great beast, shouting at the top of his lungs, "Ratha! Ratha!"

The huge lizard jerked its head back, startled, its frosted eyes with terror, then quickly launched into the sky, flying with incredible speed back into the heart of the land.

Roy watched as the black beast became a speck that finally disappeared. As it vanished into the morning sky, the weary professor began to shake. He let go of the staff and fell onto the sands, where moments before the giant lizard had been, and laughed until he cried.

❖ CHAPTER THREE ❖

Lord Mordeth

The leather-faced guard straightened slightly as his master brushed past him. Lord Mordeth seemed preoccupied today, Drogan thought. It was a stroke of luck, that, since he was at the end of twelve hours of guard duty and had been unaware of the lord's approach. Nearly too late, he had asked the password, Mordeth mumbling a reply as he passed. Yes, a definite stroke of luck. Behind him, the double door crashed shut, and he returned to his post.

Mordeth walked quickly along the cobbled stones of the hallway, anxious to reach the interrogation room. He had waited months for the capture of this particular prisoner, and he relished the thought of personally prodding information from her. Mithra Roshanna was no ordinary prisoner; it was only through a devious series of traps that he had located her. Many of those traps had been sprung prematurely, his idiot guards too anxious to please him. Some of the traps were avoided with the uncanny ability of the fox; others she simply passed through, like smoke through the branches of a tree. But

it didn't matter, for in the end, he had outwitted her.
Mithra was his at last; silently he congratulated himself.

Mordeth entered a chamber deep beneath his hold. A
thin, pasty man, his oily black hair combed off to one
side, greeted him.

"Lord Mordeth, the prisoner is in the interrogation
cell. Would Your Grace wish that I bring her to you?"
The words sounded cold and slippery in the stone chamber.

"No," Mordeth replied. "I will go to her. I have waited too long for this." His lips curved into a sneer of contempt. "Dismiss her guard. I wish to be alone with her.

"And execute the guard at the twelfth post. He failed
to challenge soon enough, and then let me pass when I
gave the wrong password."

Krotah bowed and turned toward the door behind
him.

"And, Krotah, after you have left, see that I am not
disturbed."

Krotah nodded his head and turned back to the door
behind him, murmuring something through a narrow
slit. Soon an armored guard stepped into the chamber,
saluted Mordeth, and disappeared through the open
door. Krotah bowed again and followed him.

Mordeth stood in the antechamber, savoring the moment of victory. His mouth was overly moist, as if he
stood before a banquet table loaded with succulent
food. His desire for this moment had been a kind of
hunger, almost to the point of addiction. And now the
wait was over.

He looked once into the polished silver mirror that
hung on the broad stone wall of the room. The man that
stared back was a shadow. His hair and eyes were shaded

glimpses of night. He was dressed in black satin shirt and leather breeches, ebony buttons clasping the fabric together across his broad chest. A black cape hung heavily from his powerful shoulders, its lower edge barely brushing the tops of his polished riding boots. He smiled coldly at the reflection, satisfied. He could sense the fear his image would create.

Striding confidently across the room, Mordeth jerked the heavy cell door open, stepping into the dimly lit rectangular chamber. Two torches wavered on opposite walls, and a large brazier smoked and glowed atop the hearth that dominated the third wall. Gray, sulfuric fumes rose and exited through a funnel-shaped flue. Various lengths of chain hung from rings sunk into the walls, iron manacles attached to the ends. Scattered on the stone floor beside the brazier were several metal rods, some with their tips plunged beneath the pulsing coals. In the center of the room stood a massive table, and atop it lay a woman, her wrists and ankles fastened to the tabletop by thick, coarse rope. Only her eyes moved as Mordeth entered the room, flicking in his direction, full of contempt.

Mordeth walked over to the woman, bending low to her ear, his breath moist and hot against her cheek; her eyes, unblinking, stared at the mildewed ceiling. Her breath was slow and regular, although her tunic shook with the wild beating of her heart. Moisture formed in large drops beneath her armpits, and her palms were wet with nervous perspiration. The sweat stung the raw flesh on her wrists beneath the tight bindings. Her firm thighs and calves flexed slightly against her confinement.

The Dark Lord looked down at his captive and smiled.

"Mithra, how I have waited for this moment; since the death of your lover, I have waited. You should have seen him die, Mithra. It was a beautiful agony, his body wracked with pain, his lungs collapsing upon themselves, the fluid oozing from his gaping mouth. . . . And as he died, I thought of you, Mithra, only of you. Yes, how I wish you would have been there, too, to see your precious lover die." His lips were pressed against the lobe of her ear, his voice soft and hypnotic, like the movement of a snake.

"I was there, Morelua." The name meant "Lord of Nothing," and it leapt from her mouth like a blow, pushing Mordeth back from her. Ratha had called him that just before he died, and the name angered the Lord of Darkness. He had heard the rumors that some of the unhappy peasants had called him this behind his back, echoing the words of the dead Archmage, and now he heard it from the mage's lover. He landed a sharp blow across Mithra's mouth, the force of it jerking her head sideways across the rough wooden table.

"Insolence," Mordeth purred, "will not be tolerated. I have better plans for you than to hear you spout the praise of your dead lover, or to insult me. Tell me of the Pradatha."

"No, Morelua, I will not. I was there, Morelua, and I saw your victory, and your defeat. I saw when you struck Ratha down, and I heard his defiant voice clearly as he promised to return and rid Keshia of your ugliness. His is the voice of the Pradatha, the voice of truth. No, Morelua, I will tell you nothing, for you do not rule here."

Mordeth walked slowly toward the brazier, picking one of the red-hot pokers from the flames. He inspected it as if he expected to find a flaw in the metal, then turned and approached Mithra.

"That is where you're wrong, Mithra. I rule in all lives everywhere. I am master in their pain and defeat. Pain is always victory, Mithra. Death is but the ultimate victory for me. I am Mordra here, and in all places I am Mordeth. Fear is my ally, Mithra. Together fear and I will destroy you; we will destroy Mithra of Pradatha."

His laugh sounded like the crack of bones, and Mithra shivered. "Neither pain nor fear will help you with me, Morelua. The Pradatha are free and will remain so." Her voice was defiant, almost shrill, and Mordeth furrowed his brows in anger.

"Perhaps, Mithra. Perhaps. But to be true with you, I must confess to a plan other than your death—at least, your immediate death. Your followers are not that many. The Pradatha are a weak group of inept fighters, but they are difficult to locate, and therefore difficult to destroy. It is tedious work for my soldiers to hunt the Pradatha down.

"At first, I thought that they followed Ratha, and so I destroyed him. I miscalculated, for it is not Ratha they love, but you. So I have discovered that, if I can destroy their love for you, then I will destroy the Pradatha for all time."

"Then you miscalculate again, Morelua, for my people will not lose their love, for me or for Pradatha." Her voice was low and menacing, like the growl of a she-lion protecting her pride. She had often used the voice's power to call images into the minds of her students and to calm the beasts of the forest when she was hiding amongst them. But only after the destruction of Ratha had she tried the voice's power against a human enemy;

and when the enemy's will was weak, Mithra conquered. But when Mordeth, hearing Mithra's voice, felt the touch of fear, he quickly mastered it. No petty wizard's trick would deceive him.

"Mithra . . . dear, beautiful Mithra." Mordeth smiled down at her. "There is one thing the Pradatha hate, and you well know it. If anything becomes associated with me, Mithra, then the Pradatha will come to hate it."

"I will never bow to you, Morelua. You should know that, at least. I do not fear you, and I will never make obeisance to you. You cannot win."

Mordeth reached down his powerful hand and caressed her exposed thigh. Mithra tensed her muscles at his touch, repelled by its gentleness. Slowly he untied her sash, unbuttoning her tunic until she lay naked on the table.

"No, Mithra, lover of the dead Archmage, I do not need to kill you to destroy the Pradatha. In fact, it is what you will do that will destroy your beloved people. You will bear my child— the child that will grow to govern this world, the child that will destroy the Pradatha by its very presence. No, Mithra, I need not kill one as beautiful as you. . . ." His hand swept lightly across her body, and she trembled in revulsion.

"You bastard!" she snapped, spitting in his face. He brought his lips down to kiss her, and she bit him, her teeth sinking into the fleshy part of his cheek. Blood dripped down onto Mithra's face, stinging her eyes. She tried to bite him again, but he pulled back suddenly, flailing his arm across her jaw. The blow stunned her, and she lay motionless on the table. Mordeth licked the blood trickling from her mouth, kissing the swelling flesh.

"No, Mithra, I need not kill you," he said.

Then darkness enveloped her.

*   *   *   *   *

"My lord, a message. It's urgent," the guard said from beyond the door. He was having difficulty hiding his fear; he knew that Mordeth had given orders he was not to be disturbed.

"You heard my order, Drandor, and it is by your life you disturb me now," Mordeth hissed.

"But, my lord, Kreosoath has returned with important news. He begs audience with you immediately." The guard's voice wavered and cracked as he said the name of the great black dragon.

"Damn his insolence! I should sell his hide for shoe leather." In spite of Mordeth's curses, he rose and wrapped his soft robe about his naked body, lacing his sandals about his feet.

"See that she is well guarded. And be wary of her," Mordeth ordered the frightened guard. Then he stormed out the door and down the stone corridor.

Guards snapped to rigid attention as their lord passed; each was careful to ask for and receive the correct password. News had traveled swiftly throughout the hold of Drogan's execution that afternoon. Mordeth seemed pleased with the renewed watchfulness. Despite his confidence, he still had a mote of self-doubt and concern regarding his captive and her dead lover. He remembered the sound of Ratha's voice as he promised to rise up from the dead and tear Mordeth's throat from him. The word of an Archmage, no matter how utterly defeated, is not a thing to ignore.

The hard leather of Mordeth's sandals rang against the stone floor of the governing room. His ebony throne sat perched upon the dais at the far wall, a blood-red, crushed velvet tapestry hanging behind it. The tapestry drew most people's attention away from even Mordeth; the design was startlingly simple, a faint world, stitched in silver thread, shrouded by a perfect circle of black. In the middle of the northern wall stood a set of double-wide doors of blackened oak, cold iron binding the wood together and hinging the door. A small stand was set beside the throne, also draped in a blood-red material, supporting a fist-sized crystal that sparkled fiercely in the torchlight. As Mordeth entered the chamber, he strode quickly to the table and grasped the stone in his hand, only then turning to face the black dragon who sat patiently in the middle of the floor.

"Yes, Kreosoath, what is it? And it had best be important this time, for I have business to attend to and little time for dragonkind."

The dragon shifted its great weight slightly from one massive leg to another, evidently uncomfortable with the close confines of the hold. A few moments later, a low rumbling emitted from the beast, a sound like distant thunder. The crystal Mordeth held vibrated with the sound, its colors shifting subtly from red to violet.

"I have seen your enemy, Mordeth," said the stone.

"What enemy, fool lizard? I have no patience for riddles today."

Again the dragon rumbled and the stone translated. "Ratha lives. I have seen him."

Mordeth stopped his breath, holding it until his lungs ached, letting it out in a whisper between his clenched teeth. "You, dragon, are a fool. I have destroyed Ratha, utterly destroyed his foul, miserable self. He is my enemy no longer."

"Ratha lives," repeated the stone. "I was alone, hunting the southwestern shore forty wingbeats west of the great stone men call Shymney, when I saw a fire in the night like the eye of the Tythera, glowing and sending its sparks into the night. I know that you have forbidden any to live alone, that all so found should die. I flew with haste to the Tythera eye, and there I smelled a man. But he had hidden beyond the tide, where no dragon can follow, so I chose to return at the next sign of fire.

"It was another day before the man made fire again, and I waited until the sun came, so as to hunt during the light when I might find my prey more easily. What matter that one man should live alone one more day, since surely he would die before the next? And so I sought him in the morning, landing on the shore with the hideous tide crashing behind me. I turned to do my duty to my lord, and it is there that Ratha confronted me, with bloodlust in his eye and voice, until I could do naught but fly to you with this message." The dragon swished his long tail nervously as the stone translated the last of his story to Mordeth.

"Fool dragon!" Mordeth spat. "How is it you know that it was indeed Ratha if you fled so rapidly? Is it a coward's voice that shakes the Translating Stone?"

The dragon seemed unaffected by the insult. "By the mystic number three, which in all things speaks truth," Kreosoath replied. "First, by the verse he spoke when I first landed, before he knew I was there. I thought little of it, since the words were not ones from the Book of All, and yet, upon reflecting, I now see they were in-

deed Words of Power, somehow altered. Second, because his hair was the color of blackened iron, with
strands of silver woven into it; his eyes were blue like the
sea when the first star appears; his height and weight
and body were those I remember seeing as I sat upon
Shymney and watched your battle with the Archmage.
But third, and most chilling, Lord Master, he wielded
the Staff of Quintah, the Staff of Fire, and spoke the
hunting word of the hawk, driving terror into even
dragonkind."

Mordeth grew pale as Kreosoath enumerated the necessary three evidences which confirmed a legal truth. Ratha had returned, then, and would be plotting against
him. It made no difference how it was possible. He
cared only that direct and immediate action be taken.

"Krotah!" Mordeth shouted. Almost immediately a
side door swung open and the slippery captain of Mordeth's Elite Guard entered, his gray robes swishing
across the stone floor.

"Yes, Mordeth?"

"I want your two best scouts to accompany Kreosoath
to destroy an imposter. Prepare them immediately!"
Mordeth turned and stormed from the room.

"I will be with you presently, lord lizard," Krotah said
to Kreosoath after Mordeth was well out of earshot.

Kreosoath rumbled angrily and Krotah quickly left
the room.

* * * * *

Drandor finally relaxed as Mordeth's heels echoed
around the corner, eventually fading completely. He was
in a foul mood since he had heard the news of his cous-

in's execution. They had been friends since boyhood, some twenty years ago. It was rare these days for anyone to have a friend for twenty years. He paced to the open door of the interrogation room and looked inside.

It was true, then; Mordeth had captured Mithra Roshanna. She was even more beautiful than he had imagined. Mithra's cloak was draped loosely over her torso, but her long, muscular legs lay exposed atop the table. Drandor entered the room, hoping to get a better look at the face of Mithra, the lover of the Archmage. Although Mithra's face was puffy and slightly bruised, Drandor could see that she was as beautiful as the legends told. Her flaxen hair cascaded onto the table. She was breathing softly, as if asleep. Drandor came closer to her face; her lids fluttered and eyes of electric blue stared back at him, catching him off balance.

"Your name is Drandor, is it not?" her lilting voice wafted up to him. He couldn't deny it; he couldn't even respond. The power of her voice hugged him like a giant bear, crushing his every attempt to struggle against it.

"Untie me at once," she said, and although he tried to resist, he could not. The bindings came loose one by one, until Mithra sat up on the table and rubbed her ankles and wrists.

"Where has Morelua gone?" she commanded him, and Drandor began to tell her all he knew, although he was aware it would be his death.

"He has gone to meet with Kreosoath, the dark dragon who is now his ally. The rumors say that your lover has returned and that the dragon is the herald of Mordeth's own execution. It is a false belief, for all know that Ratha is dead, forever sent to the world of darkness where Mordeth has all power."

Mithra's heart raced with the news. Ratha. Alive. Although she had always kept a brave front before her followers, she had never dared to believe he could come back.

She took a deep breath, trying to master the power of the voice one last time. "You may sleep now, Drandor."

The weak-willed guard immediately slumped to the floor and began to snore softly. Quickly Mithra glanced around the room, looking for another exit. Finding none, she sat back upon the table and began to concentrate. Entrancing one idiot guard was a simple task, but to make her way out of the bowels of the hold could well prove beyond her powers. Yet escape she must, and quickly, before Mordeth returned. Behind her, a branch crackled in the brazier.

Mithra looked at the dying fire. The smoke drifted lazily up the flue. She walked over to it and looked up. A small circle of daylight blinked back at her some twenty yards above. Walking back to the guard, she stripped him of his cloak, cutting it into squares with his dagger. Then she wrapped the cloth around her legs, feet, arms, hands, and face, tying each piece with a length of the rope that had been used to bind her. Finally she lifted herself up into the flue and began to climb.

The heat from the fire was intense inside the confines of the chimney, and before she had gotten halfway, she felt certain she would faint. By force of will, she kept climbing. Blisters formed on her feet and back where she pressed against the heated sides. Still she climbed, the smoke gouging her lungs with every breath, threatening to choke her. Finally the cool evening air erupted around her, washing over her like a fountain, and she rolled out of the chimney to the roof.

Soon, she knew, Mordeth would return for her. In the meantime, she must make good her escape. With uncanny speed and agility, she ran along the peaks of the roofs, leaping from building to building. Fear pushed her unflaggingly, and soon she was at the edge of the hold itself, with only the high wall that surrounded it keeping her from the town and safety. She lowered herself over a darkened portion of the wall until her feet were perhaps fifteen yards from the stony ground below. She closed her eyes and uttered her Word of Power, then dropped to the earth.

A sharp pain surged through her like a dagger, jerking her breath from her lungs. She sat, panting in pain, while the night surrounded her, the stars cold flecks in the ebony sky. Moonless, she thought, and thanked the Four-That-Bind for her luck. Slowly she half-staggered through the back alleys until she came to a small inn, the lights turned low inside. She gave a peculiar series of raps on the back door and waited. After a few heart-pounding moments, it opened, and light flooded out into the alley, dispersing the darkness. A tall man, dressed in the garb of an innkeeper, stood framed against the warmth of the firelight, and he grabbed her as Mithra swooned.

"Ratha lives. He lives," she gasped, then slumped unconscious against his chest.

❖ CHAPTER FOUR ❖

The Pradatha

Mithra lay awake for several minutes without moving or opening her eyes. It was the smell that woke her: clean and wholesome, with a slight tang of frying bacon and new wine. The quilts that had been spread over her were warm and weighty, and beyond them, she could hear the quiet fire in the hearth pulsing like a heartbeat. Only after she had taken in all the sensations and assured herself that they were real did she try vainly to raise herself. A sharpness in her side forced her back down.

"Don't move, Mithra. Your ribs are broken. The healer says if you move, your lung will puncture. Be still, child."

Mithra sank back down into the soft clutch of the bed and turned her face toward the old familiar voice. Tralaina, who had been her nurse and companion for nearly all of Mithra's thirty years, stood beside her, dressed in her gray peasant's costume, wringing a clean white cloth in a basin of water. Her frame was powerful and lithe, belying her fifty years, and her hair was the color of daisy petals, but her eyes were tired, dark rings hanging like yokes beneath their rich earthiness.

"Roshah will heal you, child," Tralaina said as she gently laid the cool cloth across Mithra's fevered brow. "Let the water come as power to you. Be still and rest." Tralaina moved gracefully to an old rocking chair facing the fire. She sat down, folding her strong hands in her lap, and soon looked as if she were asleep. Mithra knew she wasn't, though, and as the wild remembrances of her flight from Morlidra, the Dark Lord's keep, came back to her, questions flooded the empty spaces of her memory.

"Tralaina? Have I dreamed it, or is it true that Ratha has returned?"

"Time enough later to discuss that, Mithra. Now you must rest," the old nurse replied sternly.

"But I must know, Tralaina. Please tell me. Was it only a dream?"

"In truth, we do not know. You gave that message to Stentor before you fainted. But rumors fly like frightened sparrows before the hunting hawk. Kreosoath has come to the city and left with two of Morelua's best huntsmen. Morelua stalks his palace like an angry Tythera, but we know his bite is weak." Tralaina smiled as she concluded, obviously pleased that Mordeth was fretful.

Mithra collapsed back onto the soft pillows that supported her weakened body. She grew more aware of other pains, upon her hands and back, and a stiffness in her jaw as she spoke. She looked at her right hand; it was bandaged with strips of linen, a yellow ointment seeping through the fabric. She remembered the climb up the chimney, the searing heat. Flexing her feet, she found that they, too, were bound with strips of cloth.

She wriggled in her bed, feeling the firm discomfort of blisters on her back. No, she decided, it had been no dream.

She fell asleep as thoughts of Ratha wandered behind her closed eyes, but those thoughts dimmed as Mordeth encroached into her subsconscious. Her dream became a tempest, with the Archmage standing bowed against an eerie wind and she hiding uselessly in the *marelock* bushes. She could see Mordeth standing erect, unchallenged by the gale, and his black eyes glistened with hate. With a horror that nearly jerked her wide awake, he looked into Mithra's face and smiled. Then, with a clenched fist, Mordeth sent Ratha into the unknown. Mithra shouted, but the wind swept her words away. A knife appeared in her hand, and without thinking, she plunged it deep into the Dark One's chest. And then the darkness consumed her. If she dreamed more, she did not remember.

* * * * *

Mithra awoke to cheerful sounds. The fire was now snapping loudly in the fireplace, a pot of stew bubbling above it. Men's voices conversed softly in an adjoining room. She heard the clatter of cookware as some of the men helped the cook in the kitchen. Most reassuring of all, there was the voice of Tralaina as she read from the Book of All.

Mithra turned her head and peered through sleepy eyes at the scene before her. Tralaina still sat in her rocking chair, pushing it slowly with her powerful legs. Around her on the floor were gathered a half-dozen children, all watching the old nurse intently. Trailana's smile was like kitten's fur, and the children wallowed in its warmth and softness.

"Tell us again the story of Ratha. Please, Tralaina!" a small boy begged.

"Yes. Tell us that one!" the others shouted in unison.

"It's a worthy story and one well learned," began Tralaina. She closed her eyes and whispered her Word of Power: "Keshia." As she did, images sprang before the eyes of the children, each image particular to the individual child, no two exactly alike but all with a common bond. She continued speaking with the voice.

"In Yelu of the Forest Black, there lived a hawkmaster named Protetha Shaleth Keshia-ne, who married a young herb tender named Manetha. They had a son, with eyes of twilight blue and a Voice of Power. The first time he cried, all of his father's hawks gathered round him, and wild birds, too: the peregrine and the red-tail, the silver and the blue. Each in turn perched beside his crib, protecting him from harm. Even the great Lord of Falcons, Moratha Rahlah-ne, the largest and swiftest of his kind, took special interest in the boy-child, never venturing far from him. The boy was called Ratha Keshia-ne, which means 'The Landborn Falcon.'

"Ratha grew tall and fair, except for his hair, which was the color of coal, unlike any of his kin. His father taught Ratha the trade of falconry. Ratha's young eyes were nearly as keen as Moratha's. Together they would hunt the fleeing rabbit and wily partridge; never a day went by when their hunt was unsuccessful. For his cunning and stamina in the hunt, Moratha loved Ratha all the more.

"In the months before Ratha's Day of Naming, an old man appeared. He was tall and slender, like a branch from a willow tree; his eyes were gold embers smoldering beneath hair of smoke gray. It was not unusual in those days, before the Dark One outlawed free travel, for travelers to pass through Yelu, since it was a large town, much larger than any of the others nearby. The villagers took little notice of the traveler and simply called him 'the stranger.'

"The stranger often sat on the edge of the forest, where he could watch Ratha and Moratha hunting. All the while he watched, the old man carved upon a long, smooth staff. Each day Ratha would stop and offer the stranger some of the bounty of that day's hunt, for it was the nature of Ratha to be generous to any who might be in need. The stranger would thank him and return to his woodwork. Sometimes Ratha would stay and watch the old man carving on his long stick of yew, smoothing the handle and carving the knot atop it. The knot fascinated Ratha, for in it, he imagined that he could see the eye of Moratha looking patiently back at him."

Now Tralaina stopped and looked at each child in turn, underscoring the importance of what she was about to say. "All things," she continued, "come from the Four-That-Bind: Keshia, the Land; Rahlah, the Air; Roshah, the Sea; and Quintah, the Fire. It is fire, my children, it is Quintah, that is the bane of darkness. Light stands alone against its evil power. The three remaining elements are strong and true, but only Quintah can banish the night.

"To each of humankind, when he has reached an age of maturity, is given one of these Words of Power; but Quintah is the rarest of all the gifts, given to but a few. It is one of the great mysteries of our world, and it makes the story of Ratha all the more exceptional. For on Ratha's day of passing, when the elders of Yelu gathered for the Ritual of Power-giving, Ratha came forward to receive his gift, and the elder of Yelu said to him:

" 'Ratha, to you is given the Word of Power Keshia, for you are landborn, living in the heart of the forest, far from the sea. Let this word be your strength and guard you through your life.'

"As the elder finished, Moratha swept down from the sky with a call wild enough to stop the hearts of even the bravest, but Ratha was not afraid. For he heard the voice of his beloved friend and understood even the speech of the great Lord of Falcons; Moratha had given him a second gift, which was the Word of Power for all beasts that fly and those that command them: Rahlah.

"And then, my children, from the forest came the old man known only as the stranger, carrying his stave of carved wood, the hawk eye alert and unblinking. To the center of the circle the stranger walked, and there he stood before the council fire, looking into the eyes of young Ratha.

" 'You are one of great power, Ratha,' the stranger said, 'and destined to do great things. The land looks to you for guidance; the beasts of the air salute you as their kin. I have searched for one like you for many years, for I see a madness soon to come, and I am afraid. So I give you one last gift.' And here the old man threw the stave into the heart of the fire. Ratha gasped, for the old man had worked for many weeks upon the staff, polishing the wood and giving it perfect balance. But the staff did not burn; instead, the hawk's eye gleamed with strength and ferocity.

" 'Take the staff,' the stranger ordered.

"Ratha bent over and retrieved the staff from the

roaring blaze. No mark had touched it, and it was cool
to the touch. Ratha looked hard into the stranger's eyes,
then simply nodded, for he recognized the stranger at
last as a powerwielder, a Master of Fire.

" 'Ratha, to you I give the power of fire, for the day
may come when you alone, among all living men, will
have Quintah to serve you.' He looked sadly at the boy,
then added, 'This is not a gift, young wizard. It is not an
easy thing I give you. And I hope, more than death is
silent, that it is a curse you will never need to bear. It is a
hard thing to stand alone as a light in the day of darkness, with night's creatures baying at your heels. And
the one against whom you must stand is terrible and
hard, and he may yet prove to be more than you can
bear. Guard well the task and strengthen your heart
against the cold night yet to come.'

"Then the stranger stepped straight into the flames.
As the old man caught fire and began to burn, exploding into a thousand dancing sparks, the people tried to
help him, but Ratha raised the staff, and the air shook
with light and thunder, forcing the villagers back. When
the eyes of the people could see once more, the old man
had vanished, with only a column of gray smoke rising
to the sky.

"And so was born Ratha, *Mor Keshia-Rahlah-
Quintah*, Master of Land and Air and Fire, the Archmage of Shaleth."

Tralaina stopped her story and looked over at Mithra.
In the firelight, tears shone in the young woman's eyes
like gemstones. Mithra had gathered the handworked
quilt about her, hugging it like a lover.

"Tell the rest, Traliana. Tell them all, for it is their
right and our responsibility to pass all knowledge to the

young." Mithra managed a hopeful smile as the children turned to look at the awakened leader.

The old nurse shook her head. "Not now, my child, not now. Now it is time for bed. Tomorrow I will tell the remainder of the story, I promise. Tomorrow." She reached out a wrinkled hand and picked up a red clay mug from the table beside Mithra's bed. "Drink this down, child."

Reluctantly Mithra took the cup and slowly raised it to her lips. She didn't want to sleep. Sleep and darkness were the realms of the Dark One, and she silently feared what might be found there. Her face grew hot as she remembered once more the vicious rape she had been forced to endure half-consciously. But her trust for Tralaina won out in the end, and Mithra took a large gulp of the warm, brown liquid. She felt its medicine warm her throat and belly, and she closed her eyes and savored its numbing quality.

Tralaina reached out her hand and softly stroked Mithra's forehead, then began to hum softly an ancient melody. She stayed beside her ward long after the song was finished and the children had scurried off to bed, until only Mithra's soft, rhythmic breathing broke the silence.

* * * * *

Mithra woke with a single thought framing her mind. She had spent the entire night embraced in dreamless sleep, and waking from it, she realized more than ever that the Dark One's influence was not unlimited. How long had she believed that the destruction of Ratha had come at the hands of the ultimate power? Within Morelua's keep, she had felt his arms wrap around her, his weight press down on her, and had accepted the inevitability of his control. But in Tralaina's house and under the protection of her magic, she had managed to evade the Dark One's cold touch.

That revelation alone nearly overwhelmed her. If Mordeth was not all-powerful, then perhaps she could have stopped him, could have found his weakness and used it to destroy him before she became tainted. But she had failed. And now she wondered if her life were destined for little more than failure.

It was guilt that met her in the morning. She was convinced that Mordeth could be beaten, but she had assumed she herself was powerless against him. And now she had to pay the price of lifelong shame. Mithra lightly touched her thighs, letting her fingers move slowly up to her stomach and breasts.

"What are you thinking about, child?" Tralaina's soft voice brought Mithra out of her reverie. "Are you in any pain?"

Mithra laughed once, unconvincingly. "No. Your medicine seems to have taken that burden away." Mithra closed her eyes and remembered again the hard weight of darkness that had pressed down on her.

Tralaina's heart thickened in her breast as she looked at Mithra. The old nurse knew that Mithra ached, but not solely from physical pain. Yet there was no way her magic could sooth a heartfelt wound.

"Dear Mithra," she said gently, "I bless the Four-That-Bind that you've come home to us again. However you made it here, whatever you had to do, it doesn't matter. What matters is that you outwitted him and made it back safely."

Mithra was stunned. She had been able to outwit him in the end, had escaped and eluded him, even in the realms of darkness and sleep. But it was all too late. Too late for Ratha. Too late for herself. The revelation spurred on her feelings of guilt.

"Come, child. There's news to tell, and the fire's burning warm in the other room. Can you walk?"

"I can walk."

Together they moved into an empty taproom and sat down at the rough wooden table in front of the hearth. A fire crackled gaily and warmed Mithra's flesh, but inside she remained cold and gray.

"The Dark One is looking for you. His spies are up and down the streets like dogs on a hunt. We've managed to meet a few ourselves and give them something they didn't bargain on finding." Tralaina ran her thumbnail across her throat and smiled unnaturally.

"Then we're in danger here," Mithra said.

"We're in danger everywhere," Tralaina answered. "We cannot move openly on the roads, since Morelua has closed them to free travel. Only his traders are allowed wagons to move their goods. We couldn't leave Lorlita without being noticed, unless we kept to the forests and fens. And they contain dangers enough, with the black dragon doing the Dark One's bidding. No, child, you're as safe here as anywhere, where our kind can defend you."

"And the book?" Mithra questioned.

"It's safe. But paper's as rare as dragon's teeth, so you'd best stave off that hunger somewhere else."

"No, Tralaina. That's one promise I must keep no matter what. Ratha swore me to it, and I will not fail him." Mithra stared into the fire, remembering how her husband had made her promise to write down all the lore of her people, to save it against a time when the Dark One would try to ban it from Keshia. "The words of the people carry truth and power. Without our stories, how can our children know Pradatha? And with Morelua wringing the stories from our people's lives, how can we hope to go on?"

Tralaina snorted angrily. "I know, child. Morelua has even taken some of the children and scattered them amongst the tribes so that they would lose track of their family's lore. But we find them and remind them."

"And what if the Dark One finds us? Without the stories, who will remind the children? Who, Tralaina? Who?"

The old nurse shook her head. "I'll find you paper, then, child, even if I have to search to the bowels of the Pit itself."

Mithra placed her hand upon her belly, then looked across the table into the nurse's eyes. "And I will see that the stories are told to any child who will hear."

* * * * *

Mithra gathered the old quilts around her and nestled deeper into the soft bedding. Night had come again, and Tralaina's medicine was working hard. Mithra struggled to keep her eyes open.

"Tell them everything, Tralaina. They must know everything. That's the way of truth. That is Pradatha's way."

Tralaina nodded in agreement, then, with eyes transfixed on some distant personal memory, she began where she had finished the night before. "Ratha's power became a legend throughout Keshia, and the king called him to court in the city of Lorlita, which means 'The City of Enlightenment.' Here Ratha was asked to instruct the youth of the city in the ways of power. This he did gladly and with great love and gentleness. Children loved him and often came to his home with baskets of herbs and berries that they themselves had picked, giving them to the young Archmage. In return, he would encourage them to speak with Moratha, his constant companion. The great falcon would leap from the broad shoulders of the Archmage and circle the group in playful display, then land again and speak into his ear, and the Archmage would laugh.

"In those days, the Lord of the City and Patriarch of Keshia was King Gondsped, a wise ruler, swift with justice and generous in giving. He desired that all Keshia would one day come to master the Words of Power for the benefit of all humankind. It is for that reason that he had called for Ratha and made him the Archmage Counselor. Gondsped had a son by his wife Rachala, whom they named Porthera. It was Gondsped's hope that Ratha would one day pass his knowledge along to the king's son.

"But Gondsped was blind in some regards, perhaps because he was so good and trusting. Along with Ratha, he called the Mage Morlin, who was wise in the ways of governing. No sooner had Morlin entered Lorlita when he set about to capture the love of Gondsped away from the Archmage. Into the king's ears, he whispered lies and deceits, telling of how Ratha corrupted the children of Lorlita, inviting them to his home and seducing them. At first Gondsped would not believe the stories, but as he watched the children coming and going from

Ratha's home at all hours and the Archmage laughing and touching first one child, then another, or wrapping his strong arms around yet a third, the seed of doubt began to grow into a noxious weed. That, my children, is the way of lies, that even good men and women fall into their grasp if they are not always on guard.

"So, my children, Morlin took advantage of the king's doubts, nurturing that seed he had planted and insisting that Gondsped should place upon him the title of Regent, so that should Ratha indeed be evil and somehow do harm to the king, power would pass to Porthera through Morlin's Regency. The king immediately made the decree, his fears blinding him to truth, for it is always fear that darkens Pradatha, that darkens the path of truth.

"Within days of the decree, Gondsped became ill. Morlin was quick to accuse Ratha of poisoning the king, but those who loved the Archmage believed it was Morlin who caused his death. Gondsped died a painful death, and Morlin seized power, proclaiming Ratha an outlaw and placing the sentence of death upon him. Ratha, fearing the bloodletting of a revolt should he be arrested, fled southwestward to the sea and soon arrived in Westport.

"Westport is far from Yelu and Lorlita, so no one there knew the Archmage. Still, he came disguised as a traveling teacher, fearing capture by the Regent's guards. Chiath, a fisherman of the village, offered to lodge Ratha in return for instruction for his daughter, who would soon be ready for her rite of passage. Mithra was a fair and comely girl, taller than most with hair the color of sea foam and eyes like the *ciandith*, the most precious of mountain flowers.

"For two months, Ratha taught Mithra the lore of Keshia. The power of his Voice moved her, and she begged him to teach her the control of it. Many afternoons they sat together and practiced upon the flocks. Moratha, the falcon, would sweep down among the sheep and startle them, and Mithra would use her voice to instantly calm their fears. Ratha admitted openly that here, in Mithra, he had found the most adept pupil of the land.

"When at last her time of passage came, it was Ratha who gave her her Word of Power: Roshah, which is the sea, for Mithra was as constant as the tides and as pliable as water. A fortnight later, much to the joy of everyone who knew them, Ratha and Mithra were wed. And on their wedding night, Ratha shared with her the truth of who he was.

"Through all this, Morlin had not forgotten the Archmage, and he set about to find and destroy Ratha, sending scouts to every village to look for him. It was at Westport that Krotah—Krotah, the toad, whose poison drips from his mouth, the Captain of the Dark One's Elite Guard—saw Ratha and Mithra sitting in the shade of a large elm, eating the fruit of the keyth tree. Krotah recognized Ratha by the large falcon that remained perched in the branches of the tree above the two young lovers. He sent two of his guards with a message for Morlin to come, for Ratha had been found."

Tralaina paused and looked around the room. The children's eyes were wide and unfocused. Each one leaned forward heavily, as if pressing against some invisible barrier. The old nurse smiled ruefully, remembering briefly how she, too, had felt the fear for the Archmage when she had first heard the story. She cast a quick look over at Mithra, who lay buried and unmoving beneath the layers of quilts.

"Listen, my children," Tralaina continued, "for it is a great truth I'm telling you. Lies and deceit travel far and fast, but truth moves quickly, too. A merchant entering Westport that very afternoon brought among his pots and pans the latest news from the capital. Morlin had seized the throne, and he had sent spies out into all the provinces to search for the renegade Archmage, whom Morlin accused of poisoning the king. What was more, the merchant had seen a man riding hard back along the road toward Lorlita, riding so hard that he didn't even pause to bid the man good day.

"Ratha heard these things and knew at once he'd been discovered. Hastily Ratha readied himself for flight, for he feared that those he loved would be harmed should he and Morlin do battle within the town. Mithra pleaded to go with him, but Ratha, knowing the Dark One's nature and strength, refused. Before the first light of morning, Ratha had left his family and love."

Tralaina paused to moisten her lips. Only that small movement broke the stillness in the room.

"To the great stone monolith of the central mountains Ratha ran," she continued, "to the place of prophecy and power, where order was set among the tribes and promises run deep. Moratha guided him with his falcon-sight until at last Shymney rose like a giant hand of warning, the gray stone austere in the light of dusk. Ratha found the catacombs of Shymney, where the falcons nest and raise their young, and there he hid himself.

"Morlin arrived in Westport within a week of Krotah's message, but Ratha had long since fled. Krotah told his lord of the Archmage's lover, and Morlin immediately sought her out. Morlin lusted for Mithra, not only because of her great beauty but also because her love belonged to Ratha. Nevertheless, his attempts to pry information from her were in vain. Morlin was forced to take his scouts and try to find the trail that Ratha had left. Mithra, fearing for her love, followed."

Tralaina looked over to where Mithra rested. The younger woman had kicked off some of her covers and lay staring at the ceiling. Her right hand rested lightly on her stomach, as if she felt some invisible pain deep inside. Tralaina wondered for a moment if she should bring a quick end to the story and tend to Mithra, but thought better of it. If Mithra wanted that, she would surely tell her.

"Morlin's scouts were successful in locating Ratha," she said, "and soon the Dark One could see the stone finger of Shymney pointing upward to the sky. As darkness draped the mountains, Morlin made his move, sweeping down upon his prey like a panther. Ratha might have been caught unaware but for the cry of the falcon alerting him. He lifted his staff into the sky and the darkness evaporated like dew before the fire of sunlight. Before him, he could see Morlin and his guards, and Ratha knew that the time to fight had come.

"And he was ready. Calling the cry of the hunt, Ratha summoned the great hawks from their nests within Shymney. The mighty birds swarmed upon the guards, slashing at their eyes and throats. There were few soldiers to begin with, for Morlin was arrogant of his power, and most of them fled in fear of the birds and the fire-wielding Archmage. Those that remained died a painful death from beak and talon. When no others stood against them, the raptors swept down at Morlin himself, but the falcons could not reach him, for a fey wind emerged from Morlin's presence and swept them away.

"At last only the two remained standing at Shymney's foot, at the very center of the world, with the falcons looking on from above. Ratha watched as Morlin reached into his cloak and withdrew a crystal orb, holding it aloft and saying mystic words that Ratha could not comprehend. Night crept around them like a corpse, cold and unyielding, and in the distance, Ratha thought he could hear the faint beat of wings. A downdraft slithered down his collar, and he looked up and met the eyes of Kreosoath, the Lord of Black Dragons. The falcons turned and attacked, managing to drive the beast away from their friend.

"The Archmage turned back to Morlin and raised his staff skyward. The dark of night was pushed farther back, but Morlin waved his hand and the darkness once again inched toward Ratha, casting shadows on the stone around him.

"It was his face, my children—it was his face that told the story then. For with the Dark One's single gesture, the Archmage felt defeat. His brows knotted with inner pain, and the color drained from his skin. He fought on, but his face was painted with defeat. When Morlin opened his palm toward him, the darkness crept forward, a staff length from the Archmage.

"Ratha uttered a weakened gasp, then struck his heel against the ground, uttering the Word of Power *Keshia* as he did. The ground shook and Morlin stumbled, only barely keeping his balance. Morlin waved his arm high above his head and shrieked like a man possessed, and the darkness swept over Ratha like a flooded stream. A small sound was heard in the heart of the darkness, and Ratha reappeared, the light about him feeble and small. He looked across the abyss at Morlin, and there he promised to return and banish the Dark One forever. Then the darkness swallowed Ratha, Archmage of Keshsia."

Tralaina reached out her hand and received a proffered cup of juice from a small child who offered it in thanks. She drank it greedily, for her mouth was dry from the telling. She glanced over at her ward; Mithra's eyes were hidden behind the quilt. For Mithra, the story always brought pain, for it was she, hiding in the bushes behind Morlin, who had witnessed these events and who recalled the final days of the Archmage. Although she had sought her lover for days, she found no sign of him. The Book of Knowledge he had promised to write was lost, as was the Staff of Quintah, all of it succumbing to the darkness that shrouded the dying Ratha.

"Beneath the shadow of Shymney," Tralaina murmured, "Morlin, the murderer of King Gondsped and usurper of his throne, uttered the blasphemous words declaring himself Mordeth, lord over the fifth power, which is darkness, never before chosen by humankind. Mordeth returned to Lorlita, and under the guise of lawful regency, began his rule.

"Mordeth dared not destroy the boy Porthera, choosing instead to lock him away in an infirmary, declaring that the boy was ill and needed time to recover. No news has come of the boy since those first days, and many believe that he is now dead, although Mordeth claims he is not. Soon after this, Mordeth began the many changes that have defiled the land in the ten years since his rule began.

"The schools of Lorlita and Hagsface were systematically disbanded, and the masters were sent to the far corners of Keshia under the guise of educating the barbarians at the kingdom's edge. Those students who gained knowledge of Quintah from the Archmage were hunted down like vile animals, for fire and light are the bane of darkness. None have been heard from in many years. A decree went out that no man or woman may live outside the villages or cities, and none may travel openly without permit. To do so is to invite the penalty of death. This was for our protection, the Regent said, but we know that it was fear of revolt that caused Mordeth to make the proclamation. Finally Mordeth forbade that any might learn to read or write, and that family histories and our folk legends and tales be forever erased. Mordeth said that it was because Ratha had contaminated them with his evil, and to read or listen to such stories was to walk in the path of Ratha.

"Many have listened to Mordeth and have chosen to follow him, but some, those who knew Ratha, are loath to obey. Mordeth purged the cities of those who disobeyed his decree, and it became dangerous to keep any old records, deadly to openly defy him.

"It was Mithra who came again to Lorlita to seek those who knew her dead husband. It was Mithra who collected the many stories and wrote them into the book, so that the stories and lore of our people would not be lost forever. For the knowledge of the Archmage was truth, which we call Pradatha, and those that follow his ways are the Pradatha-ne. We who know the truth will not bow to Mordeth and the Dark Realm. We will await the return of the Archmage and the utter destruction of evil."

Tralaina finished her story and sent the children to bed, kissing each one on the forehead as he passed.

When the room was at last empty, Tralaina turned toward Mithra and spoke. "He will return, Mithra." Tralaina said the words so quietly that they were almost lost in the hush of the fire.

But if Mithra heard her beneath the covers, she chose not to answer.

❖ CHAPTER FIVE ❖

The Citadel

"Get your arse movin', man. I ain't 'bout t' be found on th' wrong side of his lor'ship today."

Grev turned sullenly toward the speaker and gave him a dour look. Although Jelom was his sergeant and at least five years older, and Grev was only a twenty-year-old corporal, the younger man found it difficult to take orders from him. Jelom had been raised in a small village far to the south, and his ways, unlike Grev's polished Lorlitan manner, were rustic and often ignorant, not to mention prone to exaggeration and heavy drink. Such a superior could only limit Grev's ambition—unless it was possible to undermine his authority. A sudden smile curved the edges of Grev's thin lips.

"Do you mind, Jelom? All things at the proper time. And sure as the Pit is going to swallow you and your beer-guzzling ways, it'll be a long haul to anywhere looking like a town when we get where we're going. I intend to be ready."

"An' just where is that? The Toad be tellin' you an' not me?" Color rose into Jelom's rough-shaven face as he thought of the apparent slight. Grev was a full rank below him, but Jelom knew that Krotah, the captain of Mordeth's elite troops, had a reputation for ignoring protocol, especially if the one ignored was under suspicion.

"Take it easy, Jelom," Grev answered, not wanting to push his advantage too far too soon. "I've heard as much as you have. But there's a buzz out on the street. That blasted black dragon's in town, and his lordship is always on edge when Kreosoath visits. Last time the lizard was here, Mordeth sent a dozen crack troops to scour the northern forests for traitors. They were gone three weeks and never saw a thing."

"Yeah, I 'member. Levit pulled that patrol. Says Kreosoath ate 'em, bones an' all, an' never e'en stopped t' lick his chops." Jelom made a quick sign to ward off evil.

Grev raised an eyebrow. "Superstition. And you'd best not let his lordship see you making such signs. At least, not around me. If you want your head and shoulders separated, do it elsewhere."

Jelom looked nervously around the room. "A'right, a'right. Let's get movin'. His lordship won't like waitin' if we be late."

Without answering, Grev grabbed his small, neatly stuffed pack and followed Jelom out the door.

*   *   *   *   *

Chill morning air, pushed by an easterly breeze, shook the fragile leaves of the tree above Roy's camp. The tide rushed across the sands, surrounding the driftwood pile until it looked like a tiny island. Shadows crept across the thin finger of sand like a hand grasping at the sea. Roy kicked earth over the last of his fire and tried to suppress a feeling of loss. Fire had been his friend and companion in this foreign world. The smoke quieted like a dying breath, wafting heavenward.

Fear was Roy's companion now. He was all too aware of it as he hastily gathered what useful items he could. It was a stroke of unbelievable fortune that the great lizard had fled, but there was no point in risking a second encounter. He resolved to head inland, toward the great stone monolith and the haunting sound of the hunting voice, far from the lizard creature. He filled his tunic with *qomrah*—the only palatable food he'd managed to find—slung the folded garment over his shoulder, hefted his staff in his free hand, and took the first step of what he expected to be a long trek. He ambled down the beach, hugging the forest, until he reached the little stream. There Roy bent down, setting his staff and sack on the ground, then cupped his hands and dipped them into the cold, cleansing water for a last refreshing drink. His eyes searched the sky to the south and north for any hint of the beast's return. Satisfied the creature was nowhere about, Roy turned east toward the hidden mountains and began to climb.

Trudging through the thick undergrowth was monotonous, the heavy clog of his shoes as he stumbled from bush to bush the only sound to keep him company. More than once Roy began to quote aloud old rhymes to pass the time and allow his mind respite from the permeating fear of the lizard's return. But that fear led him into a more discreet silence, until even his mumbled verse died away in the still air. He longed for company—for Gwen, for anyone, anything—to help him focus his thoughts on something rational and coherent. But there was nothing, human or animal, to fill the void.

Again a sudden image of Gwen filled his mind, but Roy found it difficult to focus on the details of her face. He could see her brows arching as she laughed, but the color of her eyes escaped him. He squinted as he tried to recall the sound of her laughter, but it was lost in the steady tramp of his boots against the soil.

Thoughts of Gwen eventually filtered away to his last hour at the university. Roy had long ago accepted that he was either mad or had been thrown into a foreign world, and it seemed to him to matter little which one. But his creative instinct lingered with the idea of a new world, a world to which he felt uncannily called. He recalled the sudden surge of power as the lightning struck, the face that looked so much like his own, and yet subtly different. Vectors, he thought, and remembered his own mental wanderings. Could it be that he had somehow leaped from his own life line into that of another life, somehow similar, yet tangent to his own and in an alien world?

He stumbled on a twisted root and landed hard. "Damn," he muttered, cursing the steep, tangled terrain. He recalled a time when he and his father had walked across a small forest, making their way along the many criss-crossed game trails that stretched across the hills. But here there were no game trails through the thick brush of the forest, and he struggled to make his way. Giving up thoughts of his old life, he picked himself up and forced himself to concentrate on the long, tedious walk.

Twice before the sun was high in the hidden sky, Roy had to climb trees to gain his bearings. The first time, he climbed an oaklike tree only to discover that the perverse nature of the forest had forced him back toward the sea, leading him north of his old camp several miles, but no farther inland. The second time, Roy climbed a tall, thin tree with silver bark that towered several yards above its neighbors. The bright sun slashed against the treetop, the midafternoon breeze rippling the leaves about him. Far to the west, he could see the blue and white undulations of the sea, the bay that had been his home now only a neat footprint in the land. Nearer and to the east stood the stone finger that rose before the magenta mountains. Roy studied the giant monolith as it rose regally before him, surrounded by its mountain robes; for a moment, he thought he could discern a faint movement about the head of the stone. Fear of the great lizard washed over him like a sudden, violent storm, but the movement, if indeed there was any, vanished with a blink, and his resolve to reach the pinnacle returned.

By the time Roy reached the foothills, the sun was low in the west. He climbed another tree to scout the terrain. A vast green blanket of sea spread atop the western horizon. To the east, the monolith erupted from the earth, so near that he could see the shades of gray and black pocking the sand-white surface. To the north, Roy could see a rainbow scintillating in the evening light. As he strained to listen, he briefly imagined he could detect the sound of distant falling water.

With evening approaching, Roy began to look for suitable shelter. A fallen log, smelling of rich, pungent decay, lay seductively across his path. He gathered dead branches and grass, piling them against the windward side of the deadfall until he had erected a crude lean-to. He ate the last few *qomrah*, buttoned his tunic around his torso for warmth against the growing mountain chill, then began to hunt for food.

Night crept quickly upon the wearied outlander. His search for food in a dark, unfamiliar place was futile. Feeling fortunate to have relocated his temporary shelter, he snuggled beneath it into a pile of dry heather. Hunger rattled his stomach, but fatigue had long since turned to exhaustion, and soon he was asleep.

Morning came cold and wet, a heavy dew condensing on his shelter and dripping onto his exposed face. The morning was weak and washed, the sun stillborn in the eastern sky; even the clouds were powerless, high, hazy parodies of earlier storms. The dew puddled on the ground along the edges of Roy's shelter, awakening his thirst. He dipped a hand into the thin stream running off the roof, sipped it, and rubbed the wetness across his face, arousing himself from his exhausted sleep. His muscles ached from overuse and the unpleasant thought of yet another day of climbing. Roy lifted himself to his feet and stamped them on the ground in a little jig, stretching his arms behind his back like a runner preparing for a race.

"Well, no dragons, anyway," he told himself, inspecting the sky. His sudden concern over the presence of the lizard beast awoke in him a memory of an old Chaucerian tale of a group of fools who went hunting for Death, only to find it. He murmured a few remembered lines: "*Now, sires,' quod he, 'if that yow be so leef to fynde Deeth, turne up this croked wey; for in the grove I lafte hym, by my fey, under a tree, and there he wole abyde.*" Roy looked up at the tree above him, sweeping his eyes across the tangled branches, then turned and looked toward the direction of the monolith and began to walk.

* * * * *

Grev patted the thick hide of the black dragon. Kreosoath's massive head turned back to look at him; the dragon's eyes seemed to spin in the midmorning light, like a prismatic top rotating in the two deep sockets. The lizard's mouth was slightly agape, showing its long, needle-sharp ebon teeth. Grev tried to swallow and found he couldn't. Quickly he turned his head away and allowed himself to be hefted onto the creature's front shoulders.

Jelom watched obliquely, not daring to set his eyes on the great lizard. All the rumors he'd heard about Kreosoath hadn't prepared him for the awful confrontation. And then to find that he was to ride the great beast, in flight . . . Jelom made a quick sign, then looked around the square to see if he had been noticed. Beside the dragon, a single gray-clad soldier, his silver insignia marking him as one of the city's infantry, turned his face away and silently filed Jelom's name.

"You're certain you understand?" Krotah asked. Mordeth's first captain was dressed in black silken robes, tightened about his waist with a silver cord. His soft boots scuffed lightly against the plaza's red flagstones. Jelom heard them like the sound of sandstone sharpening steel. He lowered his eyes to look at Krotah's pointed chin, not daring to stare his superior in the eye.

"We're t' find th' man what's hidin' near th' Falcon Falls an' take 'im by force," Jelom answered.

"You're to find the imposter," Krotah corrected, venom glistening in his voice. "The imposter. And Mordeth wants him alive. No mistakes."

"No, sir," Jelom replied. "No mistakes, sir." Silently

he wondered who this imposter was imitating and why Mordeth's first captain was so intent on his capture. More than that, Jelom wondered why any description of the imposter had seemed to be withheld—Jelom could not but think purposefully—and why the imposing figure of the black dragon Kreosoath was to be their guide. He decided to take a chance. "Sir, beggin' your pardon, but how's we t' know we be findin' 'im? I means t' say, sir, what sorta' man be this imposter?"

"You've been told all you need to know. Find him. The dragon will help. And bring him to Mordeth. Alive." With that, Krotah turned briskly and made his way back into the shadowed halls that led to the main fortress, leaving Jelom dissatisfied and filled with questions.

"G'me a leg up . . ." Jelom ordered the gray-clad soldier who stood beside the great black dragon.

"Yessir," he replied, but all Flanx could think as he hefted the sergeant onto the beast's back was that Mithra needed to know of this.

* * * * *

By midmorning, the sun had burned through the overcast and sprinkled through the boughs until a kaleidoscope of light danced along Roy's path. The sunlight cheered him, and as his depression lifted, hunger swept in to take its place. Roy had eaten the last of his qomrah the day before and had seen none since he had left the beach area. Around him, the trees grew straight and moderately tall, with waxy leaves and pointed needles clinging to the branches, but no fruit. The underbrush was beginning to thin slightly, but it was still mostly berryless brambles and stiff grass. He considered digging for tubers, but his hunger was not yet so strong as to override his common sense.

By late afternoon, the trees had all but disappeared, until those remaining were little more than dwarf cousins of their lowland neighbors. The citadel-like rock thrust its head above the crowd of brush and miniature pines, and Roy tried to march a straight path toward it. The ground steepened into an incline of crumbling shale that tumbled into the distant gorge below as he climbed, the rattling of the flat stones sounding a hollow applause in the high, thin air. He crested a saddle and began a sloping descent to a valley below.

The opposite wall of the valley was an alpine meadow, with pale blue flowers pocking the dull green carpet of grass. Roy sat in a thick patch of the blue flowers, savoring their delicate fragrance and trying to imagine what the meadow would sound like if it were full of the sound of buzzing bees. Above, a single cloud glinted silver in the sunlight.

"*I wandered lonely as a Cloud/ That floats on high o'er vales and hills*," he quoted to a tiny blossom, its head bobbing in the light mountain breeze. "I wonder where I'll wander, and if I get there, I wonder if I'll know it." He picked the dainty flower and gently put it into his shirt pocket and continued up the hill. The dust puffed beneath his feet with every step; the sun poured down upon his exposed neck like an inquisitor's lantern.

Loneliness began to absorb his thoughts, and again they returned to Gwen, but the harder he tried to capture her face or voice, the more successfully they eluded him. He thought again of those last moments at the university, recalling with vivid detail the smell of ozone and the ear-splitting crack of lightning. Prior to that instant, his life was becoming increasingly less clear. Roy looked again at the tall stone monolith, a giant Citadel of hope and comfort. For the first time, he considered what it might be that was drawing him to it. Surely the hope of finding—much less being struck by—lightning was without rational merit. Even if he could manage to find a storm and be struck, what guarantee would there be that he wouldn't end up with a hole in his chest?

The stone finger of the monolith rose before him like a silencing gesture. Peace, it seemed to tell him. Peace and silence. Roy struggled with his own doubts, then finally, with a small shake of his head, surrendered to the quiet urge that drew him toward the stone. He trudged onward, trying not to think at all.

As Roy crested the ridge, the Citadel appeared like a solemn soldier guarding the surrounding mountains, the sinking sun shining upon the glossy granite and casting a long shadow deep into the east. He hurried his pace, his heart racing in the excitement of at last arriving at his destination. The land around the Citadel was a flat shelf full of shattered stones strewn across gray dirt. Short, gnarled trees formed a ring around the monolith, or perhaps the falling rock from the monolith had cleared a circle in the midst of the trees.

Roy stumbled through the dusk to the base of the giant stone, looking up at the pinnacle some two hundred yards above him. The sun dipped toward the western horizon, sliding elegantly toward the distant sea; the monolith stood as silent as a headstone in the wasteland circle. Roy's hunger gnawed inside of him like acid, driving a hole in his consciousness, forbidding him to concentrate. After circling the mammoth rock twice, he stood staring up at it until the sky was a frozen sphere of night riddled with starlight. Finally he slumped down with his back against the stone and slept.

Roy awoke from a dream of food and comfort and the distant sound of the now-familiar dream cry, a hunting scream that echoed in the morning silence. He opened his eyes and looked around at the empty sky, then closed his eyes again, trying to recapture his vision of two days before, to see again the monolith through the eyes of a dream. Nothing came, and yet he heard again the sound ringing off the granite before him, the harsh, killing sound of a bird of prey. He opened his eyes and looked again at the top of the Citadel.

A small silhouette circled high above him, brushing near to the side of the giant stone, then slowly circling like a falling leaf, coming nearer to Roy. A frightening memory leaped before Roy as he half expected the giant dragon to swoop down from the sky and slash his life from him. He raised his staff in an involuntary response, and hope returned to him: This falling object was no dragon, but a bird, albeit a fairly large one. Again the predator's call echoed through the air like a hunter's shaft, piercing into Roy's heart and making it ache with an unfamiliar, unexplainable joy. The bird continued to circle until it was only a few yards above his head, then gracefully steered in a large ellipse away from Roy, turning slowly, exposing its back to him. The falcon had something grasped in its golden talons. Roy noticed it and envied the bird, who at least had found his dinner. His stomach growled a sympathetic response.

Roy was unprepared for what happened next. The great bird continued his smooth descent, then veered toward Roy, head-high, crying again its victorious salute:

Ratha! The voice caused Roy to tremble, and he raised his staff in defense as the great bird rushed past his head. A rustling noise burst from behind him, and at first he thought he had struck the bird and brought him down. He turned and saw the bird a scant yard away, perched on the ground, a bloody rabbit clutched in its talons. The bird looked at Roy with an uncanny stare that seemed both intelligent and benevolent, then launched into the air with a powerful thrust.

The rabbit lay motionless at Roy's feet; he stooped and stroked the white and brown fur, matted in places with moist blood and still warm with body heat. The smell of blood tickled his nostrils as he bent over the rabbit, and his stomach tightened in hungry desire. His mouth watered with the thought of food—there, lying on the ground. Would the falcon return to claim its kill? Or was it a gift? Roy made his decision and plucked the rabbit from the ground, carrying it to the base of the Citadel. He craved a fire, loathing the thought of eating raw flesh, but fear of the hunting dragon dispersed any idea of building a cookfire; besides, Roy simply didn't have the energy to invest in building a fire with two dry sticks. He ripped the hide open with a sharp shale stone, pulling the skin away from the meat. Then, tearing a lean thigh from the carcass, he bit into the flesh. The blood dripped down his chin; the meat tasted surprisingly sweet, although thicker than he expected, as if the juices were a rich, succulent, meaty syrup.

Soon only white bones lay scattered at Roy's feet, with tiny bits of red flesh attached near the joints. The hide was stretched across a nearby stone, drying in the evening sunlight. For the first time in days, Roy could concentrate on something besides his own hunger and need for food; his thoughts immediately turned to the strange and peculiar hawk. He could imagine the blue-black feathers of the creature's back, the white speckled breast, the wings spread wide and filled with air as it sped toward him. How easily he could conjure the sound of the bird as it cried its hunting call: *Ratha!* The name was becoming familiar, the only living sound he had heard in a week. And it was a name, more than a sound, a name that brought an image instantly to mind, a memory—his own bizarre accident that had sent him spinning into this alien world, and that world seen through the eyes of another being. Roy spoke the name aloud, as if he were talking to an old friend: "Ratha."

Almost magically, the falcon swept down out of the sky even as the word died upon his lips.

* * * * *

"Milady, the Toad seems unconcerned. But the dragon's very presence speaks otherwise." The speaker was dressed in a soldier's gray, bearing the silver insignia of the Lorlitan infantry.

Mithra considered for a moment before answering. "And you're certain the only description Krotah gave was that the man was an imposter, Flanx?"

"Yes, milady. I was right there when he said it, not two arms' lengths away."

"A trick," Mithra whispered through clenched teeth.

"Perhaps," Stentor interjected. The old barkeep had kept his peace throughout the entire interview, but now he felt the need to speak out for caution. "The Toad is slippery and often hard to hold, and this is likely a trick, as you say. But the trick is not designed to disguise the return of Ratha. It is more likely he hopes to flush the Pradatha from hiding, hoping we will follow him to Shymney to find our salvation, but finding only our destruction."

"No!" Mithra snapped. In her heart, she knew that what Stentor said was likely to be true, but she yearned for the return of her love. Fifteen years of waiting for a promise to be fulfilled, and now it seemed so close. She grasped at the hope and held fast.

"We must consider all possibilities," Stentor said softly. "We must look for the trap and hope for the truth. It is who we are, Mithra."

Mithra turned and looked severely at the older man. "It is who we are," she repeated, then turned to the gray-clad soldier. "Thank you, Flanx. Come again as soon as you hear more."

"Yes, milady," Flanx replied, then turned and exited the room.

"What shall we do, Stentor? What shall we do?"

Stentor gently rocked the mug of ale he held in his hand, looking into the soft, foamy head as it swirled. "Be cautious, Mithra. But be ready. Send out the news that the time may be near. And then wait."

"Wait," Mithra repeated, the word all too familiar. "Wait . . ."

*   *   *   *   *

Ratha.

The falcon looked longingly at the startled English professor. Roy repeated the name: "Ratha." The bird's head bobbed up and down in earnest approval.

"Your name is Ratha?" Roy asked hopefully.

The bird stretched out its wings and, with a single beat, launched into the air and sped away. Before many moments had gone by, the falcon returned, dropping to the ground and pacing in front of Roy in an anxious waddle, bobbing its head and clucking in an urgent manner.

Without conscious thought, Roy looked up at the apex of the Citadel, his bastion of hope, as if it had called to him. He looked again at the bird, watching him with the motionless patience of a raptor. Once more Roy was filled with the memory of his fall from the bell tower, the cry of *Ratha* piercing his mind and soul, and the all-absorbing eyes of the falcon floating before him. *Ratha*, the voice had called. *Ratha Keshia-ne*.

His mouth was dry and he licked his lips uselessly. The voice claimed his presence, demanded him to come. He could sense that now and knew that he could not refuse. *Ratha*, it had said, *Ratha Keshia-ne*, and somehow the voice had called him, Roy Arthre, and brought him to this place. And now it demanded that he speak the words aloud.

"Ratha," Roy rasped. "Ratha Keshia-ne." And with a suddenness that rivaled the burst of lightning that had sent him into this alien world, his mind erupted with a thousand foreign images.

Ratha, the bird repeated.

Roy looked up and smiled with instant surprise. "Yes, I understand you," he replied, both shocked and delighted.

Ratha! the bird spoke, and Roy's mind was instantly filled with a new vision.

"Yes, I'll follow you. I see it's not far."

The falcon launched into the air and landed on an

outstretched limb of a small fir tree. Roy followed and found hidden in the undergrowth a shaft dug into the living stone, wide enough for two men to enter alongside each other.

"Well, then, let's go," he ordered and began to climb down into the pit.

Roy's first surprise was finding worn, steplike protuberances along the stone wall of the hole. He discovered he could climb down the steps much like descending a ladder. After several meters of climbing, his feet touched upon firm ground. Roy tapped the floor with his staff and heard the crisp sound of wood on stone. The falcon scuffed the stone beside him.

"So what now? I'm blind down here."

Ratha, the bird replied. As the sound rattled in the hollow chamber, a replay of the accident that had sent him to this world echoed through Roy's mind. The bird's voice reverberated off a distant wall and came back to him with the sound of the final words of his strange vision: *Ratha. Ratha Keshia-ne*. The sound startled him from his reverie.

"Ratha. It's a *name*. Ratha Keshia-ne." As he whispered the words, a faint tremble rocked the walls and floors of the dark cavern.

"*And the very Stones will shout!*" he said with a nervous laugh. "Bird, I'm not so sure I like it here. Which is worse? To be crushed underground in an earthquake, or to be eaten by a hungry dragon?"

The falcon screamed an angry protest when Roy mentioned the word "dragon." He could hear the agitated movement of the bird in the close confines of the dark cavern.

"I'm sorry, bird," Roy said, suppressing a shudder.

"I'm not fond of the beast, either, but I still need some kind of light."

The falcon was silent for several moments. Then, in as near a whisper as is possible for a bird, Roy heard it say, *Ratha*.

An image floated into Roy's peripheral vision, fleeing as he turned to view it. His eyes darted through the total darkness, trying to capture a firm look at it. Frustrated, he closed his eyes and quit resisting, letting the falcon's voice lead his mind, and the image came directly to him.

Roy saw a fire, burning large and bright in the warmth of a summer day. Dozens of men—tall, gaunt, sinewy men—stood around the fire staring at an old man and a young boy, the boy standing with a large falcon on his shoulder, staring into the fire. The old man spoke many words that Roy could not quite catch, but suddenly his voice erupted like a peal of thunder: "Quintah!" Then the boy reached into the fire and pulled a long piece of wood from it.

"It's me," Roy whispered. "I swear, it's me I see there. Or who I was, a long time ago. So many years," he said, sweeping his fingers through his graying hair. "But how could it be me? That's not something I've ever done. Bird, I'm going crazy."

The falcon flapped his wings and the image vanished, leaving Roy again in the penetrating darkness of the underground chamber.

"Was that you—with the boy, I mean? And who was the old man?" Roy closed his eyes in a vain attempt to regain the vision. "What was it all about? What was the stick he pulled from the fire?" Roy squeezed the staff in his own hand.

Ratha, the bird answered, and Roy knew that the staff

he held was the same one the boy had pulled from the fire.

"Yes, and the word the old man said. That I remember. Quintah." As Roy spoke the word, his staff began to vibrate softly, then the hawk eye began to glow with golden light. He threw the staff from him in terror. Immediately the light disappeared.

"Christ! What the hell was that?" he asked. Silence answered him. "Are you there, bird?" Now the silence scolded.

"Bird?" A minute sound rose up to him, thick and disdaining.

Ratha, the bird replied, and Roy sensed the falcon considered the glowing staff no danger at all.

"Fine. Help me find it, will you?" Roy listened for the sound of the bird as it moved toward the staff and moved slowly in that direction himself, groping along the floor until he felt the smooth wood against his hand.

"Okay, we'll try again." He sucked a ragged breath and squeezed the staff. "Quintah," he said, and the staff quivered in his hand, the warm glow spreading across the hawk eye until the chamber was flooded with delicious light.

Roy shook his head incredulously, then laughed aloud. "I suppose 'Quintah' means 'flashlight.' I don't suppose you know the words for 'steak' and 'lobster.' " The falcon cocked his head to one side and looked back at Roy, his eyes glinting humorously in the amber light. "No, I thought not."

Roy turned slowly around, inspecting for the first time the stone chamber in which he stood. The walls were smooth, polished granite, with chips of mica glistening against the white rock; the floor was a stone slab

that squared perfectly with the walls. He could see no
seams in either surface. The atmosphere of the corridor
reeked of antiquity, and Roy felt the urge to kneel and
pray, as if he sensed he were in a holy place. Roy silently
wondered if the place held some kind of power, power
enough to call him, to draw him here for some hidden
purpose.

"The inner sanctum," Roy whispered, and the soft
sounds echoed lightly down the hall. "It rings in here
like a bell." Thoughts of the high belfry in the heart of
the university came back to Roy, thoughts that merged
almost immediately into the young, brown-haired woman whom he had never told he loved. Poor Gwen, he
thought. Poor me.

"Lead on, my friend," he said to the bird, and it fluttered and hopped down the corridor, Roy following
closely behind.

The hallway led in a straight line that Roy guessed to
be west. The ease with which he walked gave him the
impression that it led downward. The corridor had several intersecting halls leading into it, but the falcon continued on straight ahead. They had walked for several
minutes, traveling some two hundred yards, when the
falcon suddenly left the main hall and veered into a side
passage. This passage was narrower than the first, and
the walls were not as polished, but there was still ample
room for two men to walk abreast. After another twenty-
five yards, the hallway intersected a stairway leading
down. The falcon launched itself into the air and flew to
the base of the steps, waiting there for Roy to catch up,
then taking off again when Roy finally made it to the
bottom.

The bird led Roy through several more turns, down

another flight of stairs, then through more turns before they emerged in a large, round room. Roy guessed that it was even larger than the regency room back at State, although it had the same quiet austerity that that room had. The walls glistened in the light from the staff. Then Roy felt movement, like a breath upon his neck. Quickly he looked up at the ceiling of the room, only to find that there was none there. Above him, three stars blinked coldly in the black of night.

The falcon didn't stop to view the constellations, however, and Roy had to trot to catch up with it again. Through at least a dozen more twists and turns, Roy followed the impatient bird, until at last the corridor ended in a stone compartment about two yards square. The remains of some decayed material were piled on one side, and a tattered, dusty blanket sat folded in a corner.

"People," Roy managed to utter. "People have lived here! But who?"

Ratha, said the bird, and Roy released his mind to the flood of wordless pictures that instantly appeared. Roy could see a man hunched over a book, scribbling frantically into it. Nestled into the crook of the man's arm was a glowing staff. The man looked up, and Roy saw his own face.

"Me? I've been here before?"

The falcon chirped, and Roy felt the definite no of his answer.

Roy walked over to the blanket and picked it up. Although old, it seemed to be in good shape, though the dust billowed from it like ocean fog. As he shook the dust from the blanket, his foot kicked against a solid object. Roy looked down at the floor and felt his stomach lurch as he recognized the familiar shape.

"The book." He bent to retrieve his treasure. Instant disappointment crashed upon him as he opened it to the title page and saw an unfamiliar script.

"I don't understand," he muttered, holding the book out to the falcon.

Ratha, the bird replied, and Roy envisioned an entire lifetime of learning. He could see himself in a small room, an old, unfamiliar man reading to him from a large, well-worn tome. Roy looked again at the letters on the page, and slowly, steadily, each became more familiar, until at last the word on the title page became clear.

Ratha, it read. *Ratha Keshia-ne*.

❖ CHAPTER SIX ❖

Discovered

Kreosoath landed on the packed sands of the western harbor. Immediately the two men jumped from his back, glad to be on the ground again. The giant dragon sniffed the air, searching for the spore of his prey. The morning breeze brought a hint of sea with it, causing Kreosoath to shudder in distaste. He inched closer to the forest.

Roy's camp lay abandoned beneath the lee of the *cocantha* tree, the fire pit a cold, black imprint on the ground. Kreosoath sniffed the ashes, trying to estimate how long it had been since there had been a fire. Two days, he thought, growling his low rumble that raised the hair on the necks of Grev and Jelom, Krotah's two scouts. Too long of a head start in this country.

Kreosoath waddled up the beach, keeping well away from the tide line, smelling the trail between the camp and the tiny stream. The scent could only be found between the two landmarks. Neither north nor south, the dragon thought. He glanced furtively at the jam of logs that made an island in the high tide. Kreosoath emitted a low rumble, tossing his head in the direction of the pile, until one of the scouts waded through the swirling tide and searched the area unsuccessfully.

Gone. But where would Ratha go? the dragon wondered. He became visibly agitated, pacing in large, sweeping circles, the guards giving the dangerous dragon generous space. Kreosoath looked out to sea, wondering momentarily if the wily wizard had dared to cross the channel to the island some ten miles to the west. No, he thought. It was a fool's errand to hazard the sea and its currents without a ship. The dragon turned and faced east.

The black eyes of the dragon sparkled like the sharp edge of a knife in the rising sun, penetrating the thick forest. He saw the great stone monolith, that which men called Shymney, rising solitary from the desolate earth. No, the Archmage would not return there, to the place of his defeat. The dragon swept the image away with a shake of his huge head.

Kreosoath pressed his great body through the densely packed trees, walking parallel to the shore, his nostrils flaring as he scented the ground. Near the stream, a faint odor was discernible, and the dragon followed it eastward, toward the distant mountains. The two scouts followed closely behind.

The trail continued inland for several miles, then began a long, sweeping curve back toward the sea. Devious wizard, the dragon thought, to turn inland, then back to the sea.

The dragon continued to follow the trail, crushing the underbrush and small trees that blocked his way. The progress was slow, for even the strength of the dragon diminished with the arduous work. By late evening, the great lizard collapsed from exhaustion and slept in the midst of the forest.

Early the next morning, the rising sun slashed through the trees and pierced the closed eyes of the two scouts. They awoke to find themselves alone in the quiet forest, the dragon gone, a wide path crushed through the forest. They hastily followed, catching up to the dragon by midmorning. The giant beast was sitting next to a *benetha* tree, looking to the east. As the soldiers approached, the dragon uttered an angry roar that sent them diving into the nearby bush.

Kreosoath was angry, for the foxy wizard had led him in a circle, beginning inland, then toward the sea, and now back toward the mountains. It was difficult for him to walk, since his body was used to flying. His huge legs ached with cramps, and his talons were tattered with the abuse. Now he must walk some more, and more, then perhaps even more, and still the mage would elude him. Another bellow rocked the silent forest.

Kreosoath lumbered forward, following the trail farther inland. His movement slowed as the pain increased in his legs. By late afternoon, the pace was as slow as the steady plod of a *rencha* beast, the heavy-footed plow animal of the lowland farms. The guards, unable to understand the dragon's rumblings, thought that they were closing in on their prey and were bewildered when the dragon folded himself into a mound and fell asleep, the sun still high in the west. They sat a respectful distance from the beast, digging through their packs and retrieving dried meat. They slowly chewed the jerky until the darkness came and brought sleep with it.

For two more days, the dragon acted the bloodhound and the guards followed, ever higher into the mountains. Neither Grev nor Jelom dared to say a word in the dragon's presence. Krotah's orders had been specific on that count.

Progress slowed as the trail grew colder, the dragon more weary. The fifth day after leaving Roy's camp, Shymney rose high above the horizon, the blue sky accenting its white walls. Jelom made a quick sign of protection. He had heard the story of the place, of their master's victory over the great Archmage Ratha and his subsequent claim of the power of darkness. It was not a place that men chose to go, especially in the company of the Lord of Dragons.

In the late afternoon of the sixth day of the chase, nine days after Kreosoath had last seen Ratha on the beach, the three hunters breached the final hill and stood inside the desolate ring of vegetation that surrounded Shymney. The smell of the quarry was thick in the circle, and the dragon snarled a contented sound, the scouts uncertain of its meaning. Kreosoath suddenly sprang into the air, circling the giant monolith, savoring the delicious feeling of flight. The guards stood watching him in the gathering dusk. As they did, a puff of white smoke wafted from atop the monolith. Each scout turned silently and looked at the other.

*　*　*　*　*

Roy sat beside his cookfire in the large room in the heart of the stone monolith, smoke and the smell of roasting meat spiraling up and out through the opening high above. Moratha, the Lord of Falcons, sat next to Roy, chewing a piece of rabbit flesh as he watched the professor-turned-mage study the book before him.

"Moratha, from what I can understand from this, this mage, Ratha, was your friend, and he married a woman named Mithra. He seems to have worked for a man named Gondsped. Am I right?"

The falcon tilted its head, a piece of meat dangling from its beak, and chirped. A picture formed in Roy's mind, a portrait of him and a beautiful woman sitting beneath a tree, the falcon resting in the branches. The picture soon dissolved and another formed, a picture of him standing before a crowned figure, then kneeling before him and finally rising to exit the chamber.

"I thought so," Roy replied. The curious method of talking with pictures disturbed Roy, but as he communicated more frequently with the intelligent bird, the pictures became more commonplace, until at last Roy could treat them like any other form of communication, not unlike the holograms of the regency room.

"You have taught me well, Moratha, my friend," Roy said, scratching the great bird on the back of its head. "But back to business. This book is a sort of diary, it appears to me, written by a magician named Ratha. He was your master." The great hawk twisted its regal head and blinked. Roy quickly corrected himself. "He was your friend. But am I to glean from this that I've been called to take his place? Is that why the picture images you send me always have my face superimposed on his?"

Moratha blinked at Roy, then turned and waddled over to the thick, heavy book and pecked at the open page.

"Okay, so back to the book before I can get the answer. Tell me where you want me to stop." Roy leafed slowly through the pages until the falcon's voice ordered him to stop. Roy began to read.

"*Morlin has had me banished,*" Roy read aloud, "*and I have left Mithra at Westport, fleeing to Shymney, hoping there to gather my power and wage a reluctant war against the murderous Regent. I have spent many hours trying to contact another plane of existence in order to bring an ally to this world to help us in the war. I fear I will either be too late or otherwise unable to accomplish this task, and that Morlin will discover me and my plan.*"

"It's true, then. I *am* the person Ratha brought to this world. But why? I'm no warrior. I have no magic of my own, and this world seems to abound in magic of one sort or another. Why call me and not someone else, someone with the skill to fight this Morlin?"

The bird looked up at Roy, a plaintive expression on its hawkish face. Roy wished the the bird could talk to him in other than the picture language. Although it was more than sufficient to relay a story, the picture language was inadequate for some things. It simply could not deal with conjecture or the realm of ideas. As far as Roy could tell, all that Moratha could show him were vivid glimpses of actual events.

"I'm tired, Moratha," he said, yawning and stretching his arms. "I'll sleep now. Later, perhaps, we can struggle through this tome and find more answers." He left the falcon resting alone in the warmth of the dying fire.

* * * * *

Morning stirred its warm breath over the circle of desolation, eddies of dust waltzing slowly across the open area. The black dragon emerged from the shadowed recesses of the forest, the two scouts walking tentatively behind him. The dragon growled and tossed his head toward his back, signaling the two men to mount. Reluctantly they climbed up on the tough, leathery back and clung to a spiny ridge. The dragon unfurled its wings and launched itself gracefully into the air.

Kreosoath circled the stone monolith, gaining altitude in a slow, steady arc. The two guards pressed their frightened bodies down against the unyielding hide of the dragon. Jelom murmured a prayer of protection, gaining little more than a dour look from his companion. The dragon glided across the sky, sweeping toward the head of the granite pillar, its great wings opening to slow itself as the stone grew closer. With a barely audible sound, the dragon alighted and perched on the peak of Shymney.

The two guards looked at the ground several hundred yards below, then at the narrow ledge atop the monolith. In the center of the flat landing atop the monolith was a hole, apparently drilled into the heart of the stone, perhaps a yard across and nearly perfectly round. The dragon turned its head toward the two men, then looked disdainfully at the hole. The meaning was clear. The dragon wanted them to go down the hole and hunt for their quarry. The scouts dismounted, and Kreosoath launched away from the stone, leaving the two men stranded.

"Who goes first?" Grev asked.

Jelom looked down the chimney and shuddered involuntarily. "How's about we goes together?"

Grev looked again into the hole. "How about I just go first?" Silently he was pleased to see Jelom show fear. He hoped that he could find some way to use it to his advantage.

Pressing his back against one side and his booted feet against the other, Grev began his slow descent through the smoke-filled hole with Jelom following. Soon Grev could make out what appeared to be a red eye glaring out of the darkness of the spiraling smoke.

The shaft extended deep into the stone. One after the other, the two scouts scuttled down the chimney until the red eye, which Grev now recognized as a fire, was only ten yards below, but they could go no farther, since the shaft ended at the ceiling of a large, round room. The cathedral-like silence of the room echoed and re-echoed the slightest sound they made until they couldn't trust their senses. They dangled above the ground, waiting for a telltale movement. The fire glowed a dull and hostile red, its smoke curling past them up to the blue sky above. Finally Grev gave a signal to Jelom, then let loose his grip and dropped to the floor with a heavy thud. Jelom followed as Grev strung his bow and nocked an arrow.

A sharp pain shot through Jelom's body as he hit the floor, his ankle twisting awkwardly beneath him. Sprawling headlong across the floor, he writhed in agony, his ankle a searing knot of flame. He tried to suppress a moan but could not, and the sound echoed through the chamber and down the corridors into the surrounding darknesss. Grev pressed a rough hand over the injured man's mouth, pressing so hard that Jelom turned a ghostly white in the wavering light. Tears formed in Jelom's eyes, but finally he relaxed slightly and Grev released his grip.

With an abrupt motion, Grev indicated that Jelom should remain behind him. He was feeling pleased with the turn of events; when the imposter was captured, Grev could take all the credit. He dug through his pack, withdrew a small hooded lantern, and lit it with a smoldering brand from the fire. Then he stood and walked toward a darkened corridor.

Silence smothered Grev like a wet, heavy blanket. At every junction, he stopped to listen, and when he was satisfied he heard nothing, he took a piece of chalk from his pocket and made a small symbol on the stone floor. Slowly he wove his way through the oppressive passages, the lantern held high in one hand, his bow in the other. Quietly he stalked his prey, trusting his instincts to find the place where the imposter hid.

The thoughts that passed through Grev's mind were mostly of the hunt, but as in the mind of a mongrel dog, one thought persisted, begging for attention, no matter how often he tried to drive it away. Who was he hunting? Krotah had said only that an imposter was living in the western forests. He had not said who this man was or whom he was impersonating. The dragon, curse him, was useless as an informant. And Krotah's orders had been few and explicit: no talking on the journey, for words might be their death; find the imposter; and bring him back to Mordeth— alive.

Hours passed as he paced through the empty hallways, wandering through the honeycombed corridors, vainly looking for his elusive prey. He gauged that the time must be getting near sunset, but it was only a guess, perhaps distorted by the darkness and the silence. He bent to draw another symbol on the floor, then turned down yet another passage.

*　*　*　*　*

Kreosoath sunned himself on a flat stretch of stone pressed into the surrounding mountains. Occasionally he flipped dust on his back, but one eye was always watching the top of the Citadel. The two scouts had been deposited atop the monolith, and all the great dragon could do now was wait and rest his aching muscles. Although he had never been inside the catacombs—his own body too bulky to fit through the passages—he had heard the tales of ancient men, the ones who claimed to have built the granite structure, and he well knew the vast expanse of paths that tunneled beneath the surrounding mountains. To find one man in the midst of such a place would take time. Considerable time. And Kreosoath was not opposed to the rest such time would afford him.

A distant voice startled the great dragon, a human voice, familiar and frightening to him. He tried to disperse the fear, a feeling not often felt by his kind, but the voice held such power that the effort was useless. He hurriedly ambled into the shadows of the forest, a motionless heap of blackness in the deep green of trees, and waited as the voice approached.

"Did he ever tell you who I was?" asked the voice.

Ratha, came the answer. The dragon was instantly alert, recognizing the sound of the Lord of Falcons.

"No? And you have no vision of my world? No way to see into it? Then it was simply by chance that I, and not someone else, was summoned. It was little more than a cosmic accident—or joke."

The falcon responded with a short series of chirps and whistles, and Roy envisioned a book and a group of strangers gathered about it, taking turns reading from it.

"I know that's not the Archmage's diary, but I can't seem to focus on what exactly it is. Is it some sort of book of law?" Even as he asked, Roy knew that his assumption was wrong. There was a feeling of love, as well as awe, attached to the book. The sensation reminded him of home.

"In my world," Roy said wistfully, "we have poetry. Of course, we aren't allowed to teach it, except as historical fact. For my people, poetry is a colossal waste of time, having no intrinsic value since it is only art. Science is vastly more important. Anyway, poetry is difficult to describe. Sometimes it's metered verse, while other times it's free from the confines of meter. Some poetry has rhyming lines, while others avoid rhyme. Most poetry, though, has imagery. It paints pictures inside your mind, much like the pictures you create for me. Do you have poetry on Keshia?"

Ratha, said the bird.

"I thought not. Well, I thoroughly enjoy it. I'd like to teach it as a regular subject, but the Regents won't allow such trivial use of time by one of their staff. We have problems with Regents where I come from, too."

Ratha, the falcon replied.

"Yes, well, I suppose a demonstration would be more useful than an explanation. Let me think. Ah, yes, here's one you might like.

"*The rainbow comes and goes,*
And lovely is the rose.
The moon doth with delight
Look round her when the heavens are bare.
Waters on a starry night
Are beautiful and fair;

The sunshine is a glorious birth;
But yet I know, where'er I go,
That there hath passed away a glory from the earth.

"It goes on for pages. It was written by a man named Wordsworth, who is one of the favorite poets of my friend, Gwen. You'd like her, Moratha."

Ratha, the falcon replied.

Kreosoath shuddered involuntarily at the mention of the Archmage's familiar, Moratha, the Lord of Falcons. Surely the Archmage had returned, then. Kreosoath sank deeper into the shadows, waiting silently. The moments ground by as the voice of the Archmage spoke of strange and exotic things. The dragon listened to the poetry, words that held a mysterious, alien power, lulling the lizard with their musical quality. Soon—too soon, thought the dragon—the Archmage and falcon moved away, leaving Kreosoath both relieved and somehow oddly disappointed.

Roy strolled through the dwarf forest, Moratha on his shoulder, the thick brush licking his legs, the dusk of evening dissolving the colors of the day. He looked up at the towering silhouette of the monolith and felt again the strange, alien power that radiated from it. He could feel it seeping into his heart, into his mind, mingling with his own past, somehow creating a new future, and with it a new person. Roy couldn't help feel that he was being subtly altered by the force of that stone, or what the stone represented. He only wished he could understand all the strange visions that Moratha sent him.

Roy stepped through the *marelock* bushes and into the entrance to the catacombs, his staff pulsing light as he spoke the Word of Power. The network of passages had become familiar to Roy, who had taken it upon himself to explore the myriads of intertwining halls. He felt as if he could guide himself through their many turns in total darkness, although he was happy enough to have the light of his staff. Roy had gotten into the habit of reading as he walked, the staff casting light upon the open pages of the mage's diary, Moratha nestled next to his ear, watching as the former professor read each word aloud. Roy was reading the passage about the use of the Staff of Quintah when the falcon let out a startled cry.

Roy looked up just in time to see a short, sturdy man with coal-black hair looking back at him down the shaft of a drawn arrow. Reflexively Roy jumped aside, clutched the book against his chest, and raised his staff before him. The arrow flew toward his heart, the sharp twang of the bowstring singing in the stone corridor.

Grev cursed aloud, thinking he had inadvertently killed the man he was supposed to capture. But such thoughts were short-lived.

Instantly Moratha leapt into the air, screaming an angry threat. The arrow struck the thick volume pressed against Roy's chest, piercing the cover and first few pages, stopping a finger's length from his heart.

Then the power of the monolith, with its queer life-warping ability, took over. Roy had a sudden vision of himself raising the staff and shouting.

"Quintah!" Roy called out, surprising even himself, and immediately his staff glowed fiercely, exploding in a rhythm of color. The brilliant light flew across the space between him and the scout, who let out a scream, then collapsed in a motionless heap. The falcon lit upon him, standing sentry upon the attacker, watching warily for any sign of further ambush.

"Is he . . . dead?" Roy needn't have asked the question. He had felt the power surge through his body and out the staff like a bolt of lightning.

Moratha's only reply was the slow swivel of his head as his eyes penetrated the surrounding shadows. Now Roy began to be aware of the possibility of other attackers, and his senses pricked to full alert. In his mind, he pictured a softer, less conspicuous light, and the staff dimmed until the light glowed feebly.

"Who is he?" Roy asked.

Ratha, replied Moratha, and the image of a dark lord sprang instantly into his mind.

"Are there more of them?" he asked, his voice full of dread and expectation.

Moratha turned his head like a turret, inspecting the halls with his keen sight. Apparently satisfied, the falcon clucked softly.

"Yes, it is always better to be the hunter than the hunted," Roy answered. "Where do we search?"

The falcon launched into a slow flight, and Roy began to jog to keep up with it. They raced down the halls, stopping at each junction to allow Moratha a chance to inspect the area, looking for signs of other intruders. The bird's keen eyes spotted a mark on the floor, and he beckoned to Roy to come and look.

"It appears to be some kind of signaling device, probably to help him find his way back. Best not to leave it; others might follow." Roy rubbed the chalk symbol from the floor with the heel of his boot.

The two companions retraced the path of the dead scout, with Roy erasing each symbol as they came upon it. The path led through a tangled maze toward the heart of the stone, finally stopping at the great chamber, where the fire was now merely a black spot on the granite floor. Beside the dead fire was a wounded scout, his ankle thick with swelling and his face ashen with pain and fear. Roy could sense the fear and decided to use it, igniting his staff in radiant color, the light piercing the shadows and putting them to flight.

"Who are you? How many others are with you?" Roy's voice boomed in the hall. The scout shook as if stricken by a blow.

"Two. Myself an' one more. We come from Mordeth's keep." Jelom's voice cracked with nervousness, and he quickly made a sign to ward off evil.

"Who is Mordeth?" Roy demanded.

Jelom looked astonished that Roy needed to ask. "Why, 'e's Mordeth, the Dark Lord. 'E's th' Regent." Jelom looked at the pulsing staff Roy held aloft. "As surely as you be th' great Archmage. I've heard th' tales. Please spare me."

Roy stood looking at the injured man, wondering what to do next. He had no heart for killing; the blood of one man was already eating at his conscience. Mordeth was a name he hadn't seen in the Archmage's diary. Who was he? Roy was sure that the name of the Regent was Morlin. Roy shook his head, trying to dislodge some of the confusion.

Finally he straightened and glared at the injured man, taking his cue from the man's own fear. "If you fear me, by your life, flee this place and go to your master. Tell him that the Archmage is dead. Leave us!" Roy's voice echoed like a peal of thunder, shaking the frightened man even more.

"But I cannot climb; my leg . . ."

"Then we will guide you to the exit," Roy responded,

approaching the injured man. He took the man's dagger and ripped a long strip of cloth from the scout's dirty tunic, binding his eyes with the rough blindlfold. Roy jerked him roughly to his feet, and they began the slow journey through the catacombs to the southern exit. Roy literally dragged the crippled man through the brush and deposited him outside the Citadel. As he looked up at the monolith, Roy's mind was momentarily flooded with a strange vision. He hoped he understood its meaning.

Roy turned sharply and walked over to the edge of the brush, where he spotted two fairly straight pieces of deadwood. He brought them back to the injured man and knelt down beside him.

"I don't know if this will do any good, but I can't just send you off on that injured leg." Without further explanation, Roy positioned one piece of wood on each side of the man's leg, then removed his blindfold and wrapped it tightly around the man's leg to form a makeshift splint. Finally he touched his staff gently to the injured ankle and whispered a single word: "Quintah."

Jelom felt a sudden coolness wash over the ankle. Although it still ached, the jagged pain that had been there moments earlier had vanished.

"Now go!" Roy ordered, and the man stood up and hobbled down the hill, away from the monolith and the frightening Archmage.

"Well, I guess that should take care of that," Roy said to Moratha. The bird looked unhappy.

"I couldn't kill him. I just couldn't," Roy replied, trying to convince himself as much as his friend. He was frightened at how easily he had accepted the killing of the first man, the first human he had seen in nearly two weeks. He looked at Moratha doubtfully. The falcon blinked thoughtfully but offered no solace. Without another word, Roy turned and went back into the heart of the mountain.

*   *   *   *   *

Jelom stumbled down the hill about a hundred yards, barely glancing behind to see if the angry Archmage followed. The pain in his ankle had diminished at the touch of the staff, but it hadn't healed the break, and he couldn't move quickly without putting weight on it. He entered a small clearing in the forest and whistled. Soon a shadow spread before him, blackening the sun. Dust kicked into the air as the dragon landed beside him.

"It be Ratha! By your dragon's brood, it were! Quick, back to Mordeth," he ordered the dragon. If Jelom's fear of the Archmage had been less, he might have noticed the dragon's peculiar expression or the fact that he didn't even growl at him when he dared to issue orders. But his fear of the Archmage blinded him and overcame his fear of Kreosoath and the long flight to Morlidra. He climbed gingerly upon the dragon's back.

The dragon lifted off the ground and sped north to Lorlita, the City of Light.

❖ CHAPTER SEVEN ❖

The Falcon Sighted

"Imbecile!" Jelom flinched at the acid in his master's voice. "You dare return to me without the imposter? Coward! Idiot!" Mordeth struck a vicious blow across the man's lowered head, then turned sharply and marched back to his ebon throne.

Mordeth's face was without emotion as he sank slowly onto the black stone chair. "Krotah," he said, his voice chill, "have him executed at once."

The frightened scout fell to his knees, sobbing. "Lord, I beg o' ye', have mercy. Grev vanished, I tell ye', left me alone, and me wi' my poor ankle burnin' and twisted-like. He ne'er came back. What was I t' do? I couldn't fight 'im, Master, not alone, and him wi' that bird flutterin' round about. An' he had a killin' stick, Master, a staff that glowed and burned. I didst the bes' a man could do, Master, and I got myself back here t' tell ye' jus' wha' I saw. For mercy's sake, Master, have pity!"

Mordeth stared unblinking at Jelom's prostrate form. His mouth barely moved when he pronounced his decision. "Execute him," he repeated.

Krotah nodded at the three palace guards standing by the door. Quickly they marched over to the quivering scout and dragged him out of the room, leaving Mordeth alone with Krotah and Kreosoath. The giant dragon lay in his customary spot, his tail curled around his sinuous body, wings folded in the relatively close confines of the palace receiving room. His languorous appearance belied his alert senses. The dragon watched as Krotah flitted around his master like a fly on a dung heap. Mordeth dropped heavily onto his throne and plucked the Translating Stone from the adjoining table, turning to address the lizard.

"Tell me, O weak and treacherous beast, why did you return without the imposter?"

"He is no imposter, Mordeth," rumbled Kreosoath's voice through the stone. "It was surely Ratha. The scout told you not, and now his head is severed from his body and cannot, but this he told me: The mage held a book of gilded pages and blackened leather, an arrow shaft broken in the cover. The book itself protected the wordly wizard. He held the staff. Fire spat from his staff, and the falcon crooned into his ear.

"You know Ratha's weakness. The scout was injured, and the mage let him go free, unable to destroy a defenseless man, unable to wield his power to do what must be done. You also know the mage's strength: He is master of the Three-That-Bind. He held the book. He allowed your servant to live. He is no imposter."

"You were deceived, dragon. He is an imposter. I know Ratha's power. I can sense it. It is finished."

"Then know this, Lord of Darkness," translated the stone. "I heard the mage's voice and felt the power's chains wrap about me. Only one who masters the Three-

That-Bind can claim dragonkind as servant. He has that power; I fear that he will enslave my kind. Be wary.

"Know also this: I am and remain your ally of necessity, not of love. Be twice wary." Even the stone's monotone voice carried Kreosoath's contempt.

"Do not threaten me, worthless lizard." The light in the chamber grew visibly dim as the Regent spoke, and even the great Lord of Dragons trembled at the power in the voice. "Now leave, before I sell your hide for boot leather. Go!"

Kreosoath stood glaring at the Regent as if he wished to say something more. Instead he turned quickly and exited through the wide double doors, his flanks brushing the jambs as he went.

"Krotah," Mordeth whispered when the beast had left the room.

"Yes, Mordeth?"

"Let your spies spread some news for all to hear. I want it known that Mordeth plans to personally train his troops. It's not good for an army to become soft with too much easy city life. I plan to lead them on a march, perhaps to the western harbor—or even better, to Shymney, so that the ranks can once again swear their allegiance to me at the foot of the Archmage's tombstone."

Krotah smiled weakly. "Yes, my lord. When shall they say we depart?"

"Within the week," Mordeth replied as he turned and left the hall.

"Yes, my lord," Krotah murmured, waiting until the dull click of Mordeth's boots against the stone floor had vanished before calling for servants to begin the preparations.

* * * * *

"Mordeth prepares to move," the man began. He sat at the rough wooden table of Stentor's inn, staring down at a half-filled mug of ale. The meats on the platter before him remained largely untouched, the conversation too important to consider eating.

"You are certain of this, Flanx? We must be certain."

"Mithra, I tell you, the word is out that we are to begin maneuvers. Rumor says we head for Shymney by week's end. Milady, you know as well as I that the armies of the Dark Lord have never been summoned together to one place since the fall of Ratha. What else can it be?"

Mithra looked back into the pale blue eyes of the man across the table from her. He was a loyal follower, a spy deep in the heart of the Regent's camp. She needed to trust him, and yet there was a dark worry that pressed upon her: Could this be another trap that the devious traitor had plotted for her capture and the destruction of the Pradatha?

"Flanx, you must find out the true intent of the marshaling. I fear a trap. But if Ratha has indeed returned—and it is my fervent prayer that he has—then he will need us with him to help him defeat Mordeth. Return to Morlidra and keep your ears open. Truth keep you, my friend."

"And Pradatha you, Mithra," Flanx responded. He stood up and set a small silver coin on the table, conscious of the possibility that he was being watched, then turned and left the inn.

"What do you think, Mithra?" Stentor had been standing nearby, waiting for the conversation to end.

"I think that the Dark Lord baits us. I hope it is true that Ratha has returned, but it may be a trick. In either event, the Pradatha underground must be alerted. Have messengers sent to our leaders. Prepare them. They must be ready."

"Right away, milady." Stentor nodded in the direction of one of the inn's patrons standing at the bar. The man turned and left through the door. The movement did not go unnoticed by Mithra.

"You know me too well, Stentor. You always have planned for every contingency."

Her gentle laugh coaxed a half-smile from the grim innkeeper. "Then I should also inform you that my good wife humbly suggests that you should go directly to bed and sleep for not less than twelve hours."

"Ah, Tralaina always thinks I should be asleep. If she had her way, I would doze through the Third Age!" Mithra laughed, and her eyes sparkled with the warmth of the banked fire pulsing on the inn's great stone hearth.

"On this particular occasion, I must agree with her. But for the love of the book, don't tell her I said so. She might begin to expect me to always agree with her." Stentor's face was so grim in the red glow of the fire that Mithra laughed again, but she stood and headed toward the stairs leading to the upper floor's sleeping rooms.

"Awaken me when your messengers return." The leader of Keshia's Pradatha disappeared into the shadows.

"As you will, milady," Stentor whispered as her steps evaporated into the night.

* * * * *

Lorlita clanged and clattered with the sound of wagons being loaded and soldiers trying to find their units. Horses stomped the ground nervously as the streets swirled around them, the snap of wind-whipped pennants a crisp counterpoint to the sounds of the restless animals. The late-spring sky burned down upon the hapless creatures with an early and vicious heat. The dust of the streets permeated the air and made everyone choke with thirst. Business was brisk for the inns, and several of the ones closest to Morlidra quickly ran out of provisions. Soldiers soon sought out those inns where ale still ran freely.

"Ale here," a red-clad soldier grunted to his companion, his voice barely rising over the din of the streets. "Benetar told me this morning that Stentor's inn hasn't run out yet. Not the highest quality, mind you, but right now I could drink Tythera piss."

"Let's hope he's right," replied his friend, and the two soldiers entered the inn.

Inside, it was nearly as crowded as the street, the common room crammed with well over two dozen soldiers and a few regulars milling about the bar. The only two tables in the inn were already filled with the empty mugs of dusty soldiers clad in the black uniforms of Krotah's Elite Guard. The two newcomers ignored them and waded through the crowd to the bar, where a stout, middle-aged man was busy pouring ale into pewter flagons.

"Two," the first soldier ordered abruptly. "And don't skimp."

"Right away, sir," Stentor replied. The Pradathan barkeep turned his back to them and poured two flagons of brown liquid from a wooden cask, then set the mugs of ale before the two men. "Would you be desiring anything else, sirs?"

"Not unless you have women here," the second soldier said with a grin.

Stentor looked back at the man, noticing the lieutenant's insignia on his shoulder. "Up the stairs, second door."

The lieutenant turned to his comrade, a plaintive look on his face.

"Please, Captain? Who knows when we'll get back from these maneuvers."

"How much?" the captain asked, turning to Stentor.

Stentor shrugged, implying that the price was negotiable. "I only rent rooms," he said, picking up the empty flagon with one great, meaty hand. "Another?"

The captain frowned at the empty mug Stentor waved before him. "Send it upstairs," he said and dropped a coin onto the bar.

The two officers elbowed their way through the knot of customers around the bar, most of whom were civilians and poorly dressed. The captain kept one hand on his money pouch, not trusting the rabble. Finally they made it across the room to the stairs and bounded up. The lieutenant knocked on the second door, a plain wooden plank with an iron ring for a handle. A woman opened it, her hair the color of seafoam, her mouth full and seductive, her eyes blue and hard, a counterpoint to the soft curve of her bare shoulders.

"Yes?"

"I—I understand you have services for hire," stammered the young lieutenant, stricken by the beauty of the woman before him.

"Yes," the woman replied, reaching out her hand and

letting her finger run down the young officer's chest. "Please come in."

The two officers followed her into the room, a small cubicle with a large square mattress in the center. A second door stood closed on a side wall.

"Ten silver. You can undress here. I'll go into the other room"—she smiled coyly—"to prepare." Her voice was hypnotic, exciting. Lightly she turned and exited through the connecting door.

The sound of sword belts unbuckling and falling to the floor drifted through the crack beneath the door. Mithra reappeared, looking at the two naked soldiers. The grim nature of her business made her stomach twist, but her face remained impassive. Behind her, two of her Pradathan followers appeared, armed with swords and longbows, an arrow nocked in each and aimed at the surprised officers.

"We will begin now," she said, using the power of her Voice. "We require information. Where are your units from?"

"S-S-Silth," stammered the lieutenant. "The leeward desert area."

"Shut up!" ordered the captain and started toward his companion, but before he could take two steps, he was rewarded with an arrow through his throat. The dull thud of his body as it hit the floor was barely discernible over the noise of the inn below.

The lieutenant swallowed hard, imagining sharp steel piercing his own windpipe. His eyes flickered between the drawn bows and Mithra's eyes, as cold as steel.

"Where are the armies heading?" Mithra asked, forcing her voice to remain calm, not daring to look at the man bleeding on the floor.

"To Shymney."

"Why are they going to the Citadel?"

"Mordeth requires it. It's said that he believes his troops have gotten soft and the two-hundred-mile forced march will toughen us up. We are supposed to give him thanks for the favor and repledge our allegiance at the giant stone, there to remember that darkness is supreme in power."

"Who is going?"

"The entire army's been summoned. Half of the Elite Guard will be left behind to protect Morlida. Half that many would be enough, for the fort is well protected and the Elite are worth four of any other company. Mordeth himself will lead us. Krotah will ride vanguard with the remaining Elite. This is all I know."

"No, I'm afraid that is not entirely true," Mithra replied, and for the first time, her voice held compassion. The young lieutenant felt a brief flutter of hope until the woman spoke again. "You know of this place, and that the Pradatha are here. For this, you must join your comrade." The arrow sped across the room, a period marking the end of her sentence and the young lieutenant's life.

"See that they are well hidden," she ordered. "Make certain the dogs cannot find their bodies. We will not treat even Mordeth's men without honor." A small pang of guilt tugged at her conscience, but she reminded herself that this was war. Righteousness is often cruel.

Her two companions dragged the bodies from the room, and she poured water over the fresh blood and blotted it from the floor. After several moments, another knock came at the door, and Mithra straightened her frock and opened the door. Stentor stood framed in the flickering hall light. Mithra quickly ushered him inside, closing and barring the door behind him.

As the latch clicked behind them, Stentor took Mithra in his arms and gave her a fatherly hug. He could feel Mithra begin to tremble, and he held her as the tears came. Only when the quiet sobbing ended did he let go and step away, looking into her red, anguished face.

"Damn him!" she whispered through clenched teeth. "Damn him to the Pit forever!" She took a deep breath and let it out in a long sigh. Her eyes drifted up to the ceiling, staring blankly at nothing in particular. Stentor didn't notice her right hand, tracing slowly over her stomach.

Finally she spoke. "Two lives, my friend. Two. So we could hear more of the same. Mordeth is moving the day after tomorrow at the latest. His army will meet him at Dragon's Lair, and they will start across the mountain. This late in the spring, the pass will probably be clear. It's also the quickest way to Shymney."

"Do you know why they go, Mithra? We pray each night for the truth. Has Ratha returned?"

"I don't know, my friend. I doubt that weak excuse Mordeth has let circulate. To strengthen his troops! Against what? No army stands a chance against his army. Oh, to know the truth and damn his lies! Either this marshaling of forces is the greatest trap of all time, or my love has indeed returned. These are the only options I can see. We must prepare to move at once. If Mordeth is to use the pass at Dragon's Lair, we must circumvent it, either by way of Westport or around the Guardian. I think Westport is best, for I have no desire to skirt the desert, even in the spring. Tell your men we leave in the morning."

"As you say, Mithra." Stentor turned to leave, then paused and turned back toward the Pradatha leader. "Mithra, don't blame yourself for the death of Mordeth's soldiers. This is war. We cannot wear the mantle of guilt as well as fight to win. And win we must, for the sake of our children and our world."

"For the sake of our children," she repeated, not daring to let her voice rise above a whisper. "Ratha would forgive me, too, I'm sure. But he had no taste for killing, and his ways run deep in me. I wish there were some other way."

"Our people will be ready at first light, milady," Stentor said, trying to sound confident and reassuring. "See that you get some sleep," he added with a smile that seemed more a grimace. The door closed behind him, leaving Mithra alone with her tortured thoughts.

*   *   *   *   *

The morning came before the dawn as Mithra was startled from her sleep by a soft knock at her chamber door. Stentor entered and informed her that the Lorlita Pradatha were ready, and that messengers had sent the word throughout the western provinces that other Pradatha should meet at Westport in two days' time. The few horses they could muster were saddled and ready outside the city, and provisions were prepared and packed, ready to be strapped to sturdy backs. The Pradatha awaited their leader.

Mithra rubbed the crusted sleep from her eyes, stretching her aching muscles and trying to massage life into them. Her injured ribs, so carefully tended by Tralaina, ached dully. She had slept but lightly, and only for a few hours. There had been much preparation, silent preparation so different from the grand marshaling that Mordeth performed on the broad streets of her beloved city. She had seen that the Pradatha's preparations were undertaken with care, although both Stentor and Tralaina had reassured her that they would personally oversee the operation. Although she knew that it might appear insulting to her two good friends, she insisted on staying. She couldn't tell them that she was afraid, that it was fear that kept her awake and threatened to crush her spirits.

Stentor looked at the weary leader, all too aware of the pressure she felt. He understood that she was ill suited for war, too gentle and trusting and loving. It was her nature, and there was no way to change that. But the people needed someone, someone real and physical, to lead them. And Mithra had risen like a tree in the desert, personifying their hope with her vision and resolve. But each act of violence she performed seemed to wrench something from her, like some cruel child tearing apart a delicate flower. Stentor had a strong urge to reach out and embrace her, cradling her like the child his wife had never borne, protecting her from the hostile world.

The two friends remained silent as they descended the stairs to the quiet inn below. Half a dozen men milled about, eating bits of bread or meat, their swords sheathed and hanging from heavy leather belts. Another half-dozen women stood beside them, their bows strung and quivers filled with arrows. The absence of children rang like a sour note, and Mithra nearly repented her order that no one under the age of passage would be allowed to accompany the party. There had been no grumbling from the well-trained older children; they had accepted the responsibility that they had to contribute to the effort by staying behind and tending the smaller children.

"All is in readiness?" she asked.

"Everything, milady," Stentor replied. Tralaina stood beside him, dressed in travel gear, her yew bow strung and ready.

A last-minute thought occurred to Mithra. "What about the inn? Surely someone will think it peculiar that it's closed."

"We have posted a sign on the door, Mithra. It says that our provisions have run out at last, like so many of the other inns in town. We have simply gone to purchase more. It's not unusual."

Mithra heaved a ragged sigh. "Very well, Stentor. Forgive me. I'm a bit uneasy. It's not every day that a wife goes to meet her husband come back from the grave." She managed a weak smile.

"No, not every day," Tralaina answered softly, reaching one thick arm around the shoulders of the slender woman. They stood together for several moments, eyes locked, thinking the same thought. Finally Mithra struck her open palm loudly against the bartop.

"To Shymney," she said firmly, and the band of Pradatha filed out the back door of the inn and into the waning darkness.

* * * * *

"Mordeth's as angry as an August storm," the soldier whispered to the man beside him. "By the Pit, what could be causing it?"

The soldier beside him remained silent, his eyes straight forward, standing perfectly spaced with the forty-nine other soldiers in his unit. His eyebrows barely raised when a member of the Elite Guard approached from behind his talkative companion, lifted him by the collar of his tunic, and carried him in the direction of the Regent.

"This one was speaking in the ranks," the Elite Guard said, his voice like a stiletto.

"Flog him," Mordeth replied. "There will be no disobeying of orders. Then return him to his unit and make sure he makes the march."

"Yes, my lord."

Mordeth rode upon a jet-black stallion, its shod hooves polished like the midnight sky. The nostrils of the stallion flared as Mordeth reigned him in, keeping the beast under control amidst the crowd of soldiers. Mordeth himself blended into the dark predawn sky, his steed, his dark complexion, and robe mere shadows upon the horse's back.

"Krotah," he said with a nod. Krotah turned on his gray gelding and shouted an order that echoed down the long column, until the collected army of the Dark Lord jerked out of its stupor and churned forward like a great machine. Mordeth rode before his army with Krotah beside him. A half-dozen Elite Guards were gathered around them, watching the road and forested land for signs of an ambush. Behind the vanguard rode a seventh guard, the black and silver banner of the Regent flapping lightly in the early morning breeze.

"It goes well, Mordeth," Krotah said.

"It will go better when the Staff of Quintah consumes itself and I have the false mage's head spitted and placed above the walls of Morlidra." With a quick turn, Mordeth spun his stallion around and charged toward the rear of his troops, carefully inspecting them as he rode past.

Krotah watched his master disappear into the billowing dust, then turned and croaked an order to the guards.

"To Shymney. And by thy lives, go quickly."

❖ CHAPTER EIGHT ❖

Encounter

"It's been three weeks, Moratha. Don't you think it's about time I meet some of these people I've read so much about?"

The gray falcon stared unblinkingly back at the man from another world. Moratha had spent the past three weeks insuring that Roy had mastered the language and customs of Keshia. Even though the outsider seemed to have a command of the human tongue, he lacked all sense of nuance and subtlety. As for the customs, well, it was difficult work, but Ratha had prepared him for the contingency of someone being called from a foreign plane and had instructed the Lord of Falcons to carefully teach the outworlder whatever was necessary.

Ratha, the bird said, and deep in Roy's mind erupted a vision of more studying.

"Yes, well, that may be, but I personally think I've spent more than enough time studying. I've already told you that the language is just a variant of my own native tongue, with a slightly different vocabulary. From what I gather, the current historical age is quite similar to our own European feudal systems of the thirteenth and fourteenth centuries. It's really remarkably similar to the so-called Dark Ages of my own world. Frankly, though, I'm lonesome. Truly I enjoy your company, but I long for the sound of human voices and the taste of something besides rabbits and qomrah!"

Ratha, the falcon replied, and the vision returned to Roy with greater intensity.

"No, I don't agree. It's true that there are natural laws that have no parallel in my world, and the mastery of them is of some import. But I see no reason why I should master the deadly arts of this staff, or any of the other Words of Power. If your friend Ratha called me here, and it would appear that he did, I cannot believe that he intended me to be a general or great warrior. I'm a teacher, not a killer."

Ratha, Moratha squawked complainingly, and Roy instantly remembered, as vividly as if it were occurring again at that moment, the death of the soldier in the cavern.

"That was an accident," Roy replied. "I didn't mean to kill that man; the power was too great for me to handle. It leaped out of the staff when I became frightened. All the more reason for me not to tamper with the art. Besides, you saw that I let the other one go. Nothing has come of it; no one has returned. Let it be, bird. I will not become your warrior leader."

Moratha looked impatiently at Roy but made no reply. Instead, the great falcon continued to stare into the professor's eyes, penetrating ever deeper into the imagination of the Archmage's double. Suddenly Roy's head snapped erect, his eyes wide with terror.

"You make your point, friend bird. There is the dragon. I need to be able to protect myself from wild beasts. But I will not be your military leader. I cannot."

Ratha, the bird replied.

"Intelligent?" Roy was surprised, and instantly wondered why. He had considered the dragon dangerous, but not inherently evil. If the beast had made a choice, it was doubly deadly. And although Roy's instincts had saved him once, there was no guarantee they would again. Roy was a rational man, as much as he might hate to admit it. Instincts and feelings might have been sufficient in a romantic world, but Roy had long ago concluded there was nothing romantic about where he now found himself. Barely suppressing a shudder, Roy began his study again in earnest.

Rolling the smooth staff between his palms, Roy studied the dun-colored eye that perched upon the top of it like a watchful hawk. He closed his eyes and concentrated; he could sense the energy seeking his hands, attempting to leap into the staff and through it. Light, he thought, and the word formed upon his lips, gentle like a kiss.

"Quintah," he whispered softly. Through his closed eyelids, he could see the brilliant flash, then the harsh light that intensified until he had to raise his open hand before his eyes, shielding them from the blinding glare.

"Quintah," he said, louder than before, and the air around him crackled with the tiny streaks of lightning that leaked from the atmosphere. He could smell something burning and wanted to open his eyes to look, but instead he continued to concentrate on the word that swelled within his head and threatened to render him unconscious.

"Quintah!" he shouted, and the red flames pierced

through to his retina, ignoring the vain shielding of his hand. The pain in his eyes was excruciating, and he gasped aloud, nearly losing his grip on the Staff of Quintah. The heat seared his body, and he could feel the hair crisping on his skin. His lungs ached with every breath, his throat dry from the effort.

Finally he was unable to bear any more, and he tossed the staff aside, opening his eyes as the world dimmed. From atop the monolith, Moratha swept down to greet him.

"Not even a dragon could withstand that, Moratha," Roy gasped, panting heavily.

Ratha, the falcon replied.

Roy looked down at his arms, expecting to see the charred remains of hair or the red inflammation of burned skin. Instead, his arms were their usual pale tan, covered with the fine black hair that had been there since he was fourteen.

But—but I *felt* the flames. I was burning. I know I was," Roy stammered, unable to fathom what was happening.

Ratha, the bird replied.

"I'm impervious to fire? I'll feel it, but I won't be affected by it? Why? I don't understand."

Ratha, the falcon intoned, and Roy sensed the bird's meaning.

"I am the Master of the Three-That-Bind: Air, Fire, Land. The Words of Power serve me and can do no harm. Only the combination of two can destroy me: water and darkness. Moratha, this is too weird. Look, I need some time to consider these things. In the meantime, please consider bringing me near other people. I'm still lonely." Roy turned and headed toward the cavern opening, leaving the falcon to sit and watch, tearing a scrap of rabbit meat from the bone that lay before him.

The cycle of night and day repeated, and Roy arose to the inky blackness of the catacombs, his fire long since dissolved to ash. Instinctively he reached out an invisible hand for the familiar staff, the reassuring feel of the wood like a cup of morning coffee, a necessary and assumed ritual of the new day. The thought of coffee rumbled through Roy's mind as he ignited the staff, the warm glow of it removing the morning chill. He missed the once familiar conveniences of his old home, the bitter taste of the coffee and the warm pelting of a hot shower, the poignant loneliness of his apartment's reading room and the lively conversation of his fellow professors. Thoughts of Gwen mulled amongst the other thoughts, leaving a hollowness in his stomach that no breakfast of this new world could fill. He rose to his feet, stretched, and began the long walk through the stone corridors to the surface and the bright, sunlit world.

Roy read as he walked, a sullen habit that he had carried with him from his own distant world—the only thing, it seemed to him, that he was allowed to bring. The massive diary of the Archmage flopped open to a passage about Mithra, the beautiful wife and companion of the dead magician. Sometimes Roy found himself in the role of voyeur, staring in at the lives of the two lovers. Today he was surprised and pleased to feel the nearness of the woman, the distinctive human touch that he so longed for. Roy sighed and continued reading as he climbed the stairs to the surface.

A crisp sound caught his attention, and he expected to find Moratha lounging in a tree. Instead, the unmistakable movement of another human being darted from one tree to another, some forty yards away. The sight jerked the breath from him, and his mind automatically sent out a warning to his falcon friend, a mental image of danger lurking in the shadows of the morning forest. His keen eyes swept the landscape, searching for another clue, any movement that was out of place. His swift perception was rewarded with the awkward shadows of a dozen men, crouching behind the marelock and cocantha, ducking behind the great granite boulders. Slowly Roy backed down into the stairwell, keeping his eyes just above the level of the earth.

Another noise, barely perceptible, fluttered behind him as Moratha sped to his side, landing on his shoulder. The gray falcon was nearly invisible in the half-light of the stairwell, but Roy could hear the short breaths and light click of his sharp beak as the bird tested the air, sensing the spores that had invaded the area. Moratha sent the images to Roy's mind.

"Mordeth's army? How many? Is he here, too?" The questions were thick as they left Roy's mouth, nearly choking him as he spoke.

Moratha silently nodded his falcon equivalent of yes.

Roy gripped his staff more tightly, silently swearing that he hadn't been more persistent about learning its use. His instincts told him to flee, but his reason overrode emotion. Where could he go? He had been summoned to this insane world for a purpose, but from all that Roy had been able to learn, the summoner had died years ago. What was he supposed to do?

The falcon answered his unspoken questions by launching from Roy's shoulder and hurling himself, like a well-fletched arrow, straight at one of the closest soldiers hiding in the forest. It wasn't much of a battle. Mordeth's soldier had been trained to stand against a man, to protect himself from the slash of sword and club. Against Moratha's fluttering, three-pointed attack, darting about his head, he was next to useless. The man screamed as the hawk lacerated his face with the sharp talons, the blood dripping down his forehead and into his eyes. Roy was encouraged as the falcon dipped and attacked yet another hidden assassin, striking him cleanly in the temple with outstretched talons, the man falling, stunned, where he had stood.

Old stories emerged from the recesses of the soldiers' memories, stories banned by Mordeth but not forgotten. The Archmage alone could summon the forces of the hunting birds. Several of the remaining soldiers began to flee, the great war hawk's voice a piercing battle cry that sent fear into their hearts. Roy ventured outside the cavern again, still watching for movement.

Moratha was an effective hunter, and the great falcon had successfully chased the few scattered soldiers from the immediate area. Roy moved quietly through the underbrush, navigating the thickets with the aid of weeks of experience he'd had in the area. Soon he was standing along the perimeter of the circle of desolation, the great stone monolith rearing its hoary head in the morning light. He watched for several moments, the stillness of the area seeming uncanny and wrong, the uneasiness of the situation gnawing at him like a bad breakfast, until his stomach ached with discomfort.

After an hour, Roy began to relax, convincing himself that the army Moratha had feared was only a product of the bird's overactive imagination, and that the few soldiers who had been there that morning had long since

fled to the safety of lower country, perhaps even returning to Morlidra. But the still coldness of the day belied
him, and in spite of his own reassurances, he couldn't
relax completely. The sun slid along the sky with the de-
liberateness of a funeral, slowly dragging the dead orb
across the pale carpet of blue. The sun failed to heat
him, and he shivered in its feeble glow. By noon, Roy's
teeth chattered with the chill of the day; still he had seen
no more movement.

The shadows had just begun to stretch toward the east
when he heard the voice, speaking a word he could not
fathom but that drove a chill deep into Roy's chest, jerking a ragged breath from him, striking his heart and daring it to be still, once and for all. Roy leaned hard upon
his staff, trying not to collapse even as his knees buckled. A numbness spread through his extremities, seeping toward his chest and head, threatening to drag him
under into the cold, austere world of death. The numbness had continued moving up his legs and arms, reaching his shoulders and hips, when he recalled the staff.

"Quintah," he breathed, his lips and tongue, his entire being so cold he could barely speak the word. The
staff began to pulse with its golden light, the heat radiating from it like a stove, cracking the cold in his hand.
Roy could feel his own energy returning and seeking the
staff, feeding the fire, warming the area. With the
numbness dispelled, he looked about him at his surroundings. Darkness, like the world beneath an eclipse,
draped over the stones and trees. He looked to the sky
and saw the sun, a silver parody of the star he remembered.

"Quintah," he said again, his voice barely audible.
The word gave him back his substance, drew warmth

and life back into his chest. He could hear his own voice crackling with energy. The shadows disappeared around him, and the silver gloom of the mountainside began to dissolve like ice beside a fire. Then he heard the voice again.

The world of shadow pressed in toward him, and he fought to gain his breath. His eyes narrowed and began to lose their focus, his peripheral vision narrowing to pinpoints. The cold began to clamber up his legs again, and he tried to stamp his feet to regain the lost feeling. He clutched the staff tighter, lifting it slightly off the ground.

"Quintah!" This time he shouted the word with all the force he could muster, and the staff vibrated in his hand. Light bounced off the granite all about him, the leaves of the nearby trees curling with the heat. The force of light sped from him, piercing the dim world. Then Roy saw the source of the voice.

Mordeth stood upon a large granite boulder, looking down at Roy. Roy immediately recognized him as the man Morlin from the falcon's visions. The man before him was as dark as the month's first night, his hair a gleaming mass of ebony; he wore a black cloak and breeches, his polished boots riding up to just below his knee. Everything about the man spoke power—austere, repulsive power—like nothing Roy had ever known. He realized he had to fight this man, this thing that emulated all darkness.

"We meet at last, imposter," Mordeth laughed, the half-bright sun glinting off his teeth as he spoke. "Come and speak to me; come and know me. I have many questions for you."

Roy kept staring at the dark vision of a man standing

fifty yards from him. The voice was hypnotic, fluid, like the swelling tide or a river passing by. Roy soon began to become absorbed by it, into it.

The staff pulsed and Roy came back to himself. "I don't think that's a good idea, Morlin. We can speak from where we are." Roy managed to sound almost confident as he spoke.

"Fool!" Mordeth shouted. "You will do only what I say, only what I want."

The voice seemed vaguely familiar to Roy, and as he considered where he had heard it, the trance began to break. With a movement that surprised even Mordeth, Roy lifted his staff and shouted his Word of Power. The landside exploded with thunder, rocks falling from the surrounding cliffs. The clear blue electric light arced across the distance between the two men and struck Mordeth full in the chest, the intensity of the light making his sharp features washed and flat. The valley rumbled and complained with the impact of the blow, and the smell of ozone caused Roy to sneeze. When his eyes refocused, Mordeth still stood upon the granite stone, staring malevolently down at Roy.

Darkness swept like a flood across a barren plain, enveloping Roy before he could flee its path. The liquid darkness covered him, soaked through him, until he could feel nothing but the iciness of its touch. He tried to speak but could not, the abyss filling even his lungs and mouth. His tongue remained numb as he tried to articulate a sound, but nothing came out. In fearful desperation, he concentrated on the Word of Power, willing the staff to dispell the darkness that choked him.

A tiny sliver of light etched the periphery of the blackness about him, and the sight of it encouraged Roy to press harder. He concentrated on the word, oblivious to time, his entire mind perfectly focused. Three times he tried to speak the word aloud without success. On the fourth attempt, it happened. With the suddenness of a collision, his own voice rattled through the abyss and led light back into the world. The brilliance of the surge pulsed through the mountainside, driving the darkness from even the deepest corner. Mordeth still stood upon the rock, but he seemed tired, pained by some force that drained life from him.

Had Roy been any other kind of man, he might have swept down upon Mordeth with vengeance and blood-lust, destroying the Dark Lord on the spot with the power of his staff. But Roy was filled with compassion and the dread of killing, even for this man who epitomized evil incarnate. He stared at the man before him, buckled over with pain, the man who moments before had nearly submerged him in eternal night. The moral dilemma hung before his eyes like a festering wound, needing immediate attention. Roy could not decide.

Instead, the decision was made for him. Mordeth recovered, and with a faint wave of his clenched fist, he pressed the darkness down upon Roy once more. Again Roy tried to utter his Word of Power, but the darkness swept into his open throat and strangled him. He tried to concentrate upon his staff, to urge the power to funnel through it and out toward his foe, but his strength had been drained from him, and the power of the Lord of Darkness was too much for him. Roy felt himself floundering in an abyss of nothingness, unable to reach back through it to the world about him.

Like a still, soft voice whispering across a mountain meadow, he heard his answer: *I am the Master of the*

Three-That-Bind: Fire, Air, and Land.

His mind refocused, searching for some way to use the power within him. Fire was of no use, but land . . . He remembered the earthquake he had started when the assassin had startled him in the catacombs. He concentrated on his foot, trying to sense any feeling in his extremity. He felt nothing. The darkness continued to crush him, sweeping him deeper into the vacuum of nothingness; he imagined himself stamping his foot hard upon the dust of the circle of desolation, picturing the rocks tumbling from the mountains, the trees swaying with the abrupt motion, the Citadel rocking with the force. Again and again he pictured the stamping, each time more violently than before. Then, with the fourth attempt, light shot out through the perpetual night and erased the darkness, coloring the world with familiar shades. Roy stood with one foot planted in the dust of the circle of desolation, his staff a flaming lantern blazing in the midday.

Mordeth lay sprawled across the top of the granite stone, his black robe like a shroud about his powerful body. Roy told himself that the Regent was dead, but a nagging doubt prodded him. He raised his staff as if for the final, killing blow, then lowered it, unable to deliver its death sentence to an unconscious man. He closed his eyes, pondering his options, trying to renew his strength.

Suddenly the voice of Moratha broke into his silent world. He saw the falcon land in a nearby tree, then survey the scene before him. The Lord of Falcons knew what he must do, and he had no such reservations about killing. Moratha sped from the tree, his sharp talons ready to tear at the throat of the unmoving Regent. The hunting cry of the hawk echoed in the valley.

The sound of the cry died as darkness again welled up from Mordeth's prone body. The Regent stirred, then stood, a small rivulet of bright red blood oozing from one nostril, a sharp counterpoint to his chalk-white complexion. The darkness hurtled toward the flying falcon, who banked hard to his right, then climbed into the higher reaches of the mountain. Roy turned and began to run through the woods, the darkness stalking him like an angry tiger.

Roy didn't dare turn to look back at the pursuing darkness. Instead, he ran, the staff gripped tightly in one hand, the Archmage's diary in the other, the tangled mass of branches and vines trying to trip him with every stride, grabbing maliciously at his bare arms and face. He ran until his breath burned in his chest and his knees quivered with the exertion. His heartbeat pounded in his ears, deafening him to any sounds of movement. He was nearly spent when a heavy grip jerked his shoulder around. Bile churned into his throat as he turned toward his assailant.

"Damn you, Moratha! You nearly scared the life out of me!" Roy shouted to the falcon on his shoulder. "But you'll never know how glad I am to see you. Let's get going!"

The two companions again began their evasion, the professor running through the dense forest, the falcon flying above, scanning the territory. Several times Moratha returned to Roy's shoulder, directing him away from the presence of Mordeth's troops. Hours passed and night began to creep across the land, the sun slipping relentlessly into the west. Roy and Moratha continued their flight, heading due south along the ridge of mountains, stopping only long enough for Roy to catch his breath, not daring to let fatigue defeat them when Mordeth had not. When the sky became well dotted with stars, the two fugitives turned west, toward the sea, the downslope of the foothills urging them to a faster pace. By morning, the Citadel was a distant stone finger pointing up out of the earth.

"Let's . . . rest here, Moratha," Roy puffed breathlessly. "They couldn't have . . . followed us . . . all night . . . through the dark. Even if they could . . . they'd be well behind us. We can afford . . . a couple of hours' rest, at any rate."

Ratha, replied the falcon and tucked his head under his wing, almost immediately falling into the regular breathing pattern that Roy recognized as the hawk's sleep.

"Sleep well, my friend," Roy whispered, then curled into a ball on the leafy forest floor.

Roy's sleep was suddenly interrupted by the touch of cold steel against his throat. Swartled, he opened his eyes to see four jerkin-clad soldiers standing over him, their swords drawn and pointed down at him. Moratha was nowhere to be seen, and a sense of panic overwhelmed him. He began to reach for his staff, but it wasn't there. Then he noticed that one of the four had slung it over his back.

Roy scrutinized his closest enemy. He appeared to be the leader, judging by his stature and the way the others reacted to him. He appeared no older than one of Roy's students might have been, judging from the dull fuzz of adolescence still clinging to his chin. But Roy had no time to consider the youth of his captors. One of the group abruptly jerked him to his feet, while the remaining two bound him with a thick, rough rope. Too young to be soldiers, Roy thought, even in this world.

The leader shoved Roy ahead of him down a faint path, and the other three walked behind, swords ready. Roy hung his head, too tired to resist. What he saw as his eyes focused on the path reached into his chest and squeezed his heart, for on the ground at his feet, Roy saw a single, gray-brown feather of a hawk.

❖ CHAPTER NINE ❖

Search

The Pradatha inched along the narrow trail single file, their heads pressed down against the howling wind. Around them, the sharp peaks of the Western Range stabbed upward to the boiling sky, the snow-capped head of the Guardian invisible behind its mantle of scudding gray clouds. Mithra watched her feet as she placed one step before the last, the wind pressing her against the stone face of the mountainside, the rain pelting her with its stinging cold. Her ribs still throbbed with each ragged breath.

Mithra's people had been delayed a full day at West-port. The Pradatha from Yelu and Shaleth had met one of Mordeth's patrols along the road and had had to skirt wide around them to avoid discovery. By the time the Yeluan Pradatha arrived in Westport, Mithra's group, as impatient as a dog when the hunting horn sounds, were pacing up and down the hard-packed earthen floor of Mithra's family home. They set out toward Shymney even as the town crier chanted his midnight ritual.

The Pradatha hurried along in the storm toward

Shymney, along the western foothills of the great Keshian mountains. They followed the winding trails toward Elvathain, the Mount of Tears, which rose quietly in the east, encircled by the pulsing gold of sunrise. But prevailing winds sucked the warmth from the morning, and by midday, the gray clouds rained sleet down upon their backs, and the hoary head of the Mount of Tears disappeared into the black thunderheads that had overtaken them.

For two more days, Mithra drove her companions toward the Citadel, resting only long enough to grab a few hours of sleep, eating on the march. On the eve of the third day out of Westport, the storm relented. The evening sky was dark and cloudless, the light from the stars piercingly sharp in the thin mountain air. Those among the Pradatha that were Rahlah-ne informed their mistress that the stars told of another two days' hard march to reach Shymney, provided the weather held and their strength did not give out. Mithra looked into the weary eyes of the Pradatha standing beside her, but she would not relent; she sensed the importance of haste in reaching the Citadel.

Words were rare as the march progressed, giving Mithra time to remember. And to listen.

"She's blinded 'erself, she has," one jerkin-clad farmer said, and though his tone was conspiratorial, his voice traveled easily in the stone-edged pathways of the mountains. "Ratha's dead, or else where's he been all these years past? I tell ye, we be marchin' all this distance for naught."

"Hush, man," came the whispered reply.

The farmer's voice climbed higher with obstinancy, as one who has found something that creates uneasiness and won't let go. "Hush, ye say? Hush? Why, I once met the Archmage m'self, I did, and I tell ye, he weren't one t' lay low for no man. No, sir. But that Mordeth, he's a keen one, an' I wouldn't bet my last year's crop against this bein' a trap he's laid for us. You mark my words."

Other words followed, but Mithra didn't hear them, lost in the struggle within her own mind. Could it be, she thought, that she was indeed a woman possessed, a woman so afraid to go on alone that she willed her dead lover's return? Had Mordeth's abuse won at last? She looked down at her flat stomach, girded with a leather belt pulled taut. And for the first time since she saw Ratha die at Shymney, she doubted.

Such thoughts haunted her as much as her memory. Had it really been twelve years since she'd first met him, a stranger in her small port town? She recalled those easy, early memories of her love. A gentle man with tremendous patience, Ratha had been admired by most of the townspeople. She had loved him from the moment she first heard him speak, teaching the stories of power, weaving the Three-That-Bind into their lives. She had loved his strangeness, his dark hair and hard blue eyes, the way he spoke to the birds, especially the great falcon, his constant companion.

The first day they had met, the clouds scuttled across an azure sky, sweeping low against the ocean's green horizon. She had walked down along the beach, savoring the delicious salt spray as the breakers beat upon the sands. Ratha had followed her, as she had hoped, and together they had walked for hours along the ocean shore. Mithra remembered turning back regretfully and seeing the seemingly endless stretch of their intertwining footprints, two paths becoming one, exciting and new.

Before Ratha came to Westport, Mithra was destined to follow the path of her mother, and her mother's mother, and her mother before her. She would mend the nets, practice some minor healing, and never travel more than a day's journey from the town in which she was born. But after he came, she was filled with a sense of great purpose, a desire to travel and see those distant sights he spoke of in his stories. Her parents thought her indolent on more than one occasion, disturbed by her constant pestering to do things that were not her lot. But Ratha understood, allowing her the freedom to become her own person, to choose her own destiny. Except once.

When Ratha had arrived in her small village, he had withheld news of the Regent's search for him, of his plan for the Archmage's destruction. She had heard stories that Ratha had been advisor to the king, but of Morlin's hatred for him she had heard nothing. News from Lorlita came infrequently to Westport. Mithra was content to simply have Ratha there, and when she heard others speaking of the great danger he had fled and the massive hunt that the Regent was conducting for him, she needed only to look at his passive face and her worry faded.

Inevitably they had married. Her joy swelled like a tide, rushing in and filling her once parched world. But the rumors had proved true, and Morelua had come searching, his spies locating Ratha in Westport. Ratha was unwilling to jeopardize the small village, and he left. Mithra had begged to come with him, but he had felt it was too dangerous and refused her. He left in the night, believing that she would sleep until morning and then would find the note he'd left. But she knew.

She sent one of the village lads to follow, and he had returned to report to her that Ratha had headed south along the mountain trail. She knew that he would go to Shymney, the great monolith that held strange secrets. He had told her of some of the powers hidden within the stone Citadel. It was not difficult for her to decipher Ratha's intent; they were as one.

Now she remembered watching the deadly battle through the *marelock* bush; she witnessed the hideous event, too frightened to move. But no longer was she the girl of seventeen. Now she was strong, too strong to sit idly by while her love faced danger. Now she was ready to come to his aid, to fight for him and be his strength. Never again would she allow the man she loved to walk into Morelua's deadly traps alone. The thought increased her determination to reach Shymney as quickly as possible.

With sunrise, the mountains swelled to the east, and Mithra saw the Guardian rising majestically above the magenta hills. The wind brought the quiet music of the sea with it, and she turned and looked to the west, sweeping her eyes across the vast expanse of aquamarine ocean that spread along the horizon. The sky was blue and undefiled, but the land was quiet and empty of life. A coldness crept into her. Mithra shook off the chill and pushed the Pradatha onward to their goal.

Good weather became their ally and companion, and the hearty Pradatha made swift progress across the western foothills. By nightfall of the sixth day, the laughing music of Falcon Falls echoed across the darkening air. Mithra was loath to sleep another night so near her destination, but Stentor and Tralaina convinced her that a

well-rested army was of far more value than an exhausted one. The Pradatha slept the sixth night with the gentle music of the falls echoing about them.

Before the sun had crested the eastern mountains,
Mithra had awakened the group for the final day of
march. They forded the river below Falcon Falls, march-
ing a short way inland from the Great Western Bay of
the Windward Sea. The silver sun climbed in the sky,
and the scouts shouted down from the tops of trees that
Shymney lay a dozen miles in the southeast. The band
of rebels turned toward the granite spire.

As the sun began its slow descent, Mithra sensed the
first of several low rumblings in the earth. The trees still
rose thick and full across the foothills, making it impossible to view Shymney without first climbing one of the
tall cocantha trees. A scout was sent into the branches
and called down a disturbing message: The Citadel was
shrouded in a veil of night.

The memory of a past battle urged Mithra and her
small army forward; the young leader became determined to cover the final miles to the granite Citadel in
all haste, but her eyes flickered with blue fear. She had
seen her love destroyed at that awful place once; she
could not bear to see the sight again.

A second scout reported that the darkness seemed to
be coming from the monolith, and Mithra's steps instantly became more determined. The air seemed warmer to her as she nearly ran up the steep incline. The briars
tugged at her woolen leggings and seemed to keep her
somehow bound to earth. Frequently, impatience hard-
ening her usually soft features, she had to stop to wait
for the others, many of whom were ten or more years
older than she. Tralaina came panting through the thin-

ning forest, sweat beading on her plump face like tiny diamond jewels. She placed a clammy hand upon Mithra's bare arm, trying to reassure her that they would arrive in time.

Reports of the battle came more frequently as runners raced back down the hill to inform their Pradatha leader. Darkness and brilliant light oscillated across the pass, first the one, then the other overwhelming the Citadel. As yet another runner completed her report to Mithra, the ground suddenly lurched and trembled, sending the small army sprawling across the hard earth. Leaves swept through the air, rattled from the branches by the earthquake, lighting on the earth motionless and dead. Then there was stillness.

A boy of fourteen, only three months from his day of naming, broke the melancholy mood, shimmying up a slender tree and gazing upon the Citadel. The boy stared intently to the east, his face expressionless but alert; moments churned into thick, unyielding minutes, culminating in the shrill, adolescent voice barking excitedly. The Citadel was alight!

Mithra again resumed her ascent, her aching legs pushing her up the narrow trail that led to Shymney. Her lungs burned as she gasped for every breath. Suddenly the granite monolith appeared above the trees, staring down at her in cold majesty. She guessed that she was only two or three miles from the pass, and she silently prayed for the strength to finish the journey. She turned and looked back at the panting line of Pradatha that strung out behind her, wondering if their small force would be enough to sway the balance in Ratha's favor. A sharp clattering of stones broke her reverie and snapped her head back toward the trail before her.

A runner burst through the thinning trees, sweat thick upon his upper lip, fear in his eyes. The boy attempted to control himself before his leader as he stood, breathing heavily, his blue eyes begging Mithra for permission to speak.

"Yes, Jerriod, what news?" Mithra asked, her voice gentle yet anxious at the same time.

"Mithra, they move." Jerriod took a deep breath before continuing. "Morelua moves. His army sweeps down upon us, less than a mile distant. There is no sign of the Archmage," he added, looking straight into Mithra's pleading eyes.

"Do they move swiftly?"

"They come as if in pursuit. Perhaps they have seen us."

"Quickly," Mithra called to the Pradatha. "We must move back down the mountain. Morelua comes. Find flat ground and prepare. Stentor! Take two of your best archers and guard our retreat. But take no chances; fall back before they overwhelm you!"

The Pradatha responded immediately, turning and moving quickly down the trail they had so laboriously climbed. They moved with an uncanny silence, and Mithra found herself feeling pride in knowing them, in leading them. She turned back to Jerriod.

"How many are there?"

"Three for every one of us, Mithra." A guilty look crossed the young man's face.

"Don't worry, Jerriod, we do not kill messengers who bear bad news," Mithra said, a warm smile sweeping across her soiled face. "And Morelua will not capture us today. Ratha lives, for light still rattles in the hills like a war cry." Her words sounded bright and hopeful, belying her own feelings. Jerriod smiled back at her, then turned and raced down the hill.

"I pray that I am right," she whispered, then followed her tiny army down the mountain.

The Pradatha camped that night near the south point of the Great Western Bay, the glimmering finger of Shymney shining gold in the light of the setting sun. They had managed to avoid the searching army of the Dark Lord, lying silently in the deep grass near the shore as Mordeth's troops passed to the south. That in itself was significant to her. If Mordeth suspected their presence, the guards would surely have been instructed to look for them in earnest. But Mordeth's soldiers appeared as if they were content to reach some other goal and only casually inspected their surroundings. The thought gave Mithra a cold chill, for she believed that nothing, absolutely nothing Mordeth did, was casual. If the Dark One's army wasn't searching for them, they were up to something else that was foul. But if they were truly unaware of the presence of the Pradatha, and if she could manage it, surprise might prove an awful weapon. She only hoped that surprise would belong to the Pradatha.

Night blanketed the coastal forest with a warm westerly breeze, the smell of the sea heavy in the air. The Pradatha ate a cold supper, sitting huddled in fireless circles, finding small pleasure in the taste of the juicy keyth they had managed to gather before the sun set. Mithra, fear staving off sleep, watched her people fidget in the dark. The sound of the surf pounding rhythmically just on the edge of her perception both tensed and reassured her. It reminded her of the rhythm of life, that her time—the Pradathan time—would come eventually.

Truth would win out, she told herself.

She placed one hand on her belly and rubbed it lightly. "Truth will win out," she said aloud, and she shuddered at what that might mean. For the hundredth time, she wondered if she were deluded, if all she had hoped for was nothing more than the mad babblings of a love-lust child. A bulky movement caught her eye, and she turned to see Stentor approaching.

"Mithra, we should make plans for tomorrow. Daylight will find us discovered, for Morelua's scouts are cunning. We cannot wait here for the Archmage to come."

"You are right, my friend," Mithra replied, "but what plan is there? We must find Ratha if we are to aid him. Shymney was our main hope, but I sense he's no longer there. The Windward Sea speaks a sad refrain tonight, for once again my love is lost."

"Have no fear, Mithra. Ratha lives. It is his word. And we will find him." His words were as comforting as firelight in the still darkness of the forest.

"You're right, old friend." Mithra placed her hand inside of Stentor's, folding his fingers over her own with her other hand. "So you tell me—what plan shall we create tonight?" Her smile was a soft white gleam in the dark.

"I have our own scouts watching Morelua's army. Wherever they go, we shall know about it. So far, they seem unaware of our presence. Perhaps it's a trap. Perhaps they're not chasing us at all. I hope that they seek the Archmage, too. If so, Morelua will aid us in finding Ratha."

"Good." Mithra was glad to hear someone speaking with such confidence, and she clung to it. "We'll strengthen our odds, though. Send six archers into the woods to harry the Dark One's flanks. They must be careful not to draw attention to us, but for each one of the Dark One's army we kill, the balance tips toward our favor."

"As you say, Mithra," Stentor said seriously. He stood and walked toward the shadowy ring of trees that surrounded Mithra's camp, then suddenly stopped and turned back to the young woman as if he had forgotten something.

"And, Mithra, my wife tells me that you are to go to sleep. If you don't, she says she'll come here personally . . ." Stentor left the threat unspoken. Both he and Mithra knew Tralaina's ire—and her love.

"As you say, my lord," Mithra replied with mock seriousness. Stentor's soft chuckle disappeared into the night, and Mithra lay her head down upon the coarse woolen blanket on the ground, thinking that even so she would not sleep.

Mithra soon found herself enveloped by darkness as thick as tar. Somewhere within her, she felt the feeble kick of life, and as she pressed her hand against her abdomen, her thoughts turned unwittingly to death. Far out of her sight, she could sense Ratha looking down at her, his staff glowing angrily, the Archmage shaking his head in disapproval. The voices of the Pradatha joined his in sad and solemn reprimand.

Sleep scattered from her like grasshoppers before the hawk. Suddenly Mithra sat up, nocking an arrow as she moved. The dream dissolved instantly, but her fear remained. The woods around her were lit with early morning light, but still she strained her eyes to capture any sign of movement, sniffed the air to locate any unfamiliar scent. The silence pressed against her lungs tightly, and she held her breath, waiting. The moments stretched until a shrill, familiar voice broke the silence.

Ratha, the falcon said.

"Moratha? Is it you?" Mithra was up on her feet instantly, moving swiftly toward the great falcon perched in a nearby tree.

Ratha, replied the hawk.

"Is he with you, old friend?" Her heart beat wildly at the sight of Ratha's familiar.

An image of Roy flashed into Mithra's mind, a picture of a hawk flying side by side with a man running down the mountain toward the sea. In her mind, she saw the battle between Roy and Mordeth, witnessed the darkness overcoming Roy, then exploding into light as the mountains shook and the stones struck the Dark Lord. Joy and fear shot through Mithra like heated arrows, and tears poured down her cheeks.

"He lives! Ratha lives!" she gasped between her sobs.

Ratha, said the falcon, and Mithra sensed the wrongness of her words.

"Ratha dead? No!" she shouted. "*No!* You showed him to me. He escaped. He lives!" Her voice was at once imploring and commanding.

Ratha, said the bird.

"I don't understand. He lives? He's dead? Which one, Moratha?"

Ratha, replied Moratha.

"Oh, for the love of the Four. Why can't I understand you? If I only had Ratha's gift of birdspeech. You say he's dead, but you show him to me alive. Moratha!" she wrung her hands in exasperation.

The great falcon launched into the air with a single

beat of his powerful wings, then circled above the mistress of Pradatha, all the while his great falcon voice imploring her to follow. She gathered her cloak, bow, and quiver of arrows, then raced after the bird.

"Stentor! Moratha has returned! Wake the others! The falcon leads us to Ratha!"

The Pradatha camp came suddenly alive with movement. Stentor came trotting over to Mithra, his great, thick thumb gouging the sleep from his dark-rimmed eyes.

"Mithra, what is it? Have you heard news?"

"Stentor, Moratha has come to me. See him perched in the tree?" Mithra pointed at a slender birch in which the great falcon rested.

"Moratha?" Stentor whispered. The falcon shifted his weight on the branch.

"Come quickly. The falcon wishes us to follow." Mithra turned and sped toward the bird, leaving Stentor to organize the Pradatha to follow.

The sun hung higher in the morning sky and the sound of the sea grew nearer as she ran. Moratha flew from tree to tree, waiting patiently for the Pradatha leader to catch up to him, then lifting again into the air and landing a bow shot farther up the trail. Mithra had been running nonstop through the dense seaside forest, and her lungs and legs ached with the exertion, but the hope of soon seeing her husband pushed her forward.

Moratha lit upon a branch, facing away from the woman who followed him. Mithra caught up to the bird and looked down at the ground beneath the tree. The earth was scraped raw of vegetation, the signs of a brief struggle evident to her keen eyes. She looked at the falcon, still resting in the tree.

Ratha, said the bird, and Mithra sensed the desperation in his voice. Moratha had left the Archmage here, exhausted and sleeping, and now the man was gone. Fear shivered up her spine.

"We will find him," Mithra promised, searching the ground for clues. But the captors had been uncanny in their escape, and Mithra returned to the circle without any idea of where they had gone. She sat down on the spongy grass beneath a *chontha* tree.

Soldiers rattled noisily through the forest, but the sound of their approach didn't even stir her. Stentor came and laid a massive hand upon her shoulder, but she wouldn't look up at him. Tralaina came a few moments later, chasing Stentor away, and took the thirty-year-old woman into her arms as if she were still a child. The two women sat wordlessly for several minutes, until at last Mithra pushed the older woman away.

"We must find him," Mithra said.

"Yes, Mithra. It's being seen to. Stentor's scouts will find the trail. We must be patient."

Mithra looked into the tree above her, expecting to see Moratha perched protectively there, but the falcon had left. Someone told her that the great bird had gone with Stentor to search for the Archmage, but it didn't seem to matter to Mithra. She was being overwhelmed with the intense fatigue of failure after an extraordinary effort. She struggled vainly to fight back her hopelessness.

Stentor returned an hour later, the listless sag of his head telling more than his words could: The Archmage was gone, and the trail had vanished. Not even his best trackers could follow the carefully concealed path. Stentor dared not raise his eyes to meet Mithra's.

The three friends sat beneath the shade of the chontha tree, their heads bent as if in prayer. It was long past time for the noon meal, but no one ate. The hush of the Pradatha was profound, casting their spirits even deeper into gloom. From the north, the sound of rustling branches came to them, but they didn't turn to look. A young man, his light brown hair swept back off his forehead and stuffed beneath a leather cap, a badge of his homeland far to the south, approached the Pradatha leaders and waited for acknowledgment.

"Yes, Thenta?" Stentor said listlessly.

"We captured a prisoner," the scout said, his voice tinged with pride. "We've tried to find you all morning, but your camp was vacant. We have come full circle, returning here only now to the place of his capture."

All three leaders looked up at the young scout, staring into his beaming face, the pink of exertion showing through his tanned complexion. None dared verbalize their hope, that in this prisoner they might find a clue to the Archmage's location.

"Bring him here at once," Mithra ordered, and Thenta motioned to someone waiting in the shadows of the forest. Three other young men came into view, roughly dragging a bound and gagged body, limp and unmoving. Stentor's eyes grew wide, and Tralaina instinctively reached her hand out to her husband as Mithra gasped in recognition. For wordless moments, no one moved. Mithra was the first to gain control of the situation.

"Unbind the Archmage at once!" she commanded, then strode to the unconscious body and cradled her lover's head in her lap as the bewildered scouts cut the bonds from their prisoner.

* * * * *

Roy opened his eyes to see the face of a woman gazing down upon him. At first her pale white hair gave him the false impression that she was quite old, but as his eyes adjusted, he saw that she could not be older than he, and was in all probability younger. Her face, though unquestioningly beautiful, was mildly disfigured by a bruise that had just begun to fade, the mark extending from her determined jawline up the right side of her face to just above her soft, nearly invisible eyebrow. He focused on her eyes, an involuntary action spurred by their intensity. They were the color of a stormy sea, green and blue jumbled together in a passionate torrent. Her eyes were hypnotic, and he raised himself awkwardly on one arm, trying to break the spell.

"You must rest, Ratha," the woman said, looking down at Roy with a fierce gentleness. "You have survived much. Let the healing work."

Roy began to protest, but his body ached and shook with the effort of movement. He let his head slip slowly to the soft blankets beneath him.

"It's good to have you home, my husband," Mithra said, bending down to caress his forehead with her slender hand. Roy felt the coolness of her fingers against his flesh, and he instantly relaxed, the woman's caresses like fragrant water washing the pain from his body.

"Mithra?" Roy said, his voice feeble in the thick forest air.

"Yes. We are one, Ratha. Now rest."

The words tumbled out by their own weight. "I'm— I'm not Ratha. My name's Roy. I'm not even Keshian. I was brought here by your husband." Roy was startled by his own adamancy. He wanted to tell this woman that her husband was dead and had trapped him on this world, but her eyes stared gently at him and he felt compassion stir within him, like the first breeze of an early spring. He debated with himself for several moments as the woman continued to stare down on him with a look of deep concern. Another figure moved behind her, a stout, elderly man with slate-gray hair, his arms thick from years of heavy labor.

"How is he?" the man asked.

"He's delirious, Stentor. The Dark One has wounded his mind. He has no fever, but he speaks of absurd things, of another world."

Stentor looked down on Roy, the old man's steel-silver glance ending the useless debate.

"I know you," Roy said. "You're Stentor, the husband of Tralaina, who was Mithra's nurse before her naming. My name is Roy, and I have been called by Ratha to aid in the fight against the Regent of Many Names." Roy smiled at his invented joke, but the two Pradatha continued to look worried. "Look, I'm a teacher. I come from a place called Ashton. I work at the university there—or at least I did. I fell from a bell tower and somehow landed on a beach in this world. I met a dragon, then fled to the stone pillar that you call Shymney. I found a book there and a falcon named Moratha. He taught me what I needed to know in order to survive on this world. You must believe me!"

"I'll get the healer," Stentor said and trotted off into the forest.

"If only Moratha were here," Roy muttered.

Ratha, said the voice of the falcon. Roy turned and saw his friend perched in the lower branches of a nearby tree.

"Moratha! Thank goodness! Tell them. Explain to them who I am."

The bird's eyes narrowed, but he said nothing.

"Please, Moratha! They think I'm mad!" Suddenly the humor of everything that had happened—his arrival in a new world, the meeting with a dragon, speaking with a hawk—hit him, and he laughed uncontrollably. He stopped and cast a sideways glance at Mithra as he considered all that had happened. "Perhaps I am," he said, more serious now.

Ratha, replied the falcon, and Roy heard a thousand voices laughing.

Roy glowered at the bird. "It's not particularly funny. And I do think they deserve to hear the truth. Isn't that what Ratha was known for? His dedication to the truth?"

Ratha, replied Moratha.

"Of course! The book! Mithra, did the group that brought me here bring my things with them? A book and a staff?"

The woman had been observing the conversation between her husband and the Lord of Falcons, bewildered and frustrated that she couldn't understand the bird. She started with the suddenness of Ratha's attention. "Yes, Ratha. We're keeping them safe until you need them."

"Bring them to me now, please."

Mithra considered the request for only a moment before she stood and walked into the shadowy forest, leaving the professor alone with the Lord of Falcons.

Several minutes passed before Mithra returned, carrying the Staff of Fire in one hand and the Book of Knowledge in the other. Roy took the proffered items from her, setting the staff on the ground beside him. He opened the book to a page near the back, carefully searching for a particular passage. When he found it, he turned the book around and handed it back to Mithra.

"Read this," he ordered.

Mithra took the book gently and looked down at the open page. "*By my estimation,*" she read aloud, "*I can bring one from another world here to aid our cause. His life must somehow parallel my own, and I must use most of my power to draw him here. I know not what that parallel will be. I have no knowledge of the other's power. I know only that whoever comes will be the one to defeat the enemy. I pray that my people will follow him. It is their only hope, for the Regent grows ever more dangerous. I fear for my world. I fear their rescuer will come too late.*" Mithra clutched the open book to her chest, hugging it as if it were a lost child. Roy wanted to comfort her, but could find no words.

For a long moment, Mithra wanted to dash the book into the fire and bury it among the coals, so fiercely had she wanted this man before her to be her returned husband. Parallels! What absurdity. This man, captured by four boys, was no Archmage! All she had here was a doppelganger, without substance. She looked at the page again, read the words herself, saw how they were in Ratha's own flowing hand. She trusted her husband completely, knew he would never commit a lie to paper. As hard as it might seem to accept it, this man was sent here by her husband, by the Archmage of Keshia. She looked again into Roy's eyes but couldn't keep her gaze there and dropped them to the ground.

"The book speaks the truth," she said at last. "The

Pradatha will follow you as the Archmage wished, Mage-sent. Where will you lead us?" The woman kept her eyes on the ground before Roy's outstretched legs.

"*Whither thou goest,*" Roy quoted. "I'm not a lead-er, Mithra. It was an accident that brought me here. I have no power." He opened his empty hands to her in a futile gesture.

"My love brought you here. You wield the Staff of Fire. You defeated Morelua on the hill." She enumer-ated the facts with a fierce forcefulness that nearly con-vinced Roy of their truth.

"Morelua wasn't defeated, Mithra. We fled and he couldn't find us. Look, I'll help you if you wish, but don't make me out to be a great wizard or something. I'm nothing but an English teacher."

"We shall see," she responded, then stood and left Roy and Moratha alone.

"Don't even say it, bird," Roy snapped, looking at the smug silhouette of the great falcon perched in the tree.

*   *   *   *   *

The forest submerged into the undefined color of night as the Pradatha concluded their council. Roy had once again been called to explain his situation, showing the Book of Knowledge to the assembled leaders. No one doubted the written word in the Archmage's own hand, but an uneasy atmosphere still pervaded the group. It wasn't a simple thing to comprehend and still more difficult to accept: They had awaited the Arch-mage and received Roy instead.

"One final question," Stentor said. "You are not Ra-

tha returned, but yet you managed to escape the Dark
One. How did you manage such a feat if you are as powerless as you say?" The council turned toward Roy, waiting for his answer.

"Moratha taught me how to use the Words of Power:
Keshia, Rahlah, and Quintah. I summoned their power
under the stress of attack. I'm not exactly sure how."

The council began to murmur among themselves,
leaning toward one another and speaking rapidly in
small groups. Roy was confused by their reaction and
looked to Mithra for help, but the Pradatha leader was
engaged in discussing something with another young
woman.

"This is most encouraging," Stentor said. "You say
you have no power, and yet you admit you used the
power you have. Only a mage would answer with such a
riddle as this. You have been sent by Ratha Keshia-ne,
Master of the Three-That-Bind, and have arrived in his
image. You wield power and the Staff of Fire." Stentor
looked around the circle of the Pradatha. "If Morelua
believes that Ratha has returned, let him continue to believe so. The one sent is the voice of Ratha, and the voice
is the person. Let the news be sent to every Pradatha village that the Archmage has returned."

"Agreed," said Mithra. "The Pradatha will combine
their forces. Together we can hold Hagsface. The walls
there are sound. We dare not head north again yet,
straight into our enemy's teeth. Let our forces travel
south to Torvathain, then east along the desert's edge,
and let the Dark One follow. The Pradatha throughout
Keshia can use the time to gather at Hagsface and plan
our stand. Those in the north must be notified." Mithra
looked at the sky, marking the measure of the moon's

crescent. "Time. We need time."

She looked at the twelve assembled leaders, representing the twelve tribes, and stared into each one's face. "Do any of you dissent?" One by one, each affirmed his tribe's support. "Good. Stentor, send messengers to the Pradatha that the Archmage has returned. All will gather at Hagsface. We will skirt the mountains to the south and hope the Dark One follows. Prepare to leave tonight." The young woman stood, stretching her long legs beneath her. The others stood and began walking toward their individual camps.

Roy turned his head slightly to look at the falcon resting on his shoulder.

> *"Happy the man whose wish and care*
> *A few paternal acres bound,*
> *Content to breathe his native air*
> *In his own ground.*

"Moratha, I wish I were home."

The great bird blinked back into the professor's eyes but uttered not a sound.

❖ CHAPTER TEN ❖

Flight

The Pradatha began their slow journey south to Torvathain, the Valley of Tears, which was the southernmost pass through the Keshian mountains. It was a quiet journey for the most part, although Roy was acutely aware of the questioning eyes that lingered on him as he walked among the Pradatha and the murmurs that came once he was beyond earshot.

As he moved among them, he counted at least a hundred members, dressed in a variety of costumes but all with the unmistakable rustic appearance of farmers and villagers. None gave any appearance of being a professional. Almost as discomforting, he saw no means of transportation except a few sturdy packhorses, and those were already laboring under the heavy weight of the band's provisions. With only a single exception—himself—each person labored under a backpack containing food, a blanket, and other items of necessity. There seemed to be no discrimination between the sexes. Men and women alike shared the work, each carrying according to his or her own strength. Roy silently logged the information in his memory, another fact so different from his home world.

Thoughts of home brought Gwen to mind. Roy closed his eyes and tried for the hundredth time, unsuccessfully, to conjure up her face before him. The color of her eyes escaped him, the way her nose turned up—or did it?—the creaminess of her skin, the tint of her hair. . . . He struggled to remember.

When they made one of their infrequent stops, Roy and Mithra would sit together, nibbling on some dried bread or keyth, but never speaking, always without contact. Mithra would watch as this man, this stranger in her husband's form, drew pictures in the dust with his heel. Roy would look down at the two lines he'd formed, wondering about vectors, about the life line he'd left behind. And he wondered if he'd left it behind forever.

Several times throughout the day, one or another of a succession of young men would run panting up to Mithra with the same message: "Milady, the Dark One's armies follow, but at a distance. They seem to make no effort to overtake us."

"And Mordeth?" Mithra would ask.

As if they had been trained to make only one motion, each would shrug and shake his head. "I know not, milady." And Roy would watch as Mithra would slowly clench and unclench her fist, as if she wished to crush something inside her palm to dust.

The evening star dipped behind the western horizon, but the Pradatha continued on. Now Roy gave up his mingling with people, who invariably watched him with awe but never spoke, and walked behind Mithra as the young woman glided along the forested path, her longbow strung and nocked with a hawk-fletched arrow. Stentor traveled somewhere ahead of the group, scouting for the Dark One's army. Night crowded against Roy, jostling him into trees and brush as they walked the narrow trail southward along the mountainslopes. He looked westward through a small window in the forest, imagining he could see the glitter of moonlight on the distant sea.

The Pradatha marched on through the night, the forest sounds muffling their movement, amplifying Roy's own heartbeat. Rest came too infrequently for him; he longed to speak with these people, to fill his need for conversation. He reached one hand out to Moratha's head, stroking the bird perched on his shoulder.

Slowly the hours crept toward sunrise. Through an opening in the trees, Roy thought he could distinguish the sharp profile of the mountains to the left, a whisper of amber brushing their peaks. He looked skyward, focusing on a distant star, wondering if it could be his home. Loneliness forced its way through the heavy wool cloak that had been given him, piercing deep into his chest. He remembered some lines from Wordsworth:

> Our birth is but a sleep and a forgetting.
> The soul that rises with us, our life's star,
> Hath had elsewhere its setting
> And cometh from afar.

Roy looked back at the bald star glaring in the night. Suddenly it disappeared. He groaned as he recognized the telltale sign of the dragon.

Mithra turned and looked at him, then followed his eyes upward into the sky.

"What is it?" she whispered.

"The dragon's returned," he replied, his voice more calm than he thought it could be. He pointed at the slow, circling object not far above them. The silhouette of the dragon swept effortlessly across the brightening sky, a huge black cloud of muscle and terror. Mithra jerked impulsively, drawing a slender arrow into her bow, and quickly let it fly toward the hunting dragon, striking Kreosoath in the breast. The arrow clattered against the tough hide of the dragon and glanced harmlessly away, fluttering to the ground below. The dragon angled the rear portion of its wings downward and arched higher, out of range of the useless bows.

"By the Four," Mithra breathed, and Roy couldn't tell if she were angry or afraid. Then she shouted, "Kreosoath has come!"

The Pradatha instantly scattered, hiding beneath the boughs of trees, weapons held ready for the attack of the great dragon. No one spoke. Roy held his staff ready in one hand, although he felt anything but brave. He closed his eyes and tried to imagine the fiery assault he would try to heap upon the lizard-thing. Moratha had disappeared, presumably to hunt, and Roy instantly longed for his companion's return.

Beside him, he could hear Mithra's soft, steady breath. Oddly, it reassured him. He turned and looked at her. Her face was lifted to the heavens, her blue eyes glistening coldly in the feeble starlight. Her bow was across her lap; her right hand clenched the material of her robe above her stomach, and Roy could see, even in the half-dark of twilight, that her knuckles had become white with the strain. He turned away from her and said nothing.

The wait dragged on until morning's light spread across the green hillside and the voice of Thenta called down from his place atop a tall tree: The dragon was gone.

"Hurry! We must hurry," Mithra ordered, and the Pradatha resumed their journey south.

* * * * *

The dust scattered like frightened children beneath the downbeat of the dragon's wings. Kreosoath landed on the ground, his rough hide scraping the dirt with a sound like grinding stone. Far to the north, Shymney cast its shadow westward.

"They move south," the Translating Stone interpreted the great dragon's words. "Many dozens, including the Archmage."

The ebony horse stomped the ground impatiently, its black-cloaked rider tightening the reigns. From atop the stallion, Mordeth could look straight into the eyes of the Lord of Dragons, and the Dark One chose to do so now.

"South? Good. Krotah!" Mordeth turned in his saddle, looking for his security chief.

"Yes, Mordeth?" The slick-faced man crowded through the surrounding soldiers, stepping beside his master.

"We've got them caught between two stones now. Send our quickest riders with word to the commander at Silth. Have him assemble his troops at Oasis within a fortnight. Send word also to Bain. Have Captain Deluta guard the southern pass, then send half of his troops north. Inform him that the Pradatha move toward him."

"Yes, Mordeth."

"And Krotah . . . if the messages do not get there, I will send the new security chief to them with your head."

"Yes, Mordeth." Krotah hurried through the thick mass of guards and collared four sturdy-looking scouts, whispering fiercely to each.

"Kreosoath, continue to follow them and keep me informed. But watch them only. The kill is mine." Mordeth spun his mount away from the great dragon and rode through the parting soldiers.

The black dragon glared angrily at the disappearing rider.

*   *   *   *   *

For two days after the sighting of Kreosoath, the Pradatha continued their southern march. The jagged head of the Mount of Anger, Keshia's only active volcano, reared up before them. Roy wondered at its odd appearance, capped with snow except at the very top, which remained slate gray. If he squinted his eyes, Roy imagined he could make out steam rising in a slow, eastward arc.

The days grew noticeably warmer. Roy, used to the air-conditioned atmosphere of the university or the stone-cooled comfort of Shymney's catacombs, found it oppressive. He noticed also that his legs had begun to bulge against the synthetic material of his trousers, and the ache of the early days of the march had all but disappeared.

On the third day since the sighting of the dragon, the Pradatha turned upslope, toward the Pass of Tears, which the people of Kesh called Torvathain. The land grew coarser, the trees little more than stumps and thin twigs clinging precariously to the small cracks in the rock. A thick, wiry grass spread along the valley bottom like a broom half-buried in the earth. Vaguely it reminded Roy of home, a home that was becoming increasingly difficult to recall.

"You look thoughtful." It was Mithra, speaking to him for the first time since the night of the firelight council meeting.

Roy smiled at the small kindness. "I'm homesick, I think."

A short, ironic laugh escaped the Pradathan leader. She had been unprepared for the simplicity of Roy's emotion, but hearing him say the words brought her own loneliness to the surface.

"For a moment," she said softly, "you sounded just like . . ." She turned and inspected the man who stood beside her. "Tell me, what is it that makes you long for home?"

Roy shrugged. "I look at this place, and it's totally foreign to me. I see the ground, the mountains, the sky, and I know I don't belong here. It's not my world. It's yours."

"And you want to return to your home?" Mithra asked earnestly. She hadn't considered that this hero her husband had sent might be unwilling.

"Wouldn't you?"

Mithra considered a moment. "I have no idea how the Archmage called you here. His book is unclear about that. And if I knew, I haven't the power to send you back. I believe you are here for good reason. I trust Ratha completely." She paused and stooped beside the path, plucking a small, fragile blue flower that had managed to avoid the crush of the march. "I cannot give you back your world . . . but I think I can give you some of ours." She took a deep breath, whispered her Word of Power, and began the storytelling, weaving the picture with her voice.

"Ciandith was a sickly child," she began, and as she spoke, Roy began to see pictures, much like the ones that came to him when Moratha spoke, yet somehow more subtle. He quickly became absorbed in the storytelling, as if he were an observer of an actual event.

The child's hair was the color of sunlight on still waters, and her eyes were the reflection of the sky. Roy tried to guess her age and finally decided she must be about five or six, certainly no older than that. She was lying in a bed, a handmade quilt of red and blue pulled up to her chin. He watched as two adults entered the room. One was male, his uneven beard more gray than brown, his shoulders as thick as a plow animal's, a counterpoint to his narrow waist. The woman—Roy knew instinctively she was the man's wife—was tall, almost as tall as her husband, and ghostly-looking. Roy wasn't even certain she was alive. Her long, pearly hair was left to cascade onto her back, and her bare arms were as white as cream.

"Are you feeling better, Ciandith?" the mother asked, but the little girl didn't even blink a response.

The father put his meaty hand on the woman's shoulder, and Roy could see him fighting back tears. The mother turned to him but said nothing.

The father sucked in a huge breath, then, like an impatient child, scraped the toe of his boot against the rough wooden floor. "Mithra Rahlah," he said reverently, "Mistress of the Wind, come, for the sake of love, come; breathe again the breath of life into our child."

Then the mother spoke. "Mor Quintah, Master of Fire, come, for the sake of love, come; place again the fire of life into our child's breast."

And as Roy watched, the child seemed to fade into translucency, as if she were a glass poured out upon the ground, left empty of life.

The scene changed swiftly, and suddenly Roy was watching the father placing his dead daughter on a pyre of broken sticks. The mother took a lighted torch and touched it to the dry wood, and the flame snarled hungrily as it was fed. The wind began to blow, growing in force until Roy wanted to clasp his hands to his ears to shut out its awful, mournful howl. All at once, the earth shook, and small sparks jumped up from the blaze and were caught up in the wind. Like a thousand thousand torches, what remained of the little girl was scattered across the valley.

Roy turned to look at the father and mother, who stood silently, watching the fire consume their only child. Both faces were wet, but Roy could not tell if it was with grief or joy. For as he looked again, he noticed that wherever the small sparks landed, there immediately sprang forth a small blue flower.

"The Four-That-Bind—Earth, Water, Fire, Air— heard their prayer and knew their love. The four have commanded that these flowers remind us, for all time, of the child Ciandith and the faith of her parents. The Four-That-Bind see our suffering and they care."

Roy stooped to pick a second *ciandith* blossom, cupping his hands to cradle the delicate flower. "We have many stories on Earth, Mithra, but none more lovely than this. You live in a wise and beautiful land."

"We live in a land corrupted by Morelua." Mithra spat the words, the crisp mountain air giving them added edge. "There was a time when Kesh was filled with those who hungered for the words, the taste of stories satisfying children's curiosity." Mithra looked down at the flower she still held between her fingers. "This is the legacy the Dark One gives us. He has tried everything he can think of to keep the stories from being told. He has banned all written works. His spies live among us; the people fear to tell the old tales. But the Dark One cannot destroy all our stories. To do that, he would have to destroy the land."

Roy reached out his hand to hers, touching her softly. "We will prevail, Mithra. In my world, there are stories, too. Some we call fairy tales, and in them good always overcomes evil. It is written; it will be done."

Roy smiled at the melodramatic sound of his own voice, and Mithra mistook the gesture. She leaned toward him and kissed the startled professor, who quickly pushed her away.

They stared into each other's eyes for several labored moments. "I'm sorry, Mithra. I'm not Ratha." Roy held the woman from him with stiff arms. Her hair moved lightly in the breeze, and he could see the mountains reflected in the black pupils of her eyes. The bruise had faded to a soft brown, nearly mistakable as a smudge of dirt across her right jowl, and Roy realized how beautiful she truly was.

Mithra turned away from him, again walking up the steep slope. Her arms fell into a relaxed swing as she climbed away from him, and he saw the faint blue of the *ciandith* as it tumbled from her hand.

"Damn," Roy said to no one in particular.

Ratha, came the answering voice of the falcon from a nearby tree. How long it had been there, Roy didn't know. Apparently it had returned from whatever errand it had gone on. The bird flew across the clearing and landed on the professor's shoulder.

"You'd best stay close, my friend. I'll have more than Mordeth to deal with before this is over."

* * * * *

The Pradatha made camp when they reached the saddle of Torvathain, and the watch was set to reconnoiter each slope. Runners had reported to Mithra throughout their flight, informing her that Mordeth still followed, but they were a hard day and a half's march behind. The Dark One didn't seem overly anxious to cut the distance between the two armies, although, according to the scouts, his troops outnumbered the Pradatha by more than three to one. It irked Mithra that the Regent was so overly confident, but she was thankful that he followed at a distance. It would give her people that much more time to gather at Hagsface and to prepare.

The sun dipped into the west until the great fire sunk beneath the watery horizon. Then the sky began to burn with the hot red of sunset, a smoky haze spreading along the edge of the planet.

"*Red sky at morning, sailors take warning; red sky at night, sailor's delight,*" Roy quoted as he watched the brilliant sunset.

"Is that another poem from your great book?" Mithra had moved silently beside the professor.

"Great book?"

Mithra considered him through narrowed eyes. "The

Great Book of Knowledge."

"Where I come from, we don't have such a book. It's just an old saying that people are fond of quoting." He shifted uncomfortably. "It's a pretty sky."

"Yes." Mithra sat beside him, and Roy felt his shoulders tense.

"I'm sorry," she said. "I wanted to apologize for this afternoon. I realize you're . . ." She let the sentence hang unfinished. "You are much like the one I loved. It is difficult."

"For me also, Mithra. I find you more than beautiful. But I am not Ratha. You must remember."

The woman looked west at the last wisp of magenta that lined the horizon, but she didn't answer. "Tell me of your world."

Roy relaxed visibly. "It's good and bad, like all worlds, I guess. I taught at a university, which is a place where people gather to learn the world's knowledge."

"We had universities here once, too. One such university is at Hagsface. There we taught our children the stories of Keshia and the power of the Four."

"And now?"

Mithra's eyes flashed her anger. "Now the Regent forbids any teaching about the Four. Only darkness and emptiness are taught."

Roy smiled sourly. "So it is in many worlds. In my world, I teach the language and the stories of our people. We call it literature; the Regents of my university frown upon its teaching, too. *With infinite information, only the necessary need be taught.*"

"In Kesh, *litera* means 'volume' or 'collection.' The stories of the land are called 'literava Kesh.' It's my duty to collect them into the Book of All, to save them from forgetful minds and the dark age of Mordeth."

"Do you write in it often?" Roy asked.

Mithra shook her head. "No, not often. Other things have kept me from it." Her fingers traced their way to her belly, and she looked away from the professor. "Tell me about your literature."

"Well, there are religions on my world that center around a certain piece of literature, a certain book, or even, in some cases, a certain sentence or group of words within a book. There has been considerable fighting over how to interpret these books, how to make the stories work."

Mithra snapped around, fury in her face. The energy there surprised Roy. "I cannot see how people can fight over the meaning of a story," Mithra said. "To each person, it is personal. On Kesh, we always speak the Word of Power before we tell a story that teaches, so that each person is empowered to visualize the story for himself. What a person sees when a story is told is sacred, for it is given by the word."

"Well, it isn't that way on my world. We have no Words of Power, or if we do, we lost them long ago. In my world, we have machines called computers, which store information. They gather pictures and string them together, so that people can watch them move inside a little box. Stories are told without words, but with pictures only. We call them movies, because it is the movement, not the words, that is emphasized.

"Science is our power. We mechanize everything possible so that we no longer need to labor, to struggle. Machines give us leisure time, and we spend that leisure time watching movies, being entertained, instead of entertaining ourselves. Science has so much power that it has all but destroyed literature." Roy looked through the gathering dark at the woman beside him. She was intent, her eyes unblinking spots in the soft whiteness of her face.

"We live in sad times." Her voice came as a gentle caress across the night.

*   *   *   *   *

The Pradatha were on the move again before first light, traveling down the steep eastern slope of the Keshian mountains. Roy immediately noticed a difference in the land. The trees, once deciduous, now were primarily conifers, and the grass was brown. Before him, the mountains undulated as far as he could see, spreading out like a knotted carpet. He hastened to catch up with Mithra.

"How far to Hagsface from here?"

"We go north and east for five or six days until we reach the Fenfeder River. From there, it's a day's journey to the Great Desert. It may take another week to reach the Tranquil Sea and Hagsface once we reach the desert. A fortnight in all."

"Great," replied the professor dourly.

"Of course, you could always push that lazy bird from your shoulder and send him on ahead to prepare your bed." Mithra laughed and poked a good-natured finger at Moratha, who blinked sleepily at her.

"I think Moratha is conserving his energy for more important things. Besides," Roy added in a conspiratorial whisper, "I think he's getting pretty old." Moratha fluffed his feathers in a threatening gesture, and Roy and Mithra laughed aloud.

"Tell me more about your literature, Roy."

Roy warmed to the task, pleased to be asked to do what he most loved. His mind sifted through a myriad of stories he could tell until he found one that seemed to fit.

"A man named Ray Bradbury wrote a story about a world in which books and literature were outlawed by the government. The hero was a fireman, someone whose job was to burn the stories that had been written. People willingly died rather than give up their books, so Montague, the hero, became interested in books. He hid some in his home and began to read them. Then he was discovered and targeted for execution, but he fled, finding a new world of old-fashioned folk who still valued the stories."

"What was the government's name?" Mithra asked.

"I'm not sure it had one. Apathy, maybe."

"Here we call it Morelua. 'The Lord of Nothing.' Mordeth hates that name." She walked on in silence.

They continued their steep descent, rarely stopping to rest along the way. From time to time, one of the scouts would shout a warning, and all eyes would focus on the distant movements of the black dragon as it swept across the cloudless sky. But the beast never ventured near enough to provoke an attack. Instead, it hung back and let the fear it spread do its work. After dusk, they rested beneath the boughs of the tall conifers that spread throughout the forest, the comforting twinkle of stars filtering through the needled limbs. For six days, the routine continued unbroken. Scouts were sent out to hunt for food, while the main body continued to drive on in a northeasterly direction, talking among themselves, watching for the approach of the seemingly omnipresent dragon.

The sound of water tumbling through a narrow gorge greeted them late on the morning of the seventh day, filling the valley they were following with the music of the cataract. The Pradatha rested on the right bank of the river that they called the Fenfeder, the great river that runs eastward from the mountains into the Great Fen, the dismal swamp that borders the land south of the desert. The group sat and broke out their rations, eating dried fish, hard bread, and bits of fruit they had gathered on their journey. Roy occasionally offered a morsel of fish to Moratha, which the falcon accepted gratefully.

After the brief rest, the Pradatha followed the carefully marked trail of the forward scouts, moving westward along the rapidly flowing river. The forests of the mountains had given way to the short scrub grass of the steppe. The river they followed was contained by sheer rock walls, and Roy wondered how the people, much less their animals, would ford it. His answer came when they reached an enormous oak that once stood proudly overlooking the river, but which now, hewn and tumbled, stretched from bank to stony bank. One by one the entire group crossed the churning water, until at last only Mithra and the dozen horses, lightened of their burdens, remained on the southern shore. With a wild shout, Mithra frightened the horses away, sending them galloping through the pine forest. Then she, too, crossed the thick trunk to the other side.

Stentor divided up the supplies once carried by the horses, giving a share to each of the Pradatha. Waterskins were filled and strung across the already heavily laden backs of the stout rebels. Then the group turned north and headed for the last ridge of mountains that shrouded the dunes of the Great Desert.

Mithra turned to Roy, victory shining in her blue eyes. "Mordeth will try to follow, but he'll have to backtrack. There are no fords within a half-day of here, and no trees large enough to fell and stretch across. We'll gain a half-day or more." As she spoke, three sturdy men grasped the makeshift bridge and tossed it into the water, the current dragging the heavy mass downstream like a child's toy.

As the Fox Star rose red on the western horizon, the Pradatha crested the saddle of the final ridge and stood looking down at the great desert that spread out before them to the east. In the fading light, it appeared like a still sea spreading before Roy, like the bay to which he had been summoned on this world, only larger, so large that his legs weakened beneath him in a wash of vertigo. They camped upon the crest looking down upon the barren desert.

Roy awoke the next morning in the shadow of a rock, opening his eyes to see his steady falcon companion still asleep beside him. He propped himself up on an elbow, savoring the crisp, dry mountain air and the smell of the blooming mountain meadow in which they camped. About him, the Pradatha were preparing for the descent into the desert.

Roy ate his morning rations slowly, carefully setting aside a portion for Moratha. A fear that Moratha might be ailing gnawed at the pleasant feeling he had awakened to, and he wanted to talk to someone about it. He looked around at the busy Pradatha, silently attaching names to each one he could remember. Although he rarely spoke with anyone but Mithra, and occasionally

Stentor and Tralaina, he had come to recognize many of the assembled army. Suddenly he realized that Mithra was conspicuously absent.

Roy set a piece of jerked meat before Moratha, then stood and began to meander through the camp, searching for the Pradathan leader. He spotted Stentor adjusting a bundle for a younger man and headed toward him.

"Have you see Mithra?" Roy asked.

"No. She's missing?" Stentor's voice reflected his concern.

"Not really. I just haven't seen her yet this morning. She's probably up with the forward guards, reviewing instructions." Roy hoped he sounded more convincing than he felt, for a deep worry pinched within his chest. He turned away from the stout barkeep and walked around the outer edges of the camp, keeping his strides even so as not to arouse suspicion from Stentor. It was enough that he was worried.

As he moved up a narrow path that led east, he heard a noise in the thin brush. Roy raised his staff, whispering his mantra of Words of Power, and the falcon eye began to pulse with fierce energy. He raised the staff above the level of his eyes, poised to send the shock of light through whatever evil lurked in the bushes. He lowered his staff, the pulsing energy subdued to a faint glimmer, and spread the bush apart.

Mithra knelt upon the ground before him, dry heaves racking her slender body. Her face was paler than usual, and her arms trembled as they supported her. The weakness Roy witnessed startled him, for Mithra had always seemed a bastion of strength. The two looked at each other with a kind of grotesque fascination, the spell finally broken by the unmistakable sound of beating wings.

Ratha, said the falcon inquiringly.

"Mithra's ill," Roy replied, helping Mithra up from the ground. Roy noticed a vague look of disbelief in the glossy eyes of his friend. The professor shook his head in wonder.

"I'm not ill," Mithra replied. She met Roy's worried look with a thin smile. "Not anymore, at least. My breakfast must have gone bad. I'll be all right."

"You're sure?" Roy asked.

"I'm sure," Mithra answered.

"Perhaps we should warn the others. It wouldn't do to let them eat tainted food."

The urgency in Mithra's voice struck Roy like a slap. "No! It—it was food I brought on my own. I wasn't careful enough preparing it. There's no need to tell the others."

"But—"

"I said no." Mithra smiled once more weakly, and when she spoke again her voice was gentle and reassuring. "I'm fine. Thank you for your concern, but the others don't need to see their leader on her knees, throwing up her breakfast." The color had already returned to her cheeks, and Roy felt relieved. But as another thought came to him, he turned suddenly to the falcon and frowned.

"What made you come?" Roy asked the bird.

Ratha, he replied.

"My staff? The power surge awakened you? Moratha, you are mystery itself, but I'm glad you came. It reassures me for the future." Roy attempted a feeble smile, still embarrassed to have seen Mithra so vulnerable and to have needlessly aroused the great hawk. He turned back to the Pradathan leader. "You're sure you're all right?"

"If I weren't, I'd tell you. We'd best get back to camp."

"Stentor's probably organizing a search party to look for you by now. I asked him if anybody had seen you this morning, and he seemed awfully concerned." Roy shrugged as if trying to push away an unwelcome feeling. He wanted to pry further, but he sensed Mithra's resolve to say nothing. Without another word, he followed Mithra back to camp.

Stentor was concerned, but he hadn't yet assembled a search party. Instead, he had tried to busy himself with travel preparations, leaving Roy to search for Mithra, confident that the Archmage's messenger was competent to handle any problems. Nonetheless, he had kept an anxious eye on the distant circling shape of Kreosoath. His face showed enormous relief when Roy, Mithra, and Moratha returned to camp.

"We leave in ten minutes," Stentor called. Silently Mithra went to her pack and hefted it across her back, tying the straps securely over her shoulders and around her slim waist. Roy went to his bedroll, finding that someone had already rolled and bound it. He hefted it and slung it across his back.

"You'll need to help me watch her, Moratha," Roy whispered to his friend. "Something's not right, but she's too proud to tell me. Watch her, bird. Watch her." Then the professor fell into line at the head of the troops.

Moratha did watch the Pradathan woman, as did Roy, as the Pradathan army moved down the slope toward the

Great Desert. Mithra's face regained its healthy glow as
the march progressed, and Roy began to feel relief seep
into his tense body. He began to notice the panorama
that spread before him like an artist's easel, the chalk-
blue of the desert shadows melting into the austere
white of the sand. The desert swelled before them, and
by midday, he could feel the pulse of heat radiating
from it, a scorching, dry heat that pulled the sweat from
his body.

Mithra seemed to eat less at the midday meal, although Roy guessed that her stomach was still upset
with a meal that had not settled well. It wasn't all that
unusual that a person would spurn food after a bout
with food poisoning. But he continued to watch her as
she picked at the food before her, selecting a few choice
morsels and chewing them slowly, seemingly uninter-
ested in them.

The remainder of the day passed in the usual fashion,
the slow descent from the high country a monotony that
had become the usual fare for the group. The black silhouette of Kreosoath still could be seen hovering in the
distant sky, circling like a vulture waiting for death. It
amazed Roy how easily the presence of the dragon, even
though it was at least a mile away, had become so commonplace. He looked again at the beast, remembering
its power, its maliciousness upon the beach. A few lines
from Tennyson came to mind, and he said them aloud,
drawing the parallels between Tennyson's Merlin and
himself:

> *"Once at the croak of a raven who crossed it,*
> *A barbarous people,*
> *Blind to the magic*

And deaf to the melody,
Snarled at and cursed me.
A demon vexed me,
The light retreated, the landskip darkened,
The melody deadened,
The Master whispered,
'Follow the Gleam.' "

Mithra closed the distance between them, listening closely to the professor all the while.

"The words are unknown, but here they have power," she said, pointing to her heart. She held out her hand, and Roy took it in his own.

"Are you feeling better now, Mithra?" Roy asked, finally broaching the subject they had both avoided all day.

"I was ill this morning. The sickness seems concentrated then; I have had similar problems for the past three days. I am sure it is the food I prepared. But it would not do for the Pradatha to see their leader with her knees driven into the soil. It will pass."

"Perhaps we should tell Stentor or Tralaina. I'm concerned for you."

"No," she insisted, "trust me. It is best that they do not know." Mithra looked into the golden eyes of the reluctant mage and said simply, "I'm pregnant."

Roy felt the blood rushing to his face, the burning of his neck and ears an embarrassing irritant. He looked more critically at the woman before him, trying unsuccessfully to picture her with one of the Pradathan men who traveled with them.

"Who?"

"No one of importance," Mithra replied, her voice a

hoarse whisper, her face ashen. Inwardly she struggled not to cry, not to show weakness to this man whom her husband had sent to help her people. She bent her pain into anger, doubled it into rage. But to Roy, she said nothing more.

"Surely we should at least tell Tralaina."

"No. I'm fine. I'll be careful. For now, we have a war to prepare for. There will be time later." The woman was so adamant that Roy conceded her wishes, but he resolved to watch her closely for the remainder of the trek to Hagsface.

Even without horses, the Pradatha made good time across the southern rim of the Great Desert. Adept scouts located the few watering holes, making the journey a simpler task than expected. On the afternoon of the fifth day after leaving the cool comfort of the mountain ranges, an excited scout ran panting toward them, then knelt, exhausted, before Mithra and Roy.

"Gulls, milady, my lord. A mile away, no more." The young man attempted to catch his breath. "We near the Tranquil Sea," he panted. "By evenfall. No more." The young Pradathan continued kneeling as he sucked the dry, hot desert air into his aching lungs.

"And what of the Pradatha? Have any arrived yet?" Mithra's voice sounded tight.

"Yes, milady. From Silth and Wahala. And they tell of others on their way. According to your instructions, milady, the Pradatha are gathering and preparing for war at Hagsface."

Mithra gently stroked the boy's head, smoothing his wind-tossed hair. Then she turned and repeated the message to the Pradatha who had gathered behind her.

"We prepare now for war," she said in a clear voice,

reaching out to take Roy's hand in her own as she spoke. Roy noticed a slight tremor in her hand and squeezed it firmly, trying to abate the trembling in his own. Then they turned and began the final march to the sea.

❖ CHAPTER ELEVEN ❖

The Falcon Calls

The coarse gray stone of the merlons had long ago begun to crumble under the constant punishment of time and marine climate, leaving a ghostly pile of sand at the base of the fortress of Hagsface. Roy looked down from the parapet at the sandy slopes below, noting the fuzzy green vegetation growing there. The fortress at Hagsface was not the stuff of knightly romances. He frowned at the thought of a real battle occurring beneath these very walls.

As he thought these things, Moratha, the great falcon, returned from a successful hunt, attested to by the dark stains on his feathers and beak. Roy held up an outstretched arm to him, letting the falcon settle onto his accustomed perch. Roy was thankful for the company offered by the great bird.

"So, Moratha. Your hunt went well today, I see. Was it enjoyable?"

Ratha, the falcon replied, and the vision that came was so strong that Roy felt himself with wings, felt the hot desert air as it rose beneath him, making him lighter, more buoyant. A sudden surge of wind swept him farther from the fortress, now only a tiny dot along the horizon. Soon the dot disappeared altogether. Then an image of short, wiry grass, green with moisture and unlike anything around the fortress, engraved itself upon Roy's mind.

"Where did you go, Moratha? There's no grass like this nearby."

Ratha, replied the falcon, and Roy felt himself swept up in the raptor's flight, soaring across the desert far to the south, to the very southern edge of the desert.

Below, a hare tried vainly to scurry from one bald stone to another. The chase was short. Roy could see the darting animal below, could feel the rapid descent. He could sense the fear of the hare, the touch of the fur as powerful talons grappled the struggling form, bringing instant death. The taste of blood tinged Roy's mouth, stimulating his own saliva.

"Well, I'm not overly fond of the taste of blood, friend, but I would be grateful if you could teach me to fly!" Roy laughed as Moratha shrugged and extended his wings.

"No matter. Mithra has sent word she wants to see us. She should be ready for us soon," he said, looking down to the square below, seeking the Pradatha leader.

Mithra had been meeting with the leaders of the various groups of Pradatha that had come at her summons. It had been agreed that only those few Pradatha who had attended the first meeting, when Roy showed the Archmage's book, should know that Roy was not the true Ratha. All others were allowed to believe that he was the real Archmage, a deception that Roy reluctantly accepted.

The bright ring of metal on metal echoed across the morning as a young girl pulled the rope of the town's heavy bell, and Roy's eyes continued to scan the square below him, the bustle of activity a vague reassurance in the face of gathering despair. The Pradathan army had grown to nearly eight hundred men now, mostly rural folk who came armed with nothing more than ancient bows or half-rusted swords or spears of tarnished bronze. Many more came with less—pitchforks or stout clubs. It was a ragtag army, certainly no match for Mordeth's well-trained troops. It was mad to hope to hold the city against an obviously superior army.

The mages came as well, the men and women who mastered the one, the teachers of the legends and sagas who were banned after the Falcon's fall at Shymney some ten years past. They had fled to distant cities and villages, taking up the crafts necessary to insure their survival, meanwhile disguising their nature by becoming blacksmiths, carpenters, farmers—any trade that had as little to do with their former occupations as possible. Many of them had rarely practiced their craft in those bleak years, but a few had gathered the necessary courage to organize small schools in darkened glades or backwood caves, teaching those young boys and girls whose parents dared to secretly defy the Regent's edict. Occasionally muffled sobs of joy were heard within the fortress walls, signaling the reunion of parent and child who had been parted for many years as the child studied in an underground school, unable to return home for fear of discovery.

Roy grew familiar with the attire of the various clans: the dark forest green predominant in the Shaleth to the northwest; the yellow-accented lime green of Norshal, the eastern cousin of Shaleth; the rust brown of the desert people of Silth; the wild mosaic of colors worn by the southern people. In addition to their clothing, Roy began to recognize the lighter features of the northerners, the thicker, darker features of the nomadic desert dwellers, and the ruddy, leathery complexion of the coastal people. Many times he found himself engaged in a personal game, trying to detect the origin of someone he met along the cobbled streets.

With Moratha perched on his shoulder, Roy continued to look down into the square. The bell rang again, and for a moment, he thought he had returned to his own world. The sound he heard was the old bell ringing in the university's tower, and he was standing on the red-bricked square, beneath the veranda of Smith Tower. And was that Gwen standing there, talking to one of her students? He tried to focus on her face, but the attempt at concentration broke the spell. He was in Keshia, and he was here to stay. He looked at Moratha, already asleep on his shoulder, then gripped the staff tightly in his hand.

Mithra had told him Hagsface had been a strong fortress city many decades past, a port city halfway between the northern provinces and those of the south. The Tranquil Sea shone like a turquoise gemstone beyond the silver strands of beach that surrounded the city. Since the city lay leeward of the Keshian Mountains, the climate was dry and usually temperate, except in the heart of summer, and this, combined with the clear, bright waters and the excellent university, made the city a much-admired and joyous center for the people of Keshia—that is, until the Regent came to power.

In the heart of the fortress city was an adobe building,

octagonal in design, with large, slanting windows on the northern faces. The hardened clay tiles covering its roof looked like the scales of a desert reptile. The spacious interior was filled with row after row of pews, polished wood the color of mahogany, the soft grain gleaming a pale brown design. For centuries, the pews had been filled with students who had come to winter in the resort city. Hagsface was proud of its university, and the elders would call the best and brightest to teach and interpret the powerful stories of Keshia.

The city prospered and grew until Morlin became Regent after Gondsped's untimely death. After the edict forbidding the teaching of the Book of Knowledge, the teachers scattered like sand thrown into the desert wind, and the students no longer traveled to the eastern city. In the ten years since Mordeth had overthrown the Archmage, the city had become an abandoned shell that Keshians referred to as the "Tomb of Knowledge."

Mithra appeared in the plaza below him, wearing the heavy leather armor of battle and carrying her yew bow with a quiver strapped across her back. She hid her pregnancy well, and that singular secret had managed to break down the other barriers and bring them closer. Many times Roy found himself thinking it was no wonder the Archmage Ratha had loved her.

"Ratha," Mithra called up to him. It had been decided before they arrived that he would play the part of the Archmage, even in the midst of the Pradatha. Only a handful knew the truth, and they were trusted friends of Mithra. To all others, Roy was Ratha returned.

"I'll be right down, Mithra. Is the meeting about to begin?"

"As soon as the elders gather." Mithra smiled faintly,

for she was one of the elders herself, and her own vanity, though slight, had trouble admitting she was old enough to be an elder. Much had changed since the Regent took power.

Roy climbed down the wooden ladder to the square below, extending his hand out to Mithra and walking with her toward the university building. The meeting had been arranged for the morning, so that the Pradatha could complete their plans for battle. Reconnaissance had informed them that Mordeth's army was gathered at Oasis, more than sixty miles away. They couldn't move in force across the desert without the Pradatha knowing.

Mithra held the door open as Roy went inside the building. The cool, earthy air was a refreshing change from the heat of the parapet. He walked down the wide nave to the front of the lecture hall, feeling a sense of rightness as he did. It was good to be back in a school, no matter how far away from his own world.

The room was empty except for the two dozen Pradatha elders who sat patiently in the polished wood pews. Roy knew that they were expecting him to lead them, and the thought frightened him. He knew nothing of military ventures, even less of strategy. And the memory of the battle—and near defeat—with Mordeth at Shymney remained all too clear.

"I invoke the Four-That-Bind—Keshia, Rahlah, Roshah, Quintah—and ask their blessing. Come, Mistress of the Sea. Come, Brother Wind. Enter, Sister Earth. Be present, Master Fire. We come here now to seek thy aid. Grant us power and wisdom." Mithra intoned the liturgy that began all meetings of the Pradatha, then sat down in the front row, looking up at Roy. Although she knew he wasn't the Archmage, she still believed that Ratha had sent him to the Pradatha to help in the destruction of the Regent. Moratha perched upon the back of the pew beside her.

"By the Four, I speak," Roy began, reciting the speech he had rehearsed with Mithra. "Morelua is camped at Oasis, and his troops will be here in not less than four days, perhaps longer. I have returned to aid you. We must continue to fortify this stronghold against Morelua. I will need to prepare my power, so Mithra will be your general." A quiet murmuring rippled through the hall, quickly subsiding as Roy continued.

"Those of the mage craft among us must also prepare. Let it be done with haste, for Morelua's power is great." Roy stepped down from the dais and exchanged places with Mithra, who stood and began to instruct the Pradatha regarding fortifications.

"We know that we will be outnumbered. Our scouts tell us that Mordeth's armies from Bain and Silth will soon join him. For that reason alone, we must wait here and let them come to us. They will need to cross the desert to reach us. Once they attempt a siege, they will be without water, except for what they can carry from wells a day's march away, for the only other well is within our walls. And they must breach the walls to get to us. With the luck of the Four with us, we should be able to fend them off."

"Why does Mordeth wait? Wouldn't it be to his advantage to attack now, before we solidify our fortifications?" asked one of the elders as Mithra finished. Roy didn't recognize the woman, but she wore the light green of Norshal. The question was one that Roy had asked himself.

"I don't know, but I do know Morelua," Mithra answered, saying the name as if it were a curse. "Fear is his ally, he once said to me, and this is one truth even he speaks." Mithra paused as she remembered the dark chamber deep beneath Mordeth's hold, the fear she felt as his awful hands caressed her. When she spoke again, her words held a truth deeper than she wanted to admit.

"Time will produce a dread in us," she continued, "a dread that, if we let it fester, will destroy us. We must be wary. Know this also: Ratha gathers his own strength, and with each hour that Morelua is delayed, the Archmage's power grows. Morelua will be aware of this, and the time he makes us wait will be cut short by his own fear. We, too, can use fear as an ally."

The sounds of general consent buzzed through the room, and Mithra looked to Roy, who sat silent, studying the wood of his staff, unwilling to meet her eyes. Mithra intoned the closing words and the room emptied, leaving Mithra, Roy, and Moratha alone in the lecture hall.

"Will we be ready, Mithra?" Roy asked.

"I don't know." She reached out her hand and took his. "But we must try. And you must play the part of the Archmage, for the sake of all of us. The people must believe. And Mordeth must fear you. It is the hope that Ratha gave us. You have much to do." She paused, reconsidering. "We have much to do."

CHAPTER TWELVE

Deathstone

The heat was unrelenting, pressing upon his back like a heavy yoke, a burden he carried but resented. He had been force-marched across the scorching desert to Oasis, and now he had to wait for Mordeth to order him across more desert, to an unknown enemy. Flanx swallowed a bit of his rationed water and sat himself in the meager shade.

How had he gotten to be in this forsaken place? Mithra, of course. By the three, she was beautiful! And her voice! What a sultry temptress she could be! Four years ago—had it really been that long?—she had come to him and asked for aid. He had been about to set out from Birchwood to find his fortune when this slip of a woman found him at an inn, sat down with him, and talked of this and that and nothing at all. But she was sly and soon discovered his weakness; he, like most Keshians, hated the Regent with a passion. More than once since then, Flanx had been thankful that it was Mithra that pierced his shell and not one of the Elite Guards.

For days Mithra had met with him, sometimes in the common room of the inn, sometimes at one shop or another, and once along a beach that lapped with the cold tide of the northern sea. She spoke of everything and nothing, but always the edge of talk came sharply back to the lost stories that would never be regained, the stories Mordeth had forbidden to be told. Power, she had said, the stories had power, and Mordeth knew it. He was afraid of those stories, afraid that they might unleash the truth. Stories that belonged to the people— had not Flanx's own mother told him those very stories? And now the Regent had forbidden them. Each day his hatred for Mordeth grew, until at last Mithra told him a new story, one as powerful as the old ones, a story of how Mordeth had falsely accused Ratha, Mithra's husband, and executed him at the foot of Shymney. The stories of the battle with the Archmage were common, but to have met one who truly knew!—well, that was something indeed.

And it was easy to see how an Archmage could fall in love with Mithra. Her voice, her bearing, her attitude, all exuded power. She could have been an Archmage herself. In fact, several times Flanx had wondered if she were not, the charm she wove upon him was so strong. It wasn't that he felt compelled to do anything against his will. On the contrary, he lived for the opportunity to serve this great lady, this wielder of power. So when she came to him with the request that he join Mordeth's army to aid the cause of Pradatha, he had willingly and quickly enlisted.

Even though the Pradathan spy was more than willing to supply Mithra with information, he had difficulty adjusting himself to the hard life of one of Mordeth's troops. In the five years he had been a part of Mordeth's army, he had managed to advance through the ranks until he became a sergeant, leading a small company of men from his native Shaleth. He had been chosen to wait upon the needs of the dragon when that wretched beast had come to speak with the Regent. How he hated that black beast, with its ebon fangs glistening with the blood of murdered peasants, its eyes swirling with some unfathomable evil.

What was perhaps most astonishing of all was that he had survived those five years without being discovered or killed. Mordeth's spies were everywhere. At the thought, he gave a quick, cursory glance around him. He saw two of his men coming toward him, talking low to one another. Flanx recognized them instantly as Cimeon and Rindah, two cousins from the northeastern deserts of Kesh.

"Y' hear th' news yet, Sarge?" Cimeon asked in a conspiratorial tone when they drew close. He was a thick, dark-haired man of twenty, slow of wit, but with a surprising physical agility that had allowed him to best more than one opponent in battle.

"The water of Oasis has turned to brandy at last?" Flanx replied with a half-smile.

Cimeon considered his superior a moment, then shook his head with the dull slowness of the witless. Beside him, Rindah smiled broadly but said nothing. Cimeon finally replied, "No. What I heard was Mordeth's gonna do some prayin' or somethin' once we get to the Deathstone. He told Plentaten to gather together some of the peasants we found headin' to Hagsface. Some kinda ritual or somethin'. Leastwise, that's what I heard. From Plentaten, I mean."

"That gossip? Plentaten should be in an old woman's battalion. What do you think? Could he make corporal in such a unit?" The two cousins guffawed loudly, and Flanx snorted for effect, but the news disturbed him. All of Kesh had heard the stories of Deathstone. It was there that Mordeth had first summoned the power of night. Deathstone was an unspeakably evil place, and none ventured there voluntarily. He suppressed a shudder and summoned up a forced laugh.

"Do y' think it's true, Sarge?" Rindah asked. Rindah was Cimeon's cousin and shared the larger man's complexion, but little else. Rindah was thin and wiry, and he spoke with the drawl of the people of the desert's western edge.

"I doubt it. But if you really want to find out, why don't you go ask Mordeth? I'm sure he'll accommodate you." Flanx's smile turned into a raffish grin, and Rindah shuddered at the thought of approaching Mordeth with such a question.

"Best get some sleep now. No matter where his lordship tells us to march, in this heat, it'll feel like Deathstone." Flanx stood and left the two cousins whispering to each other.

The old sergeant fled the bludgeoning sun into the shade of his tiny tent, then stretched out on the woolen blanket sprawled across the dirt inside. His eyes stared unfocused at a tiny hole in the canvas, where light poured through and shone down upon his chest, as if to pierce his heart. Mithra needed information from him. If Mordeth was going back to the place where he found his power, if the Dark One was going to reclaim his due at the foot of the blackest altar of all Kesh, then Mithra needed to hear about it. He closed his eyes and tried to imagine some way he could escape, some means to get the word to her.

Flanx was awakened before first light, the shrill voice of his lieutenant screeching through the closed flaps of his tent. He had not meant to sleep, but fatigue had taken control and his body had submitted. Now he awoke with a start, remembering his mission. Perhaps, he told himself, there was no need to worry. Perhaps Mithra already knew.

"Prepare to march. Five minutes." The voice moved off into the night, and Flanx mechanically began to stuff his belongings into his pack. He could hear the movement of his men as they, too, prepared to march. He caught sight of Rindah, stuffing his bedroll into his pack, and ventured a quick comment to him.

"So, you talked to the man, eh? Next time ask him if we're going to have a two-month furlough."

Rindah snuffed an insolent reply, intent on packing. Within five minutes, Flanx's unit was ready to march.

They set out across the desert, the sun rising out of the flat eastern horizon, swelling the heat radiating from the sand. Heat seeped through his heavy-soled boots, and his feet sweated uncontrollably. Calluses threatened to blister if he didn't rest, but Deathstone was a full day's march, perhaps two, from Oasis. He remembered the tales of his childhood, stories he had been forbidden to hear these past ten years, of the origin of the Deathstone. The thoughts made him shudder in spite of the heat.

Deathstone was an obsidian porch, a black stone placed in the heart of the scorching desert. Tales were told of its mysterious appearance, back before the Great Desert arched across the middle of Keshia. It had soared with a fierce fire across the sky and landed with a bone-jarring crunch. Trees and bushes withered about it, and the blight spread out from the stone in all directions. Nothing lived near the stone, and through the eons, all things of inland Keshia faded like colors in the night, leaving only Oasis, its reddish waters turned brackish by the polluted stone. The western ranges blocked the evil of the stone, as did the Tranquil Sea on the east, but the legend said that the stone would rob all Keshia of life, and many believed it.

Mordeth's army marched southward to Deathstone, dust choking the tired soldiers. Mordeth rode upon his dark stallion, racing from the head of the column to the rear, scolding and threatening laggards. His mood seemed more foul to Flanx than he had ever seen before, and the sergeant despised the Regent even more. At the rear of the column were a dozen prisoners, their hands bound behind them, their mouths stuffed with filthy rags and gagged with cords. They had been stripped of their cloaks, and their skins were red and blistering in the sun. Many of the captured were children, and Flanx futilely tried to quell an angry ache in his chest.

Two hours after sunset, the army finally halted. The night was moonless, the starlight too feeble to aid in sight. The troops were mustered into a circle. At first, Flanx thought that they were about to be attacked and were forming a defensive ring, but the orders came that all were to face inward. They stood in their awkward circle, waiting for further orders.

A torch, held aloft by a wizened old mage, moved through the circle of soldiers. The men nearest him gave him wide berth as he passed into the inner circle. Flanx didn't recognize the man and couldn't remember any

elderly mage in the service of Mordeth. The circle became hushed as the mage strode into the heart of the
circle. The flickering torchlight cast a feeble glow onto a
large, flat object, several yards square. Flanx focused on
the stone, watching as the light seemed to be absorbed
into it.

A hush overcame the assembly as Mordeth appeared
through the maze of soldiers. His robes were as black as
the month's first night, except for the faint glow of the
map of Keshia stitched on his breast in silver thread. His
hands were gauntleted with heavy black leather, and his
boots, which came nearly to his knees, were of a blackness that seemed to absorb the torchlight. Mordeth
walked to the ebon stone and mounted it.

He looked down at the circle of troops surrounding
him and turned slowly, letting everyone drink in his
presence. His left hand twitched slightly, and Krotah appeared through the mass, towing the bound prisoners.
Mordeth looked down upon them as if he were selecting
a choice morsel of food. He lifted his hand and darkness
leapt from it, striking a prisoner in the chest. Flanx
heard a faint gasp, and he stretched to see what happened.

The bolt had struck a child, her blond hair thin and
limp, her narrow shoulders as yet unused to the weight
of the world. She looked to be not more than ten years
old. Flanx wondered if she had been born the very year
Mordeth had risen to power. Flanx looked on as the child
hung suspended by the power thrown at her, then collapsed soundlessly. Torchlight flickered across her naked
body. Flanx could see a very slight movement: The child
was not dead yet. He could feel his own heart beating,
measuring the moments he thought would surely never

end. Mordeth raised his arm again. The child stirred, then, pushing herself up with her rail-thin arms, stood and faced the Lord of Darkness. Flanx couldn't tear his eyes away from her face. It was as if it floated in the darkness, buoyed by the night, an expressionless mask, eyes wide and blank. He was both revolted and intrigued. He couldn't turn away, couldn't take his eyes from her lovely, horrible face.

Mordeth made a slight movement. Instantly Flanx's eyes were drawn to the Dark Lord. He stood upon the black stone, a cruel smile bending his lips. His right hand was held at waist level, his fist crunched into a ball. Then slowly, deliberately, he raised his left hand until it was high above his head. Something was there, shivering. Flanx tried to swallow but couldn't.

The girl spoke. Her voice rang in the night, like a clarion, pure but wholly unnatural. "To thee, O Lord of Night, I pledge my unending love, for this which you have given me."

Mordeth laughed, and Flanx could feel his own flesh crawl at the sound. The sergeant's eyes remained fixed on the Dark Lord's left hand, still raised above his head. A torch guttered and failed. Mordeth turned, and for the first time, Flanx recognized what he held in that black-gloved hand: the child's still-beating heart.

Flanx thought for a moment he would vomit. He tried to close his eyes to the horror, but Mordeth had woven some kind of a spell, and the sergeant was helpless to resist. The tears flooded to his open eyes as Mordeth, the Lord of Night and Darkness, brought the living organ down to his lips and bit into its flesh.

The child screamed and kept on screaming until Mordeth devoured the last bit of flesh; then, with a noble silence, she fell motionless to the earth. Flanx saw then, as if it had just appeared, the gaping hole in the child's chest as black as Mordeth's robes.

The remaining captured Pradatha stood motionless. The poor peasants that had come to the summons of Ratha's return stared at the Dark Lord, fear on their faces, but they didn't move, frozen by the sheer outrageousness of what he had done. Flanx wanted to shout at them, to urge them to fight, to flee. He was sure that many of Mordeth's troops must be as disgusted as he was. Yet he, too, felt a compulsion to remain silent and not disturb the quiet darkness of the night.

One by one the Pradatha prisoners were pushed forward and Mordeth repeated the ritual, magically ripping one heart after another from the rebels' chests. Each time the victim pledged allegiance to the Lord of Night, then watched silently as Mordeth ate the heart before his unblinking eyes, dying only after the Dark Lord had finished.

An hour later, a row of corpses lay motionless on the sands about Deathstone. Mordeth remained atop the black rock. A keening rose from the stone—no, it was Mordeth himself making the sound—and Flanx felt the heat of the desert dissipate, as if a cool breeze swirled through the assembly. The coolness changed into the steel cold of winter, freezing and penetrating. Still the cold increased, and suddenly Flanx recognized it: It was the touch of death. He tried to focus his eyes on Mordeth. The Dark Lord was staring at him—at him! He felt panic that he had been discovered as a spy, that he would now feel the wrath of Mordeth. He tore his eyes away from the Dark Lord to gaze at those around him, and he noticed that they, too, were shivering in the intense cold. The sight both relieved and frightened him. He was not alone. Even as he thought this, as suddenly as the cold had come, it left, and Flanx again felt the stifling heat of the desert. It was a sensation he appreciated for the first time in his life.

The troops were dismissed, and Flanx and the other men sought a quiet place, far from the Deathstone, to set up their camp. Without a word, each man entered his tent. Flanx wondered if any of them would be able to sleep. He knew he would not.

In the morning, Cimeon discovered the empty tent of his sergeant.

* * * * *

Mordeth sat in the shade of his command tent, looking at Krotah and Bleatha, the captain of the Elite Guard. Bleatha was picking dirt from beneath his fingernails with the sharpened point of a dagger. Beside him sat Deluta of Bain, the captain of the southern militia, and Jaspahr, the commandant of Silth.

"The imposter has some power, but not enough," said Mordeth. Bleatha stopped his primping and looked at his commander. Bleatha was half a head taller than Mordeth, but he wasn't fool enough to stir his master's ire.

"Shall we march today? The men are itching to move out. A delay might dull their edge for battle." Bleatha stroked the finely honed blade against his palm.

"Not yet," replied Mordeth, pressing his knuckles against the table. "We have several details to take care of first. This imposter is not Ratha. I sense a different power, but it is nevertheless a power to deal with." The

Dark Lord cast a disparaging glance at Krotah.

"Krotah, select your best spies and plant them in the camp of the Pradatha. Have them pose as peasants come to offer aid to the Archmage. Better yet, go with them yourself and oversee the gathering of information. I need to know their strengths and weaknesses. It must be done immediately."

"Yes, Mordeth."

"Deluta, you are to block all roads to Hagsface. I don't want an attack on our flank, and I don't want reinforcements to reach them once the battle is joined."

The swarthy commander of the forces of Bain looked back into his master's eyes, nodding curtly. Mordeth did not like Deluta, but he respected his fierceness and fearlessness. Mordeth recognized the danger in such a man, and for this reason, he had chosen not to let him join in the actual battle. It was better to keep the heroic types far from the battlefield.

"Jaspahr, you will lay siege upon the fortress itself. Have your men remain out of bow shot. Bleatha has a unit deployed to bring a siege machine to Hagsface. We will divide into three divisions, taking turns about the walls. We will harry our quarry, allowing them neither rest nor sleep."

Jaspahr grinned, flashing his bad teeth through his gray-flecked beard. He had been a powerful man five years ago, and still retained much of the original. But too many soft years at Silth had let a layer of fat encroach on his body, and that combined with the paleness of his skin and hair gave him the general appearance of an albino slug. Mordeth trusted him more than he did Deluta, but respected him less. At any rate, Jaspahr was no hero.

"My purpose is to lure the imposter out into the open. We must confine the Pradatha rebels behind the walls of Hagsface and goad the imposter into coming forth. Then I will utterly destroy him." Mordeth looked at his four captains, signifying that he would entertain questions.

"What about Moratha?" Bleatha asked. "He's like an omen to the rebels. Because of him, they believe the falcon has risen from the Pit. They follow him as soldiers follow a flag."

"Kreosoath has been sent to gather others of his kind. The Lord of Falcons is no match for a dragon. And should Kreosoath be delayed, I have a contingency plan." Mordeth smiled, pressing his knuckles more firmly into the hardwood table.

"How do you expect to lure the imposter out of Hagsface?" Deluta asked.

"That, Captain is my concern." Mordeth's voice was menacing, and the collected captains, if they had any, chose not to ask further questions.

"Krotah, are there any more prisoners?" Mordeth asked, relieving the tension in the tent.

"Yes, Mordeth."

"Good. Tonight we repeat the ritual of preparation. You and your spies leave today. In three days, we march to Hagsface."

Bleatha nodded silently, glad at last to be moving toward battle.

❖ CHAPTER THIRTEEN ❖

Quintah

Three days had passed since Flanx had returned from Mordeth's ranks, badly dehydrated and rambling with fever-induced visions. The healers had taken special interest in him, since Mithra herself had been so concerned, but little could be done to ease his tormented mind except to offer him salted water and wait. He frequently awoke screaming from the narcotic sleep, his eyes wide with terror. Mithra held herself responsible. Roy sensed a growing depression in the young woman and resolved to do what he could to alleviate some of her misery.

The bright Keshian sun heated the sands that surrounded Hagsface. Gentle waves of the Tranquil Sea lapped upon the beach. Roy found Mithra at Flanx's bedside and, taking her hand, led her out of the room into the great square.

"Will you walk with me?" he asked.

Her eyes widened with surprise. "I thought you preferred we keep our distance." She wondered what he wanted.

"I did. But you need a friend now." He looked at her beautiful face and noticed for the first time that there were small age lines crinkling the edges of her eyes. It only made her look more lovely. He tried to recall Gwen's face. It had vanished completely from memory.

"Then I can trust your honor?" she asked playfully. For a moment, looking into Roy's familiar face, Mithra imagined she was speaking to Ratha himself. She didn't resist the feeling.

"Undoubtedly, milady," Roy laughed. He, too, found it difficult not to enjoy the other's company. Her beauty and energy were infectious.

"Where to?" she asked.

"Just along the beach," he answered. When he noticed her hesitate, he added, "There are no armies nearby yet. The lookouts can warn us in ample time if danger should appear. And I have the staff." Mithra's smile dimmed at the remembrance of imminent war, but she followed him through the eastern gate of the walled fortress city.

Their footprints trailed behind them on the silken shores of the Tranquil Sea, a road into the horizon, the moist sand squishing comfortably beneath their feet. Mithra laughed as Roy removed his crusted boots and splashed barefoot through the azure water, and the sound of her laughter was a potent medicine for Roy's own sagging spirits. They walked until the fortress was but a ragged pinnacle on the northern horizon, then turned reluctantly and headed back.

Mithra savored the sunlight upon her shoulders, the gentle heat warming her without, Roy's companionship warming her more subtley from within. She turned to regard her companion, the man from a different world who was so much like her own lost love. She kept hoping to spot some defect, a flaw that would reveal to her that he wasn't Ratha, but the match was perfect. His voice, stature, movement, humor were all Ratha's; even many of his memories were those of the Archmage, although Roy insisted that they were but glimpses through the eyes of Moratha. She was somewhat dubious about this story, however, since none but Roy could see with hawk vision.

"It's a beautiful day," she said, avoiding the use of his name. "Thank you for the invitation."

"My pleasure. Beautiful, desirable women deserve the chance to be seen by everyone." Roy made a mock bow, sweeping his arm in a show of chivalry.

His words unfortunately reminded her of another man's desire, of a dark hour shrouded in Mordeth's arms. She shuddered at the memory, in spite of the heat.

"Have you ever thought . . ." Her voice trailed off into the sea breeze.

"Thought what? You might as well tell me, Mithra. I have ways of making you talk, you know," and he grabbed the woman, tickling her.

"Stop it! I'm serious." She pushed him away, and he could see that her eyes had dimmed with some dark and heavy thought.

"I'm sorry," he answered. Her back was turned to him now, and he found himself wanting to see that lovely face. "Please forgive me. What is it, Mithra?"

"Have you ever thought of having . . . children? I mean, a child of your own?"

Roy's face flushed. When he spoke, his voice was a mere whisper, barely heard over the crash of waves.

"Sometimes I wish that I had. I think of Gwen back home. I would have liked a family with her. But—" Roy's eyes glassed with an introspective despair that seemed so often to accompany thoughts of his home world—"but these days, I can't even recall her face. My old world escapes me. Those days are lost." He wondered, even as he said it, if this were really true.

She turned to face him again, her eyes bright with hope. Roy's chest constricted at the sight of those eyes. He knew before she spoke what she was about to ask. "Would you consider accepting my child as your own?" She caressed her belly with an open palm.

Roy's stomach churned. To accept her offer would be to give up all hope of return to Gwen, to his world. And the question of the child's father still disturbed him. Who was he that Mithra would so totally reject him? Had the father died? Why wouldn't Mithra broach the subject with him? He certainly could think of no graceful way to bring the matter up, and if Mithra wouldn't confide in him freely, then he had no business prying.

"Mithra . . ."

"Think about it, please. It would be for the best. I know it."

Roy grasped the words to explain. "We couldn't, Mithra. You're married to Ratha. You can't say for certain that he still won't return. You know that." It was a painful way to deflect her, and Roy was sorry he had used it.

Mithra nodded solemnly, then smiled weakly. "It was only an idea," she said. "It won't be long before people will see that I am with child. They will naturally suspect that you are the father. They think you are Ratha, whatever the truth." She stressed the last word, and Roy wondered if she still believed he was her returned lover, suffering from some odd amnesia or worse. But Mithra knew. Every time she closed her eyes, she could see Mordeth's cold face pressing down on her. That truth she could not bear to speak of.

"We'll see, Mithra, when the time comes." Mithra took the hint that Roy did not especially want to discuss the matter further, but she resolved to broach the subject again when the opportunity afforded itself.

They continued walking silently along the beach, each wrapped completely in his own worries and fears. Finally they stopped to sit among a driftwood cache. Moratha found them there and flew acrobatic maneuvers above them, but his antics had no effect on the pall that had crept over them. Mithra found herself immersed in memories of the languid days when she and Ratha had sat beneath the cocantha tree, dreaming and sharing their hopes. But now those hopes seemed hopelessly shattered.

Roy tried to recall Gwen's face again, but once again it eluded him. He fell to studying a small string of graying seaweed, dried by the sun and left dangling on a deadwood branch at high tide. He picked it off the branch to examine it more closely, then suddenly recalled a poem from his past. He dropped the twisted weed and quoted it aloud.

> "*The world is too much with us; late and soon,*
> *Getting and spending, we last waste our powers.*
> *Little we see in nature that is ours;*
> *We have given our hearts away, a sordid boon!*
> *This sea that bares her bosom to the moon,*
> *The winds that will be howling at all hours,*

And are up-gathered now like sleeping flowers,
For this, for everything, we are out of tune;
It moves us not."

"Your words mark well our mood," Mithra whispered. "Is that a prophecy?"

Roy looked at Mithra, briefly feeling again the awesome power she held in her eyes. "No. A poem by William Wordsworth. A friend read it to me once, and it came to mind."

"A friend?"

Roy smiled sourly. "Gwen."

They lapsed back into silence. Even Moratha, whose spirit was bound only by the winds, left them and returned to Hagsface.

"Mithra?" The woman did not answer, but Roy continued. "Have you ever thought about life lines?"

The Pradathan woman turned to look at the professor. "About what?"

"Life lines. The span of life a man or woman lives. I'm no physicist, but I think of time as linear, a straight line between two points. One point is where you are born; the second is where you die." Roy paused, considering. "What if Ratha understood life lines? What if he ended his own life too soon, intentionally, so that the span would be available for someone else? Someone he thought could come and save his world. What if he knew something we don't know?"

"I believe that Ratha's wisdom was without equal." For a moment, Mithra sounded like a teen-age girl again, fiercely defending her hero.

"Then why me? He might have called a general, or a statesman, or . . . anything. Why me?"

Mithra rolled over and stared hard at Roy. "You look like him. You sound like him. You have his manner. You can master the Three, even as he did."

Roy shook his head. "He had all those things, but he knew the mastery of magic much better than I do. Perhaps I came here only because of the way I look, the way I talk. Some kind of accident. Perhaps Ratha's hopes were thwarted. Perhaps he had no purpose."

"He had a purpose." A fire ignited in her voice and leapt to her eyes. "When your—" she paused, frowning—"life line, was it? When your life line ended, what were you doing?"

"I don't know. I was in the bell tower, thinking. About individuals. About how a single person can do things a mob can never do. About how the Regents of our university, our lovers of science, were trying to stop all stories from being told . . ."

Mithra slapped her hands down onto the hard sand. "The Regents stopped storytelling?" Her voice was unnaturally high, as if she were strangling. "What did you do?"

Roy looked away, staring off into the horizon at the gray belt of ocean. "I . . . I died."

Now anger crept into Mithra's voice. "No. You didn't die. You came here."

Roy made a vague gesture of noncommital. "Okay, I came here."

"So what do you bring to us? What do you have that my husband didn't? There must be something!"

"I—I don't know."

"Then tell me what you remember. I'll find it."

Roy wanted to get up and walk away, to find the safety of the walls of Hagsface, to drink from the cool fountain that bubbled in the city's center. He didn't want to talk of things he only vaguely remembered, things that only brought him pain. He didn't want to talk about the Regents, about his shame. But he looked into Mithra's eyes and found there a deepening resolve, a decision that Ratha's final act could not possibly have been in vain.

"The Regents ran the university," he began, "and their emphasis was on science. I think that if Wordsworth had known of computers, he would have directed that last bit of poetry I recited to the Regents. The Regents are really nothing more than artificial intelligences that appear humanoid through the use of holograms."

Mithra looked puzzled. "Don't worry about holograms. I don't know enough about technology to duplicate them! The Regents are programmed to regard science as an end in itself, while literature and art are mere hobbies, okay to occasionally indulge in, but not valued."

"And this science you speak of. What is it?" Mithra asked.

"An expanded form of alchemy, I suppose. Science is the elevation of thought over feeling and intuition. It's the realm of the five senses that holds contempt for the heart and soul of humankind. If you can't taste, touch, smell, or see it, then it doesn't exist. It is too much with us."

"Then science is one of the powers that bind in your world."

"Well . . . yes, I'm afraid so," Roy replied.

"Then it is not the evil that you would make it," Mithra responded adamantly. Roy looked at her and saw the deep furrows above her eyes, stubborn lines drawn in defiance to Roy. "Power is not an evil. People use power to heal, to enlighten, to defend, to save. Power is what we use it for; those who abuse power are the evil ones. The Four-That-Bind give us life and health and beauty, but all of them can destroy if misused. We drown in water and flood; our houses burn. The earth refuses to yield up food if we ask too much of it. We use the power of all four to aid our lives. We would surely be lessened by not using them. But when we do, we remember to thank the four from which the healing comes. If science is a power, we must use it."

"Perhaps, Mithra, but I would be loath to see Keshia succumbing to the lure of science. People begin to believe that they're rational when science is around; the truth is that we are not. Science would have us deny our very essence."

"Then when science demands that, we must resist, even as we resist Mordeth. And whenever possible, we must use the power against evil." Mithra pushed herself to her feet and stood above Roy, the late morning sun behind her like a fiery halo.

Together they walked back to Hagsface, approaching the seaside ramparts and being admitted through the small wooden door. Two soldiers in leather armor immediately replaced the heavy crossbeam that barred the door. Roy followed as Mithra went straight to the healer's, a building appropriated by the Pradatha for the sick and expected wounded. The walls and floors had been scrubbed with a diluted lye, and the smell was acrid but clean. Soft grasses had been piled along the walls, with heavy quilts and blankets thrown over them as makeshift beds. Inside the infirmary was a very old woman, hunched over from some degenerative disease that her skill had been unable to control. Roy recognized her as Berenta, the master healer. On the pallet beside her lay Flanx, pale and motionless.

"Is he . . . dead?" Mithra whispered.

"No, child. He sleeps," Berenta answered. "But he's lost much of his vital fluid. He must regain strength and water." The healer turned and grabbed a hollowed gourd, filling it with water from a pewter pitcher. She reached into a fold in her loose garment, retrieving a tattered pouch from which she scooped an ample portion of a silver-white powder, pouring it into the gourd. After stirring it with a whittled stick, Berenta held Flanx's head up and poured a little of the concoction into his mouth.

"What medicine is that?" Roy asked, ready to file more information into his memory.

"It's a saltlike substance, but it has none of the undesirable effects of salt. We use it for one who has lost much bodily fluids, and also to cure the meats we must take with us on long journeys."

"May I taste it?" Roy asked. Berenta held the pouch out to him, letting him dab a finger into the powder and touch it to his tongue.

"Is this a common substance?"

"The salt? It's fairly common. Every healer carries it, as do butchers and most farmers. The hills around here abound with it."

"Mithra, what do the people use for fire around here, since there are no trees?"

"*Charek*, the black, burning stone, and also peat from the Great Fen. Why?" Mithra was sensing Roy's building excitement but was unable to fathom his reasons.

"If only . . ." Roy began, his mind racing. "Do you have any yellow ore, easily powdered, bitter in taste, that smells like an egg after it's been left too long in the sun?"

Berenta wrinkled her nose in disgust. "Yes. We call it stinkstone. We have it on Keshia, but I can think of no purpose for its use. I'm sure we can gather some. It's very common."

"Then gather as much *charek*, stinkstone, and salt as you can, quickly, and bring them to the healers. Perhaps you were right, Mithra. Science may indeed be Mordeth's undoing." Roy turned and quickly left the infirmary, with Mithra close behind him.

"What is it?" she asked. "What are you going to make with these things?"

"Quintah!" he shouted over his shoulder, and his staff began to glow as he rushed down the cobbled streets of Hagsface, Mithra vainly trying to keep up.

* * * * *

It had been three hours since Roy and Mithra had stumbled, panting, into the blacksmith's building. Malek, the blacksmith, had immediately fired the forge and collared two boys to pump the bellows as Roy made rough charcoal drawings of his invention on the wall of the smithy. Malek had no idea what the purpose of such small cylindrical devices could be, but he was more than willing to perform the task of making them for the Archmage and his wife. He scraped a handful of sand together and began making a mold to cast the Archmage's invention.

Roy didn't stay to supervise the casting process, confident that the Pradatha smith would do the best he could. Besides, Roy knew nothing about the blacksmith's trade. Mithra, less confident of Malek's prowess, chose to remain to ensure that Roy's instructions were followed precisely. Roy himself raced down the street to the infirmary, finding Berenta busily directing the disposition of baskets of stinkstone, charcoal, and the silver-white sand. Four women and two men milled about the infirmary as Roy entered, their faces perplexed. Roy guessed that they were apothocaries by the many pouches they carried and their chemical-stained fingers.

"Berenta, we must work quickly. There is an invention from my . . ." Roy's voice trailed into silence as he realized he couldn't talk to these people about his own world without admitting he was not Ratha. "There is a device we must make," he corrected himself. "It has tremendous power. Have these people mix the sand with powdered *charek* and stinkstone. They'll need to experiment with the proportions . . . I can't remember them. I do recall that you'll need much more sand than the other elements. They must mix it fine, crushing it to dust, and mix it thoroughly." Berenta nodded and waited for the Archmage to finish his instructions.

"What is it we make, Ratha?"

"Quintah," Roy pronounced. "The powder is an explosive that burns very quickly and with a great deal of heat when it is ignited. If we put it inside a container, then light it, it'll explode like an earthquake. Even those without Quintah as a Word of Power may use it. It's a great power. But I don't remember the exact formula, so they'll have to experiment until it burns right."

"As you wish, Archmage," Berenta replied, then began directing the six Pradatha in their duties. Roy turned and hurried back up the street to the blacksmith's.

"The alchemists are busy with the gunpowder," Roy told Mithra. "How is Malek coming with the canisters?"

"The metal is cooling now. It is an odd shape."

"Back home they used to make these as weapons of war. They called them 'pineapples,' but the real name is hand grenades. We don't have a detonator, so we'll have to soak strips of cloth with lantern oil and light them with torches. We can drop them from the ramparts when Mordeth attacks and give him a real surprise. He won't expect the entire Pradatha to be versed in the way of Quintah."

"Let's hope the surprise works."

"It's science; it will work." Roy scowled at the thought of using science to defeat Mordeth. Mithra, too, looked worried. "Trust in the Pradatha, Mithra." And then he lied, "Truth prevails, even in my world. And gunpowder isn't the only gift that science will bring. Have you ever heard of a catapult?"

"No, but I'm sure I will." Mithra smiled hopefully at the exuberant professor.

"Mithra, one more thing. When this is over, you must promise to make me show you some ways that science is not destructive."

Mithra only smiled, then turned to the forge to help Malek.

❖ CHAPTER FOURTEEN ❖

A Stuck Toad

Krotah felt only contempt for the Pradatha. It had been easy to gain access to their fortressed city, posing as a traveling merchant from the far south hopeful of becoming a member of the underground rebel forces. There had been no inquiries, no formal checking of his story. The Pradatha were eager to take any and all who would come to their aid in the war with Mordeth.

Three of Krotah's best men, soldiers who had been assigned to guard the inner sanctuaries of Morlidra, Mordeth's hold, came with him, posing as servants to the peddler. Krotah had been worried that the Pradatha would become suspicious of a middle-class trader traveling with three obviously healthy, battle-hardened men, but their presence went unquestioned. Once within the walls of Hagsface, the four spies split, hoping to acquire information to relay to Mordeth.

Billah happened upon the smithy and stood watching as Malek poured the molten iron into the sandcast, his two apprentices busily soldering together the two halves of numerous egg-shaped objects. Crates of the peculiar objects were scattered about the smithy. The tall, dark-haired spy offered to lend the blacksmith assistance, but Malek was adamant that he and his two apprentices could handle the project. The spy had to leave from the smithy without guessing the purpose of the dull iron cones.

Tronch meandered through the red cobbled streets until he found the infirmary, entering under the guise of a minor healer. Seven Pradatha were cloistered in the confines of the building, busily grinding a gray powder he recognized as curing salts and mixing it with a large quantity of find sand. The seven were too engrossed in their task to take much notice of the stranger.

The seven alchemists continued to grind the preserving salts into a fine dust. Then they grated charcoal into the dust until there was nearly half as much charcoal as sand. Finally they sprinkled an ample amount of stinkstone powder into the concoction before hefting the bowl and taking it to a window ledge. One of the old women touched a lighted torch to the bowl, and a vile gray smoke heaved into the air, gagging the alchemists and bringing burning tears to Tronch's eyes. The alchemists muttered among themselves, then continued working silently, giving no further clue to the bewildered spy.

Bezwak surveyed the ramparts, checking each of the fortress's four walls for evidence of weakness. He quickly noted that the eastern wall, nearest the Tranquil Sea, had fewer merlons placed to hide attentive archers. Aside from this singular flaw, the architecture of Hagsface easily lent itself to protection from siege. The water source for the city stood in the center of town, but it wasn't a common well. Water poured through marble spigots planted into the stone to form an enigmatic fountain. It was an archaic construction, one lost to the current residents of Keshia. Strategically, it made poisoning the water supply impossible.

The buildings of Hagsface were of adobe or stone, while the roof tiles were made of molded clay, as were the framings for the doors and windows. The only wood evident in the entire hold was in the doors of the ceremonial buildings, probably those associated with the ancient university. The climate lent itself to open buildings, allowing the heat to disperse with the evening sea breeze. Bezwak did notice wood in use in one other location: In the heart of the city square, several carpenters were busy notching and pegging a peculiar combination of green lumber. To Bezwak, it looked like some sort of hinge.

Krotah traveled throughout the hold, judging the numbers of defenders, noting the colors of the mage robes. Mage robes had been banned in Keshia, and the sight of the blue, brown, red, and white garments brought back memories to the chief of the Elite Guard: memories of his childhood, his father wearing the blue robes of the sea mage; the laughs and taunts of the other teen-agers as he stood for his naming and received the namesake of Krotah, the Toad. Considered too arrogant and hostile, he was sent without a Word of Power into a world of mages, where even the lowest peasant could work small wonders with his Word of Power bestowed on his Day of Naming.

The sight of the mages brought back those bitter recollections now, and he comforted himself with the thought of the Pradatha's utter destruction. Krotah counted the robed mages, marking twenty wearing his father's blue, twelve Rahlah's white, another sixteen with the brown of Keshia, but only five wore the dangerous red of Quintah. All told, there were fewer than threescore wizards.

Another wizard, who wore no mage's robes, strode through the streets of Hagsface. This was the imposter, wielding the Staff of Fire, ministered to by the great falcon. Krotah's anger flared. No one should be granted mastery of three powers when the Elite Guard chief himself had been denied his right to even one. Contempt burned like acid inside Krotah as he watched the Archmage rush from building to building, giving orders and encouragement to everyone he encountered.

But it was not only the imposter who captured the attention of Krotah. Krotah's eyes also leered in the direction of the white-haired woman at the mage's side. Mithra was every bit as animated as the Archmage, but somehow the brilliance of the desert sunlight, or perhaps the nearness to the sea, added extra appeal to Mithra's beauty. The green bruise administered to her by Mordeth had completely faded from her jawline, and her hair, blown by the gentle desert breeze, frothed about her face like seafoam, softly caressing the delicate curves of her face, accenting the electric blue of her eyes. For a brief moment, Krotah envied Mordeth for his moment with the sea-born beauty.

Krotah knew that the woman was the key to the Pradatha's success. He had informed Mordeth of the allegiance that the Pradatha paid her, the unyielding loyalty that led many rebels to their deaths. Krotah had convinced Mordeth to destroy the Pradatha by using the woman; he had laughed in cruel appreciation when Mordeth told him of his plan to force Mithra to bear the child of the Dark Lord. With Ratha dead, Mithra alone stood as a symbol of the past era, a citadel of beauty and trust. The Dark Lord's plan was a stroke of brilliance that meant the certain undoing of the Pradatha, for Mordeth would quickly spread the story of their consummation. A love child produced by the union of the Lord of Darkness and the widow of the Archmage! How delicious! Yet it was all ruined by the blundering of a palace guard. Krotah had personally executed Mithra's guard. And the emergence of this imposter made things more difficult yet.

The Toad looked down at Mithra from his position atop the western wall. She was busy helping an old woman sort fruits in a wicker basket, bending over the basket, laughing as the Archmage fumbled with a bruised apple. She seemed protective of him, and Krotah noticed how she tended to hover over the people she met, a maternal image in the barren world of the desert.

Yes, maternal, he thought, and the idea crystallized like salt in a drying well. Mordeth's plan was not totally upset, for Mithra Roshanna radiated the unmistakable signs of a woman with child. Krotah laughed silently at the thought.

The four spies found little else of import within the Pradatha fortress. After the common dinner shared by those not standing watch, Mordeth's spies gathered in the tiny room assigned them by the chief steward. The room had once been part of the university dormitories, this particular section reserved for the less affluent students. The fact that he was forced to rest in the hollow dormitory of a dead university brought more dark memories to Krotah, and he was eager to finish their task and be gone.

"They're building something. It's much like a siege machine, but the type is unknown to me. From its strange construction, I doubt that it will ever work," Bezwak began. "I also noticed that the seaward wall is the least defended."

"They work like old women, doting over stinkstone and charcoal," said Tronch. "Do they expect to stink so bad that we run from them?" The three Elite Guards laughed heartily.

"Don't underestimate them," Krotah growled. "They have considerable numbers of magic-users, but I counted only five Quintah mages. Mordeth must know this, for it is they that will cause him the most problems."

"I watched as the blacksmith built metal containers of a queer design. I could glean no information as to their use," Billah offered.

"There is little more we can do here. We have a good idea of their strengths and weaknesses. We know they prepare for a siege. We'll return to Mordeth tonight." The three guards silently nodded as Krotah stood. "But first, there is one more detail I must take care of," he said, then quietly slipped through the door and down the hallway.

Krotah needed only to ask a few well-placed questions, perhaps over a mug of ale, to locate the whereabouts of the imposter. He didn't fear recognition because few people outside Morlidra knew what the Dark Lord's second-in-command looked like.

As it happened, he didn't need to find a tavern. A young boy, carrying a fagot of sticks and dressed in a rough, rustic robe that marked him as one from a southern climate, hustled down the narrow street past the shadows that hid Krotah from view. Krotah stepped from the shadows and hailed the boy.

"Young lad," he called out, letting his voice take on the lilt of the southern folk, "kindly be a-tellin' me where t' find the Archmage. I have some urgent news t' tell 'im."

The boy turned around sharply, surprised at Krotah's sudden appearance, but he found no reason not to trust someone who spoke with his own accent. "Try th' infirmary, sir," the boy answered. "Down the roadway a piece, 'n to th' right. Y' won't be havin' any trouble findin' 'im there. It's all lit up like." The boy bowed his head and swiftly headed down the road to complete his errand.

As the boy had said, Krotah had no trouble finding the infirmary. He peered through the open doorway and saw Mithra and the imposter kneeling over a man who lay awake on a pallet. The Toad's heart raced as he stole inside. Such an opportunity! The two leaders' backs were turned from him, their conversation masking the noise of his boots scuffing the well-scrubbed floor. Slowly Krotah drew his dagger, the curved steel making a low, husky whisper as it scraped out of its scabbard.

Mithra was teasing Flanx, playfully suggesting that few men would go to such lengths to get time away from their unit. Flanx chuckled, enjoying the good-natured banter after days of languishing in the care of the strict Berenta. His eyes flicked toward the motion behind the Archmage, recognition draining the recently returned color from his face. As the dagger slashed down toward the mage's back, Flanx lunged out of the bedcovers toward the former professor, knocking Roy sideways, away from the deadly blow. Krotah's blade knicked Roy's left arm, ripping through his tunic and slicing into the soft flesh beneath.

Mithra reacted a moment later, grappling with the arm that wielded the knife. Roy quickly recovered his wits, and the Staff of Fire flamed angrily, its white light leaping toward the assassin and jolting into his chest. Krotah slumped limply to the floor. Roy checked his pulse as Mithra assisted Flanx back into the pallet.

"Krotah!" Flanx whispered. "It's Krotah!"

"The Dark One's second?" Mithra asked, smiling suddenly. "Then we have happened upon a treasure indeed!" Roy was binding the man's hands behind him, making certain that the knots would not come undone. When he finished, Mithra attempted to tend to Roy's bleeding arm.

"Damn . . . that hurts," he said as she probed the ragged flesh. He bit down upon his lip.

"We'd best find Berenta," she said.

"Let me go, before you kill me with that incessant prodding." He smiled weakly at Mithra. The sight of the red fluid dripping from his arm unnerved him almost as much as the pain.

"Is he alive?" Flanx asked, nodding in Krotah's direction.

"I'm sure he is. I've learned a little in the past few weeks. I can control the staff better now."

Flanx raised a questioning brow but said nothing.

"He won't be alive for long, the bastard," Mithra was furious over the assassination attempt, and more angry at herself for letting it happen.

"Let him be. We can question him when he regains consciousness."

Mithra silently acquiesced to Roy's demand. Roy left

the infirmary and asked a passerby to help him locate the healer.

Flanx was obviously nervous about having Krotah in the same room with him, even with Mithra there. The sturdy Pradathan wriggled in his bed like a child afraid of spiders, fidgeting with the covers, casting furtive eyes about the room. He watched Krotah as the Toad's breathing became more regular and the color returned to his ashen face. Then the captive's eyelids began to flutter.

"He's coming back, the four help us," Flanx said, his voice cracking with nervousness.

"Good." Mithra was anxious to question the man who had tortured so many of her friends throughout Mordeth's long reign. She glared down at him on the floor, taking stock of his slight build, his oily black hair and pockmarked complexion, the thin excuse for a beard that smudged his face.

Krotah awoke, trembling slightly from the shock of the magical blast, and opened his eyes to see Mithra Roshanna towering above him like an angry goddess. As he tried to clear his head of the thin ringing sound there, he felt a sharp kick into his chest. Mithra wasn't going to let him move.

"Good morning, Mithra," he growled. "You look fit, I see. I seem to have run into some minor difficulty here. Pray unbind my hands."

"For you, Toad, we will keep hands bound until time rots the ropes from your corpse."

"Yes, well . . . it's as I might have expected." Krotah shrugged slightly, the ropes digging into his wrists. He tried to struggle to his feet, feeling the awkwardness of his prone position, but Mithra pushed him back with

another swift kick, knocking the wind from him. He re-
mained sprawled upon his back until Roy returned, with
Berenta and several other Pradatha following behind.
He noticed a red-stained bandage wrapped around the
Archmage's arm and grimaced at his failure.

"Make sure he's well tended," Roy ordered Berenta. It
was obvious that the old healer disdained the notion of
helping one of Mordeth's troops, especially the notori-
ous Krotah. But the Archmage had been adamant, and
she felt the need to comply.

Krotah wasted no time in taking a new tack. "I am
fine, mage. It's Mithra you should worry about."

Roy cast a quick glance at Mithra, noting her scowl
and regal demeanor. She appeared to be unharmed, although obviously angry. Roy wondered momentarily if
Krotah was unaware that he was not the Archmage.

"Mithra is fine, as am I," he answered, hoping he
sounded like Ratha. "We need only be concerned about
you, Krotah."

"Oh, but you'd better ask her first. I'm certain that
she needs some tending. It wouldn't do for the woman
carrying Mordeth's child to be wanting anything." Krotah leered at Mithra, and she struck him a vicious blow
across the jaw, sending him sprawling back against the
floor, laughing like a madman.

All of Mithra's fears rushed headlong into one another as Krotah spoke. Hearing the truth made it all the
more terrible, all the less acceptable. What if the word
should spread? What if all of Kesh learned of her secret,
learned of her shame? She couldn't live if that happened. She wouldn't.

"Liar!" she said, her voice little more than a growl.
"The child I carry is not the Dark One's." She looked

around the room at those who had gathered, then grasped at her only hope. "Ratha himself is the father of my child!" Her voice rose to a screech, reverberating in the close quarters.

Roy looked about him, all eyes of the Pradatha focused on him. He felt the blood race to his ears and neck, the redness burning and uncomfortable. Mithra had never disclosed the father's name. He had assumed it to be one of the Pradatha, but her harsh denial and blatant lie brought the ugly truth to a head. He knew the truth now. Mordeth truly was the father. He glanced quickly at Mithra, but she still glowered at Krotah. The wheels had been set in motion, and he had to respond somehow to Mithra's statement. For several moments, he said nothing at all, then answered quietly.

"It's true." He looked at Krotah, who leered back at him. "Gag him." A giant of a man stepped forward and roughly stuffed a rag into Krotah's mouth. "Take him to the smithy and have Malek shackle him," Roy ordered. "But keep him alive."

"No!" Mithra snapped, her rage taking control of her. "Destroy the dog! He's not fit to live."

"Mithra," Roy said, his voice a calm counterpoint to the tension in her own, "that's not your way; you know that."

Mithra tried to look at Roy, but she couldn't meet his eyes. Finally she answered quietly, "As you wish." She had said too much already.

Roy moved closer to her, wrapping his uninjured arm around her waist. He whispered to her the only truth he knew: "I love you." As he held her, he felt the trembling surge through her body until she was overcome with sobs.

"Take this scum to Malek," he ordered.

Four well-armed Pradatha rebels pushed the former captain of the Elite Guard out the door, unaware that even as they did, three shadowy shapes were lowering themselves over the fortress walls and stealing quietly away into the western desert.

❖ CHAPTER FIFTEEN ❖

Seductions

Tralaina was ecstatic over the news of Mithra's pregnancy, but Stentor took the news more guardedly. Mithra had been like a child to the two long-time Pradatha, and Stentor knew full well that the baby was not really Ratha's. It was Roy's, and Roy was a mere imposter. In Stentor's eyes, the child was illegitimate. Only the pleasure his wife received from the news seemed to quell his angry spirit. He kept silent, and for his wife's sake, he tried not to brood.

Tralaina had no such reservations, seeing the event as a reason to celebrate, no matter whether the father was Ratha or the outworlder. The impending war had been hanging over them, and to have Mithra, beautiful and radiant in her pregnancy, announce unexpectedly that she was over a month pregnant demanded a celebration.

The Pradatha gathered within the dormitory dining area, pushing aside the tables that were filled with warm sweetbreads, fruits, nuts, and other delicacies. Roy was surprised to see such bounty in the midst of the current crisis, but he gladly helped himself to the spiced meats and mounds of *keyth*, the small orange fruit that Roy had discovered shortly after his arrival in this new world.

Mithra, more animated than usual, danced with every young man who asked, and there were many. Roy watched as the woman spiraled across the floor, her short skirt billowing to show her shapely legs. For a moment, he relished the idea of fathering her child, but reality quickly returned, leaving him desolate. He watched the woman until she excused herself from her current dance partner and moved toward him.

"I'm glad we could have this party. We needed the respite." She smiled up at him, the soft glow of exertion glistening on her face.

"Yes, everybody needed some time away from battle preparations." In spite of his earlier proclamation of love, Roy was having second doubts, and it showed itself in his strange reluctance to speak openly with the beautiful Pradathan woman.

She leaned close and whispered, "You're distant, love," her heart racing. Roy's words had been a haven to her, his declaration of love like a potion that healed her. She clung to the gift, willing herself to believe him, to believe the lie she had created, that the child was Roy's. The awful night with Mordeth, the pain, and the humiliation, all were nothing more than a sour dream. This man before her was her love, the father of the child she carried. She sank easily into the deceit.

But Roy wouldn't let it happen. He pushed her gently away and looked into her eyes. For a moment, he thought that he might let it pass, let the lie wrap around them both. Staring into her face, he couldn't even begin to remember Gwen. But he remembered the truth.

"It's all a lie, Mithra. It's all a lie." He turned his head and watched as the swirling dancers spun past. "You know that it can't go on."

A knot tightened in Mithra's stomach, and she thought immediately of the child, strangling her from within. "It's a lie that you love me?"

Roy shrugged. "Maybe I do love you. But the child . . . you know I'm not the father. How long can that deceit last?"

"But you said—"

"What I said was to protect you. It was wrong. I'm not the father."

"I didn't mean to trap you. If you still love someone else . . ." She left the question hanging, unasked and unanswered.

"It's not that. I can't even remember Gwen's face, Mithra. I'm not sure anymore if I even want to. But this—" he let his eyes slip to her waist—"this is not mine." He looked at her again and caught her eyes. "It's Mordeth's."

She pushed herself away and struck him hard across the face. "That's a lie!" she hissed.

"No, Mithra, it is not." Roy's voice was hushed but determined. Around him, the dancers flowed, oblivious to all but the music. "I am not Ratha; I only play his part. This deception . . ." He sighed wearily. "I find you intensely beautiful, but you must face the truth!" He looked up at the ceiling, noticing for the first time that he could see the sky through the dense thatch. "The child's not mine. Please be careful, Mithra. It's a dangerous deceit. In many ways."

Mithra turned from him without answering, and soon she was swept back onto the floor. Roy noticed that in the arms of a dozen different men, she seemed alive and joyous. But he knew that, too, was a lie.

The evening wound to a late end, most of the cele-
brants having found contentment with good food and
wine and the festive atmosphere. Mithra, Stentor, and
Tralaina joined Roy as he walked back to the compound.
Nothing was said of their discussion, but Mithra's laughter as they walked was too easy, too quick. Even in this
she lied.

Stentor and Tralaina bid them a good night and left
them alone. Roy wanted to talk, to find some solution to
their problem, but Mithra excused herself and went
straight to bed, latching the door behind her. She lay
awake until she heard Roy's door creak slowly closed,
then drifted into a somber sleep.

Mithra dreamed. She saw Mordeth, black-caped and
smiling menacingly, standing over her. His grin grew
until it became a prison wall, and she found herself
standing naked within the confines of the walls. A sword
was in her hand, and she lashed out, but each time the
metal came near the wall, the sword would vanish. Then
Roy's voice echoed through the room: "It's a lie, Mithra,
it's all a lie." If she dreamed more after that, Mithra
could not remember.

Roy awoke before the sun struggled above the Tranquil Sea. His room was cool and filled with the emptiness of twilight. He whispered and the staff burned
gold, dispersing ominous shadows from the empty corners of the chamber. Moratha opened a sleepy eye, scru-
tinizing his human friend.

"Go back to sleep, old friend," Roy whispered. "No
sense in both of us being awake." Moratha's eye slipped
closed again, and the bird resumed the slow, rhythmical
breathing of sleep.

Roy dressed in the tunic and pants of his new world, pulling his ankle-high boots on with a sharp tug. His muscles were taut and his neck slightly sore from a restless night. He looked around the spartan room. Ratha's diary nestled like a black flagstone in the center of the thick wooden table. Roy hefted it, felt the familiar leather. He had read it once diligently, with the aid of Moratha. But it had kept its answers hidden, if indeed it had had any. Now he cradled it against his chest, and as the sun rose and his room filled with natural light, he took with him the only book this world had given him.

He headed immediately for the plaza, where Mithra's workmen were still trying to perfect the catapult. But Roy had done all he could to instruct the Pradatha in the ways of science. As he watched the men bend the long center pole, a thick, sour taste filled his mouth. Despite his ardent words to the contrary, using science as a means of war felt wrong—*was* wrong—and he knew it. He decided then to avoid the preparations as much as he could. What he wanted now was to walk alone and to think.

Roy meandered through the streets of Hagsface, stopping at the city fountain to get a drink of water. The water was startingly cold and reminded him of the tiny stream by his first campsite. Memories tumbled past him as he recalled the chance encounter with Kreosoath, his accidental discovery of the Staff of Fire, his first glimpse of Shymney majestically guarding the central Keshian pass. He wondered what had become of the black beast. The dragon had followed the Pradatha until they reached the fortress, circling the vanguard like a hungry vulture, always beyond bow shot—not that it mattered. He remembered Mithra's arrow bouncing harmlessly away from the beast's thick hide. Now a week had passed since Kreosoath's last appearance. Roy had easily chased Kreosoath away once, and the dragon had never seemed as vicious to him as the stories told. He shrugged away the thoughts like unwelcome rain.

Roy found himself standing at the city's east gate. The guards there made no protest when the Archmage ordered the crossbar removed and the door opened to allow him to pass. Nodding absentmindedly to the guard, he passed through the outer door and onto the vast expanse of beach, aimlessly walking through the slate gray of morning. The dull ache in his arm from Krotah's knife wound cautioned him to be wary, but he needed the solitude of the walk, the relentless crash of wave after wave reminding him that all things evened out eventually. Besides, he argued to himself, Mordeth's army was still at least a day away, and Roy wielded the staff.

He hefted the staff, feeling its comforting presence, its unusual and totally familiar balance. The staff had become a part of him, an extension of his arm and will, and Roy struggled to remember life without it. He slept with the staff nestled in the crook of his arm; he used it as a surprisingly buoyant raft when he took an occasional swim in the warm waters of the Tranquil Sea. Rarely would he burn the precious oil in a lantern when he could easily ignite his staff into cool, white flame. Despite his constant contact with the archaic device and the hundred times he'd read the Archmage's journal, he still could only guess at the extent of the staff's power as he struggled to contain it and channel its power to his own purposes.

Quintah had been foremost of Ratha's powers, and Roy had seemed to inherit it as his own, although he had not yet mastered it. He had been raised in a family surrounded by literature and the marvels of modern technology, but to the quiet professor who thought nothing of holograms created by a distant computer, it still amazed him that he could ignite a fire with a snap of his fingers.

Although not a master of Quintah, the young Pradatha Jipsom did have Quintah as his Word of Power, and he had offered to assist the Archmage in any way possible. Roy had declined the offer. Jipsom wasn't privy to the fact that Roy was but a messenger to this world. Roy had taken advantage of Jipsom's presence, however, and watched as the fiery-eyed young man instructed his pupils in the old university building. On more than one occasion, Roy had to hastily decline Jipsom's offer to have him assist in the teaching lesson, insisting that the younger man was the superior teacher. Jipsom glowed with the praise.

The university was being put to good use, especially since the mages had gathered together, seeking something to fill their idle hours as they waited for Mordeth's approach. It had been Mithra who suggested that the reestablishment of the university be their first order of business, and the parents of the children applauded the idea enthusiastically. Now the once empty hall was filled with the mellow baritone of Jipsom, or the chorus of others who came to teach and to learn. Roy longed to be a part of it, but he could do little but watch the real experts ply their trade.

Quintah was not the only power that Roy had inherited: Rahlah and Keshia had also become his. Moratha was proof that he did indeed have some command over the things of the air, but it was little consolation. Aside from the gulls and the Lord of Falcons, Kreosoath had been the only airborne creature Roy had encountered, and Roy had no desire to tempt fate by trying to control the enormous beast. Occasionally Roy did attempt to summon the gulls to him as he ambled along the beach. His success was limited, however, for the gulls would land upon the beach before him or, more often than not, simply ignore his gentle callings. Moratha had tried to explain to him that gulls were skittish and that the falcon's own presence might be cause for their distrust. Still, Roy was unimpressed with his ability with the creatures of the air.

Keshia, or power over the land, was more a power of creation than destruction. The power of Keshia was usually limited to the annual blessing of the crops to grow bountifully or the dedication of a building or other earthen structure. Only a very few of the mages could alter stone, and fewer still could cause a limited earthquake such as Roy had created while he was under attack from Mordeth. Roy had experimented with trying to cause another small earthquake, but his fear of losing control restrained him and success never came. He examined the sleeping city and admitted it was best to reserve the unleashing of the power of Keshia for a dire emergency.

It was Mithra who told him of the Dark Lord's weakness, that light held the power to overcome darkness. The conversation had been as much theological and philosophical as it had been pragmatic. Mithra was a reassuring fundamentalist who believed in the eventual triumph of good. Roy had nodded and listened as Mithra explained that day always overtakes night, that people were drawn to light. Roy thought of other things drawn to light and to their destruction, but he chose to say nothing. Perhaps on Keshia there were no moths.

Neither did he mention his own concern that sometimes things don't work out the way we expect or want them to. Thoughts of the dwindling English department at the university still haunted him, as did the lost hope of a growing relationship with Gwen. It goaded Roy that he had a bright, vivacious woman desperately in love with him here on this world, but he could only think of the might-have-been relationship that he would probably never know.

Probably? Roy felt a surge of disgust as he thought of the word. He was forever trapped on this world, unable to return to the life he once had known. And what was there for him back home? A possible relationship with a woman he had never told he loved. Certainly there was no longer a position for him at the university. Had the Regents sold his possessions after his apparent death? He remembered the clause in his contract that said any professor who died intestate would forfeit his estate to the university. He hadn't any family, but now he wished he had left his possessions to Gwen. At least she could have had that.

But he was on Keshia, facing an inevitable war with a formidable power. Mordeth reminded him of someone, something from an old poem perhaps. He raced through his memory, struggling with the recollection.

It didn't matter; what did matter were the preparations for the war. The thought of war disturbed Roy more than his inability to master any of the three powers at his disposal. The type of war they now planned would be considered archaic on his own world. To him, war was impersonal, not a conflict between personalities but between ideas alone. The enemy was bombed or shelled. Tanks and mortars lobbed shells at one another. Jets fought in the air. Never did you see your enemy's face. The only familiarity he had with the concept of face-to-face combat was through stories told to him by his grandmother. Long ago, she had served in the infantry. Roy remembered her quietly teasing his grandfather, who had been a conscientious objector during the war she fought. Grandfather never took the joke very well, and now, in the face of the approaching conflict, he could well see why.

His ready reliance on science also disturbed him. How easily he had delved into his memory and dredged up the idea of a bomb using gunpowder! There had been a time when he had felt pride that he was descended from Alfred Nobel, although it was a distant relationship. It was a particular point of honor that his famous ancestor had created the Peace Prize after discovering the awful destructive power of his invention, dynamite. Now Roy was busy recreating his kinsman's invention, readying it to render human beings lifeless or maimed.

Not that science would avail him any great advantage. The alchemists still hadn't discovered the proper proportions of the three powders. Only the day before, Roy had watched as they touched a torch to a small pile of the makeshift gunpowder. The mound had bubbled and swelled, turning black, with snakelike pillows forming where the powder had been. It had let off a terrible stench, but not the desired effect of quick, intense burning. Roy had felt disappointment as the elders turned and looked at him, waiting for his instructions. He could only tell them to keep trying.

The catapult wasn't going much better, although it

involved a simpler application of physics. The Pradatha assigned to the task of assembling the huge device had finished their task, but when they attempted to test it, drawing the great arm back with what they thought was a stout rope, the woven grass cord snapped prematurely. The catapult somersaulted wildly, and the main arm smashed into the stone plaza with a bone-jarring thud. Fortunately, no one had been injured, but the catapult was seriously damaged and needed to be repaired. It would be several days before they would have it completed. If Mordeth's troops attacked soon, the Pradatha would lack the advantage of a long-range weapon. Roy could feel only frustration with his attempts to help the Pradatha prepare for the oncoming war.

He also continued to struggle with his own objections to war. He had to admit that Mordeth's destruction was ultimately necessary. There was little that could be done to rehabilitate him. Perhaps Krotah would need to be executed in the end, too, although Roy hoped that his own views of civilization would affect the council once the war was over and Krotah was tried for his crimes. But where would it all end? A civil war was a bloody, unwanted remedy to the problems Keshia faced.

Was there an alternative to the mass destruction of Mordeth's troops? From Mithra's accounts, Mordeth had banned all use of the four powers, destroying any of his own soldiers who dared defy the edict. The Dark Lord protected his own black powers, unwilling to teach them to anyone around him. The lack of magecraft in Mordeth's army might prove to be an important factor in the war's outcome. Roy knew that he could control his staff so that he could render a man unconscious rather than dead. Would the other mages also be so inclined?

The many questions continued to brew like a storm within him, and he sought a quiet haven from the struggle. At last the haven came, the only thing he was certain he could trust: poetry. The thought startled him from his dismal reveries and gave him new hope, washing the bitterness of thoughts of war away from him. He wandered over to the protective cover of a driftwood pile, nestling himself into the leeward side of the great wooden mass of timbers. Aloud, he spoke lines from Wordsworth like a litany of hope.

> *"I wandered lonely as a Cloud*
> *That floats on high o'er vales and hills,*
> *When all at once I saw a crowd,*
> *A host, of golden Daffodils:*
> *Beside the lake, beneath the trees,*
> *Fluttering and dancing in the breeze."*

Roy looked up into the royal blue sky, catching a glimpse of the last star as it fled before the rising sun. Unfortunately the blue dome was devoid of clouds.

"It figures," he muttered. "Not a cloud in the sky. Not a flower. Why weren't there any romantic poems written about the desert?" He turned and looked out at the white-capped sea spreading across the globe.

Roy shifted his weight against the firm sand, smoothing the ruffled grains about him with the toe of his boot. He looked up and saw a gull circling over the ocean, far in the distance, the growing sunlight dripping off his back like honey. He raised himself with his staff and held his arm out from him, like a stately tree poised to receive the returning bird.

"Rahlah," he said, and he thought he could feel the

force of his voice carried by the wind into the heart of the desert.

"Rahlah," he repeated, and the circling bird altered its course, which became more eliptical, then straightened as the gull obeyed Roy's command.

"Rahlah!" he shouted, and the bird began to increase its speed, moving with the wind toward the outstretched arm of the mage. Then, as suddenly as a gust of wind, the bird swerved and fled, speeding out over the sea.

"Damn! I thought I did it." Roy's frustration with his failure gnawed at him as he slid back down into his protected corner of the driftwood pile, contemplating what had gone wrong.

A sudden, unexpected wind tossed the dry sand up into his face, and he sputtered, picking the tasteless grit from his mouth.

"At last . . . a sign," he said ruefully. "Give it up, Roy. Poetry is your only power." He traced the wood grain of his staff with his thumb.

> "*The woods decay, the woods decay and fall,*
> *The vapors sweep their burden to the ground,*
> *Man comes and tills the field and lies beneath;*
> *And after many a summer dies the swan.*
> *Me only cruel immortality consumes;*
> *I wither slowly in thine arms*
> *Here at the quiet limit of the world.*"

He looked out at the gray expanse of ocean. "It's a sad time, O imposter." He grabbed a handful of sand and let it filter through his fingers, pouring like time onto the ground below.

"Immortality must be tough," he muttered disconsolately, and for the third time that morning, thoughts of the black dragon sprang unbidden to his mind. "Kreosoath, thou art a mystery. Your only crime was that of frightening me, and that may not have been your fault. There's your blackness, but that's no more than prejudice. You've shown no cruelty, and yet they all despise you. It's a harsh world I've come to." Roy began to feel a lump of despair as he thought about the dragon, a feeling that he couldn't explain, except to say that he had some affinity with the beast that was Quintah and Rahlah, Fire and Air.

A distant shouting roused Roy from his reverie, and he looked toward Hagsface, his heart racing as he recognized the fear in the voices. He tried to make out their message but could not. Pushing his staff into the sand, he lifted himself and began to move toward the running figure. Then the sound of wingbeats brought him to a halt, and he turned, looking back at the driftwood he had so recently called his haven, and saw the great bulk of the black dragon, lifting from his perch behind the pile and flying with uncanny speed southward, above the great expanse of beach.

Roy stood staring at the retreating form of Kreosoath until the four figures he had been racing toward finally reached him, voicing their concern and asking him a myriad of questions. He turned and looked at them carefully, noting their youth; not one seemed to be older than sixteen. Roy wondered how anyone that young could have been allowed to stand duty on one of the fortress's walls.

"We felt your power, mage, and looked to see," said a lanky, towheaded young man. "We couldn't hear your words. It seemed you spoke to the wind, but then the black shape climbed into the sky behind you. We recognized the dark dragon and feared you would be attacked." The boy looked at him with a mixture of awe and concern. "Did you enchant him, sir?"

Roy was dumbfounded, unable to find words to tell the concerned guards that he had been completely unaware of the dragon's presence.

"Does anyone else know that Kreosoath was here?" he asked.

"No, my lord mage. We four were on watch at the southern wall. We came when we saw the black beast swoop down toward you. We thought you were engaged in battle with the creature, for you both disappeared from our sight." The concerned young guard eyed Roy with a dubious look.

"Tell no one what you saw today," Roy ordered, then hastily added, "There are mysteries too deep and awesome for those not of the magehood." Roy was desperately trying to create a story that sounded significantly ominous to keep the four youths in check. It wouldn't do to let Mithra hear of this near miss.

"Yes, my lord," they answered in unison.

"We'd best be getting back to Hagsface before Mithra discovers you left your posts." The ashen faces of the four young Pradatha was ample evidence to Roy that they weren't eager to defy the elders, especially him or Mithra. Together they jogged back to the fortress, closing and barring the southern door behind them.

Roy entered the safety of his own room, casting himself across his pallet with a heavy sigh. He was having difficulty dealing with the two near misses on his life in less than a week. Or had this morning been an assassination attempt? Why hadn't Kreosoath attacked? The black dragon certainly had the advantage of surprise, and even with the Staff of Fire, one quick blow from the powerful beast could easily have severed Roy's head from his shoulders.

Perhaps he really had enchanted the dragon, summoning him with the sound of his voice, but Roy quickly discarded that notion, remembering his fruitless attempt to summon even a small gull.

It distressed him that the dragon had been both so near and so much in his mind as well. Could there be some unknown affinity between the two? Perhaps he really did have power over the beast of air and fire, Kreosoath the Dragonlord. But if that were true, then why hadn't Ratha, who was much more adept at the mastery of Quintah and Rahlah, also mastered the great beast? Roy remembered the vision of the Archmage's last battle, how Kreosoath had served Mordeth and fought against the falcons. No, it didn't make sense that Roy's own puny strength could overcome a foe that even the great Ratha could not master.

"Moratha, wake up, you lazy bird," Roy said, nudging the still-sleeping falcon.

Moratha half-opened a single eye.

"I just had an encounter with Kreosoath. No, I'm all right. And, no, don't you dare tell Mithra. Listen, I don't know why, but the dragon didn't attack. He could easily have destroyed me before I even knew he was there. And that disturbs me. Something's very odd. No, I don't have time to explain. I need you to go quickly, fly and gather your kind, summon them to me. The battle with Mordeth is near, and I think we're going to need some air support. Quickly, my friend."

Moratha launched into the air and swept down the lit

hallway, exiting the compound by an open window and sailing north, his powerful wings propelling him quickly out of sight. Only one lookout upon the walls of Hagsface noted the departure of the Lord of Falcons, and he remained silent, standing atop the eastern wall, his corn silk hair tossing in the gentle morning breeze.

❖ CHAPTER SIXTEEN ❖

Hawks and Hares

Two months had passed since the lightning exploded with blue thunder, sending Roy into a world so different from his own. Two months of foraging for food, struggling through mountains, stumbling across a desert to a ruined fortress, only to wait for an inevitable war. Dragons and Dark Lords sprang unbidden and threatened to devour him. It was a world of danger and oppressive spirit. Roy longed for home.

But what home? Each sunrise faded with perfect light the memories of his people. His people? Roy fought with the idea. The people of the university, the people of another place, another time. He tried again, unsuccessfully, to dredge up Gwen's visage. He couldn't even remember the color of her hair. He slapped out at a stray insect buzzing around his head.

"What'll be bothering you now?" It was Stentor, glistening with sweat in the late afternoon, his thick chest heaving as he struggled through the heat and humidity. Roy sat in the precious shade of a parapet atop the battlements, where Stentor had come across him while making his inspection rounds.

Roy puzzled for a moment, wondering if he should answer. The look of earnest concern on Stentor's face persuaded him.

"I was thinking of home. Or trying to."

Stentor shrugged, unimpressed. "So?"

"So I'm finding it nearly impossible to remember any details about the people of my home. I can remember places. I can remember things. And ideas. But the faces have faded. I can't see them at all anymore."

Stentor considered a moment before answering, taking a deep breath. "I don't know much about magic. Mithra and Tralaina can take care of that. I've always felt best when my muscles were flexing. No, I've never been much of a one for magic."

"Meaning?" Roy tried to smile patiently, but he was in no mood for long stories. He wanted an answer.

"Meaning I don't know much about magic. But I know a bit about one thing and another."

Roy frowned but said nothing.

"When I was a lad, I met a girl named—" Stentor pursed his lips, remembering—"Majencia? Blast it all, I can't remember. But that's just the point. Was a time I was so confounded in love with her I couldn't see straight to strap my boots. She was the prettiest thing I ever laid my eyes upon. Leastwise, that's what I feel here." He pointed several inches above his flat stomach. "But here, in my head, I can't remember her face. I close my eyes and all I can see is Tralaina. And that's not all bad, son."

The two men looked at each other for several moments before Roy offered his thanks and turned away. It had been no answer for him, and the frustration gnawed at him. He couldn't remember the details of the people who had once meant so much to him, and the people who surrounded him now accepted him more as the Archmage, Ratha, than the English professor, Roy. To most of his closest friends on this lonely world, he was no more than an imposter.

Lonely and bright amidst it all was Moratha, the Lord of Falcons. The great hawk recognized that Roy was not Ratha, and their relationship had been built upon that fact. Moratha would patiently keep still, listening to Roy recall adventures of his childhood; in return, the falcon would conjure pictures into the professor's mind, allowing the man to view the Keshian world through the perceptive eyes of the falcon. Especially stimulating was the thrill of hunting, as Moratha recalled through picture language his daily adventures in the Great Fen, the hunting grounds of the hawk.

The relationship was unusual, unlike having a pet but not quite like having a human friend. Roy spoke to the bird, but Moratha could only respond in the eerie picture language. Although Roy had to admit it was a method of communication superior to mere language, vertigo often accompanied the races through trees and clouds. It was a difficult relationship, but through all the jumble of experiences, Roy grew to love the bird as brother, friend, and confidant.

Thoughts of the falcon now only made Roy miss the great bird all the more. It had been two days since he had sent the falcon to gather his kind, and no word had returned to him. A depressing shadow covered him, and he moped about the walled city with an infectious sadness. People began to worry about him, whispering about the queer mutterings of the Archmage. Somman, one of the young Pradatha guards who had hurried to Roy's aid on the beach in the episode with Kreosoath, became worried that the Archmage had been enchanted by the great beast, and his overactive imagination sent him running to Mithra. But Roy's stern words had forestalled him outside her door.

The sun expanded in the sky, raining down fierce heat, making Roy more fidgety than usual. He wandered past the fountains, dipping his palm beneath the cascading water, splashing the wetness across his face. Meandering through the city, he inspected the growing collection of small metal globes that Malek had constructed, approving their craftsmanship. Roy's melancholy doubled at the thought of using the carefully crafted objects as weapons of war.

The alchemists were still busy trying to perfect Roy's gunpowder, with limited success. They had narrowed the combination down to four parts sand, one part each of the other components. The result was a mixture that burned rapidly, but without the satisfactory crisp explosion that Roy hoped for that would be necessary to detonate Malek's iron orbs. Roy suggested that they try cutting down the amount of potassium nitrate, his term for the silver sand, and the alchemists renewed their preparations.

Roy climbed up the western rampart, walking along the narrow plank that served as a catwalk. Peering through the crenellations, he observed the wispy waves of heat that rose from the desert sands, the nearly shadowless dunes that spread across the land before him. He breathed the hot air deeply, feeling the moisture evaporate from his lips, then swept a hand across his cleanshaven face, thankful that Malek had taken time to hone a suitable blade to scrape the wiry beard from his face. Although most Keshian men wore beards, Roy was certain that the heat would have been unbearable for him beneath a heavy beard.

A sudden motion pulled at his eyes, and he turned to look at the woman perched high on the lookout tower of the western wall. She leaned forward, as if straining against some invisible barrier, her eyes narrowed against the glare of the sands. Roy followed her eyes toward the western horizon, searching for what she was observing. His eyes focused with remarkable clarity, a gift, no doubt, from his close association with the falcon. As he watched, a dark mass slowly wriggled into view, moving slowly toward the fortress.

"He comes!" the woman shouted. "Morelua comes!"

* * * * *

Moratha flew through the morning haze, his wings beating the air with incredible force. The Lord of Falcons was the greatest bird on the Keshian continent, strong and filled with stamina. He would need it to reach Norshal and the hunting grounds of his kindred.

Beneath the great bird, the land blurred into a jumble of color: browns, yellows, greens, mixed together by speed, stirring emotions within him. How long had it been since he sped above the Shaleth highlands, the trees below crimson with autumn, a rabbit frantic as it tried to escape the once keen vision of the Lord of Falcons? Now his eyes were clouded with age; soon another would be named Lord of Falcons, greatest of the birds that fly.

He had been strong when he first came to young Ratha in the fields of the boy's farm. Moratha had watched the boy work with the falcon's brothers, the lesser hawks that hunted with humankind. The boy had been gentle, stroking the creatures with delicate fingers, and generous, too, always making certain that the birds were fed well and rested after the hunt. Moratha grew to love the boy as he watched, circling beneath the highest clouds.

It had been a headstrong act for Moratha to come to the boy's naming; the boy was to be given his Word of Power, and Moratha had hoped it would be Rahlah. Disappointment swelled over the Lord of the Falcons when the elder gave him the word of Keshia, the Land. It was not right that such a boy should be bound by the hard earth. Without thought of consequences, Moratha swept down upon the boy and, as is the right of the Lord of Falcons, claimed the boy for Rahlah. The act was without precedent and had caused a flurry amongst his brethren, but it didn't matter, for Moratha loved the boy.

Of course, he was surprised when the old mage called the boy as well, bestowing upon him the power of Quintah. How the village buzzed with that bit of news! A mage with three powers was certainly destined to do great things! Bitterness soured Moratha's thoughts then as he recalled the destruction of his valued friend, the man he had stayed by for a lifetime and watched become Archmage of Kesh, destroyed at the hands of the evil one, Mordeth.

Moratha had tried to help, but his summoning of his reluctant brethren to ward off Kreosoath had been too late. The Dark One prevailed in the end, and Moratha couldn't even find Ratha's broken body to pour his laments over. The falcons had returned to Shaleth, having chased the black dragon from the land, but also having lost the ultimate battle. It was disheartening, and much of the blame was placed on Moratha himself. Many of his kind refused to acknowledge Moratha as lord afterward, but most of them were young. The elder falcons prevailed, although the margin that permitted Moratha to retain his grip as leader was narrow.

For ten years, Moratha had waited for the promised return of his friend, a desperate hope that finally culminated in the appearance of Roy. True, the man was not Ratha, but his physical appearance and the quality of gentleness were the same—and Ratha had summoned him. The bond of friendship was easily established with the otherworlder, and Moratha was more than glad to relinquish his self-imposed exile and return to the realm of humankind.

Beneath him, the land vaguely changed from the brown of sand to the lighter green of the plains of Norshal. He was weary from the long flight and his hunger ached for him to stop, to hunt the fat hares of the north. Slowly he circled, carefully inspecting the land below. Movement erupted to his left, and he veered, preparing to attack. He drove himself down toward his target, a gray blur, undoubtedly a hare. His tired eyes tried to focus. Yes, a hare, moving in circles.

Too late, Moratha saw the tether attached to the hind leg of the frightened rodent. Nets flew from all directions, tangling his wings and dropping him to the ground with a sickening thud. He screamed in defiance, his sharp beak biting the thick cords that held him, but men were upon him before he could break free. A rope pinioned his wings against his body and a leather hood quickly blocked his vision.

"A big 'un, 'tis fer sure," a voice bellowed from beyond the hood. "Fetch a price, that 'un will."

"By all darkness," another voice swore, "da ya know wha' ya gut der? 'Tis da mage's bird, 'tis. I'd rec'nize 'im anywhere. Ay use ta saw de mage in Yelu, years back. 'Tis you, ain't it, Moratha?"

Ratha! the falcon replied, hope clammering in his breast.

"By all darkness! 'Tis 'im! Aye, but ain't Mordeth gonna be pleased! We'd best send 'im fas' ta th' Regent. Git yer 'orse! By darkness, we is gonna be rich men!"

* * * * *

Mordeth's army had taken their time reaching the walled city, arriving only as the sun dipped behind them into the nether world of night. Inside the city's walls, the Pradatha spent the night waiting for an attack that didn't come. Roy realized that Mordeth had scored a small psychological victory, for his troops undoubtedly had themselves a good night's rest.

As morning approached, Mithra found Roy pacing nervously from the western wall to the fountain and back again. She approached wordlessly and walked beside him as starlight pierced the night. Roy agonized over his role as Ratha, his useless gifts of science, gifts he loathed and yet had offered freely. Mithra was content to be beside him. Finally he turned to Mithra and spoke.

"It's all a mistake. Ratha called the wrong man."

"Hush," she whispered to him, placing her slim hand on his chest. "You've done much for us. You've given us hope. And science."

Roy snorted in disgust. "Yes, I've given you that. I

hope your world will forgive me." He looked off toward the center of the square, where several shadows moved around the silhouette of the catapult. It had failed each time they had tested it, and Roy had little faith that it would ever work.

As if reading his mind, Mithra answered. "The catapult will be in working order by morning. And your other gift . . ."

"The gunpowder."

"Yes, the gunpowder. I'm sure that it will work, too. The alchemists will discover the proper proportions."

Roy stared into the sky, watching the starlight bead the nighttime canvas. Silently he hoped that his gift of science would not work.

"And you, my love." Mithra took Roy's arm and squeezed it. She had found a haven from the dark memory of her rape, had even begun to convince herself that it had never happened, that Roy was really her unborn child's father. She smiled at him with genuine warmth. "We have you. And that is something wonderful."

"Yes, wonderful," he repeated, but the words rang hollow.

Even as he spoke, the sun rose behind them, and Roy found himself looking out at the blood-red banner of Mordeth's army snapping sharply in the morning breeze, the emblazoned black symbol as hideous as a canker upon it.

Roy looked again at the bivouacked army that edged the horizon, less than a mile away. He could see signs of movement and small fires, smoke jumping as the brisk wind caught it and pushed it east over their heads. Roy caught the aroma of roasting meat, the succulent smell reminding him of holiday meals back home.

Back home. He tried again to remember Gwen; a sun-lit day in the east park, the quiet waters of the large duck pond in the park's center, a faceless body beside him. He shook his head violently, but it did no good. His mind wandered into the futile memories of the university, the Regents, and the accident that had transported him to another realm. A feeling of melancholy came over him, binding his courage and making him feel weak and worthless.

Mithra, too, felt the growing despair. It seemed to emanate from Mordeth's camp, lapping over them like the smoke from their fires, seeping into their clothes, their skin, their hearts. Courage melted beneath the hot glare of the scene before them. Her stomach growled with a hungry complaint, and she tightened the muscles of her abdomen. She wondered if the child inside her was happy or sad. Unbidden, an image of her unborn child floated before her. She could see its face—it was Mordeth's. She shut her eyes to the thought and tried to quiet her queasy stomach.

No one saw the black-clad figure standing on a boul-der, his gloved hands raised high into the morning sky. Behind him, his shadow stabbed the earth, piercing it to its heart. Mordeth's lips moved with a wordless chant, and the spell he wove grew stronger.

Along the western wall, where the spell was strongest, the sentries began to lay down their arms. Then as if on signal, the city filled with the sound of metal clanging on the flagstones. Each Pradathan felt the desolation tugging at his resolve, tempting him to lay down his arms and surrender before total annihilation enveloped him. It was Flanx, rising from his sickbed, who, having already witnessed the despair that Mordeth wrought and having survived it, broke the spell that the Dark One spun.

"Hear the truth, Pradatha!" he shouted, stumbling weakly through the streets. "Hear it and live! Mordeth is darkness and deceit! He enchants us with despair! Awake from the slumber and live!" Throughout the city, cries of defiance rang like warning bells, and the city once more began to buzz with life and vitality.

Mithra was off the wall and into the city before Roy realized his despair was not wholly natural. His mouth was dry and his chest ached. He looked out at Mordeth's gathered army, but it seemed no smaller or less ominous than before.

By noon, Mithra had sought out Roy again, finding him sitting beside the city's fountain, studying the grain of his staff.

"I cannot abide this useless waiting," she said. "Isn't there something we can do?"

"I don't know, Mithra." His voice was dull and nearly without inflection, but Mithra didn't seem to notice.

"Well, the waiting grates on me. Can't we use your catapult? The craftsmen say it is ready."

"No, not yet. The range is too great. When they are half as far away as they are now, then let it rain down on them. For all the good it will do."

"It will work," Mithra proclaimed. "And the grenades, too. I'm certain they will!" She recalled the final experiment with the grenade, after the apothecaries had perfected the gunpowder. Roy had instructed a single globe to be filled with the mixture, then placed in a hole in the ground and covered with an inverted cart. A long, twisted strip of cloth, dipped in oil, was inserted into the aperture, and when the boy touched the torch to it, he was told to run and hide. The small crater from the grenade's explosion left many jaws slack in wonder.

"Every third soldier on top of the wall will have two of the grenades," Mithra continued.

"Do they know they should use them sparingly?" Roy's displeasure of using such devices crept into his voice.

"I have told them, Archmage," Mithra replied, mocking him slightly.

Her words shook him. He looked up at her and was immediately caught by the intense blueness of her eyes. "I'm sorry, Mithra."

The woman sank down beside him, dipping her hand into the water trough and brushing the cool liquid onto her bare arm. It glistened around her wrist like a bracelet. "You are troubled, Ratha. Does Mordeth's spell still hold you?"

Roy felt suddenly apologetic. "No, I don't think so. It's more than that. I suppose war is the best thing that can happen, considering the alternatives. But I still hate the thought of it." He looked at the woman beside him. "I don't like the thought of you being directly involved in it, either."

Mithra clenched her fist. "When Mordeth dies, that will die with it."

Roy nodded sullenly. "Old habits die the hardest. Mine is a life of peace; yours is war."

Mithra fingered the coarse material of her robe. " *'Tis not too late to seek a newer world.'* " She looked up at the startled professor's face. "Do you remember telling me that?"

"It's from Tennyson," Roy replied. "I'm surprised you remembered it."

"When someone speaks with words of power and beauty, I remember." She took a deep breath. "Mordeth will die. I know it. I will fight him with my last breath. So that we—" she swept her arm in a wide arc that encompassed the entire city—"so that *they* may live."

Roy leaned back against the stone of the fountain and rested his staff across his outstretched legs.

He heard excited shouts from the west wall. A runner came to a stop before them, panting heavily.

"Movement, my lord, milady. In Mordeth's camp. The Dark One's army moves."

Roy and Mithra ran to the rampart, climbing the steep wooden stairs to the watchtower. Before them, a small contingent strode confidently across the hot sands. Roy could make out three figures, two dressed in the colors of Mordeth's Elite Guard, tunics and breeches of gray—the color of despair, Roy thought—with Mordeth's crest faded upon their breastplates. A third figure walked between and slightly ahead of them. He wore leather greaves of polished black, glistening beneath the heavy cloak that buffeted in the wind. His breastplate seemed to be of burnished iron, with the scarlet, silver and black coat-of-arms of the Regent of Keshia etched deep into the metal. His helmless head was covered with flowing black hair, and Roy could imagine the dark eyes darting beneath angry brows. Mordeth approached.

Roy continued watching as Mordeth climbed upon a basalt outcrop some two hundred yards from the west wall. The two guards stood poised behind their master; Roy noticed that they held a small crate.

"Mage imposter, are you there?" Mordeth's voice carried with the wind, sounding like a laugh as it swept over the rampart.

"Ratha's here, Morelua," Mithra shouted defiantly.

"Is that you, Mithra? Good, good. I had heard you were within the walls. Will you come out to meet with me?"

"We can talk from right where we are," she shouted back.

"Come, be reasonable. You cannot win. My forces are too strong, your despair too great. I have no desire to destroy my people. Have you that desire?"

"No, I do not want them destroyed." Roy was surprised at the strength in his own voice.

"Ah, so the imposter speaks! Good! You surprised me at Shymney, little one, but I won't be surprised when next we meet. Indeed, I would like to meet you soon, for we must finish what we began. Would you dare to come and meet me now, little imposter?"

"The time's not yet ripe for us, Morelua. But we will meet . . . sooner than you might desire." The bravado Roy mustered reminded him of another meeting he had had with a Regendt. He hoped that this one would go better.

"Hear the falcon squawk! You claim to be Ratha, the hunting falcon, the same deceitful mage I once destroyed. But know this: I have no fear of falconkind. Shall I show you, imposter?"

"I told you, we will meet soon enough."

"True. But I have a proposition—and a demonstration."

"No bargains, Morelua," Mithra shouted. "We deal only in truth."

"Really? Then tell me truthfully, Mithra, how is my child? Are you taking good care of it? Eating well? You know, imposter, she really is quite a woman. No, I don't suppose you would know, would you?"

A soft murmuring spread through the Pradatha as Mordeth's words sank in. Mithra? The mother of Mordeth's child? The Pradatha waited for her to deny it, but she said nothing.

"You mention a proposition," Roy called, hoping to refocus the attention away from Mithra. "What is it?"

"You and I, imposter, will engage in battle, winner take all. No wars . . . just a single combat. Are you agreed?"

Mordeth knew where to strike hardest, Roy thought, for the idea tempted him. He envisioned the maimed bodies of the people he had lived with for over a month, the cries of the wounded, the wails of mourning. He had nearly defeated Mordeth at Shymney; his power had grown since then. Perhaps the balance had finally tipped in his favor. He looked up from his reflections, having considered his reply.

"No!" Mithra begged. "You're not ready yet. You need more time."

"I know, Mithra. I know." Nevertheless, for one final moment, he considered the offer.

"Morelua! No, the time is not yet right. We will wait, and we will continue to listen to your lies if we must."

"Lies? You flatter yourselves. I have no need to lie; I can easily destroy you, now or later. I had only hoped you would consider the innocents behind your walls, and their sufferings. For you and for them, I offer now this demonstration." He turned and took the leather bag from the guard behind him.

"Know that I am master of Ratha, the Falcon, and all those that serve him. See here how easily I can destroy the falconkind." He reached into the box and withdrew a bound hawk, lifting it high above his head. A gasp shook through the Pradatha as they recognized Moratha, bound with black leather cords.

"Your stubbornness will do naught but destroy those around you, imposter." Roy stood breathless as Mordeth slowly circled upon the basalt porch, holding the falcon high for all to see. Then, with a brisk movement, he brought the motionless bird down upon his knee, snapping its spine and letting it tumble, lifeless, to the sand below.

"Falcons die easily," Mordeth mocked, then turned and departed for his camp.

Roy continued staring at the lifeless form lying on the hot desert sands, the brown-gray feathers fluttering in the wind, until Mithra came and put her arms around him, her soft white hair brushing against the tears on his cheek.

❖ CHAPTER SEVENTEEN ❖

War

The Pradatha waited on the walls, watching the sun descend like a dying bird into the desert, falling behind Mordeth's troops. The Dark One's scarlet pennant hung limp in the dead air, the blood-red banner a constant reminder of the fate awaiting the rebels. Shadows crept like spies into the heart of Hagsface, painting faces once lively in the sunlight with the cold gray of the corpse.

The first star appeared, an anemic parody of the bright stars Roy remembered from their flight across the Keshian mountains. The starlight sputtered in the windless night, seeming to choke on the darkness that pressed heavily down upon the waiting army of the Pradatha. Roy peered through the thick night, watching for the first wave of attack.

Beside him, one hundred and sixty Pradatha, armed with bows and spears, stood ready to repel the onslaught. Mithra had proven herself an apt general, dividing her meager troops into groups, assigning each a specific task during the expected siege. Roy turned and looked along the wall, struggling to catch a glimpse of the woman. He thought he could see her blond hair, like cool fire, about twenty yards down the wall, but so many of the Pradatha had similar features that it was difficult to tell.

Roy had tried not to waste time during the wait. Soon after Mordeth's challenge, he had gathered the Pradatha mages together and consolidated their plan of action. Mithra had suggested that the Roshah mages be set upon the eastern wall, and the idea had been reasonably well accepted, although the water wizards would rather have been stationed upon the western wall to take direct part in the battle against Mordeth. For Mithra's strategy to be successful, however, each of the mages must be willing to follow orders.

The mages of Quintah and Rahlah were more readily convinced to follow Mithra's plan. Each of the seventeen young mages had trained with Ratha and were loyal to him. Before Ratha had begun to train the youth of Keshia in the ways of Air and Fire, only one man in each generation was allowed to master the element. Ratha had felt the need to share all of his knowledge, and so a few select young people were allowed to have both the words Quintah and Rahlah. Fewer still had succeeded in becoming the mage teachers that Mordeth had hunted so meticulously for the past ten years. Now only the small band gathered at Hagsface was left to defy Mordeth.

Although the mages of Keshia had no specific powers that had been especially developed for battle, having spent the sum of their lives encouraging the growth of crops and the general well-being of the villagers, they were well respected by the peasants and rural folk who answered the Archmage's summons. Honor and responsibility were accorded them as officers of the ragtag army, each one of the sixteen men and women wearing the brown of Keshia and leading fifty Pradatha. Roy and Mithra hoped that the presence of the mages would help to overcome the fear that was sure to emerge when Mordeth cast his dark spells over the fortress.

Now there was nothing left to do but wait, to watch the interminable waves crash on the beach, watch the sun give way to a restless night. Roy was aware of the foreboding atmosphere but felt powerless to alter it. The gloom was a thick paste clinging to them. Roy shuddered in the darkness, wishing for the light of dawn to come.

"What are you thinking?" Mithra's voice pierced the night like a flickering candle.

"I wonder if we have done enough, Mithra," Roy replied. "And I also wonder if we have done too much. Perhaps I should face Mordeth alone. If I win, many unnecessary deaths could be avoided."

"And if you lose?" Mithra challenged. "If you lose, the Pradatha would be too disheartened to fight and Morelua would destroy them all. He will not allow anyone to walk away from Hagsface." The night breeze quickened momentarily, howling mournfully. "It's not your fault, Roy," Mithra whispered. "Moratha's death is on Morelua's hands, not yours."

"At Shymney, I ran when I could have stayed. Mordeth was injured. Maybe I could have defeated him there."

"You know you weren't ready for him then. You have gained much power since then."

"Not enough. The book has told me nothing more. The staff is still an enigma in most respects. And now my friend is dead." Roy shrugged, as if trying to rid himself of an ominous weight.

Mithra's voice was a mere whisper in the night. "There's a story we tell the children of the land. A farmer tended to his crops and cattle, and each day saw the sun speed across the pale blue sky, and in the evening he watched the clouds come and sweeten the ground with their moisture. He knew both the warmth of the sun and the pleasant rains caused his crops to grow, so he decided to leap to the sky and fetch them back with him, so his land could be fertile and without care, for the love he had for his land was without measure. The people watched him leaping in the midst of his fields and thought him mad, and therefore shunned him for his efforts. His task proved impossible and he finally relented, expecting the land to be angry that he had failed; but the land continued to produce and provide for his needs. I will wait with you, Archmage. Perhaps love will be the weapon you seek."

"Perhaps, Mithra. Perhaps."

* * * * *

The cell was dry, at least, and the food was better than he had expected. Krotah was continually surprised by the naivete of the Pradatha; they should have killed him or tortured him for information. Instead, they had stuffed him into a small, windowless room and set a lone guard outside the door. Twice a day food and water were brought to him, satisfying his hunger and thirst and leaving him to spend his hours plotting. The Pradatha were fools.

The guard made a shuffling sound outside the door,

and Krotah again took up the soft lament he had begun when his young jailer had assumed watch. There was yet hope, he thought, then laughed at the thought of hope being Mordeth's ally now.

Krotah placed his lips near the crack between the door and jam, hissing like an asp preparing to strike. "Your family will die soon. It's a shame, for if their son is like them, they're not bad people. The Archmage must be corrupting them, as he once corrupted the youth of Lorlita." On the other side of the door, Krotah could hear the faint brush of sandals against the floor, the sound of impatient youth.

"It won't be pleasant, you know. Traitors to Mordeth are executed. Their black hearts are torn from their chests. It's necessary, but it's a horrible sight." Krotah's voice flexed like a muscle, tightening around its prey. "But take heart, young man, for you alone can save your people." The agitated movement beyond the door quickened.

"And think of your friends. You have a special woman, no doubt. It would be tragic to see her die with all the other traitors, only because they were duped into following the false Archmage. His words are like sweet poison. Don't let the Archmage destroy all that you love." Outside, the jangling of metal rang like bells of freedom, and Krotah poised, ready to spring.

Jerriod opened the cell door, unable to put up with the prisoner's words any longer. He was completely loyal to Mithra. The young woman frequently had shown him unwarranted kindness, and Mithra loved the Archmage. No one should be allowed to slander their names without retribution. A sturdy whack on the prisoner's head would silence his foul mouth.

The strike was startlingly sudden. Krotah had used it on many an unsuspecting peasant. A brutal thrust with his knuckles into the windpipe, and Jerriod's eyes widened in fear. He couldn't scream. A moment later he lay motionless upon the stone floor, his lifeless body twisted into a grotesque shape. Krotah dragged the body into the room, slipped out of the cell, and locked the door behind him, tossing the keys into an ash-filled brazier as he moved stealthily down the hall. The building was silent, with no hint of another guard. They were probably all manning the ramparts, Krotah decided. Once outside, he strained to hear any faint sounds of breathing, of fires crackling in nearby pits. Instead, he heard only silence.

On the ramparts stood the Pradatha, watching over the crenellations. Krotah could smell their fear, a spore he recognized and loved. His nostrils flared expectantly, and he licked his thin lips as if preparing for a savory feast. Krotah understood fear.

With uncanny silence, Krotah slipped along the walls of the buildings, all the while observing the fortifications, memorizing the configuration of the troops. Hagsface would soon fall if he could manage to pinpoint its weaknesses. He sucked the breath through his teeth in silent anticipation. The walls around him beckoned steadily.

Through the musty darkness, he could see the blue-robed mages of Roshah on the seaward walls. There the fewest Pradatha were gathered, but Krotah sensed some unseen obstruction. The Pradatha upon the wall were coastal peoples, people claiming the sea as their Word of Power. A slight tremor of distress rippled through him.

The northern walls were well manned and alert, with

long lines of bowmen gripping their longbows with strong hands. Every third person upon the wall stood beside a thick sack, bulging with its contents. Small torches flickered beside the sacks, casting long shadows across the worn planks. The western wall was similarly staffed, except that above the giant doors stood a solitary figure. Even through the murk, Krotah could distinguish the strange garb of the Archmage.

A female figure in a hooded robe stalked across the walkway toward the Archmage, and Krotah guessed the hooded figure must be Mithra. The night breeze caught at her hood, and he saw a flicker of pale white hair. This was the place, then, to draw Mordeth's troops for a quick victory. He need only open the door. He scanned the area between himself and his objective, noting a large bulk partly hidden in the shadows. Shadowy figures moved silently around the vast contraption. Keeping near the building, Krotah moved like a viper through the night, quickly approaching the catapult.

The strange machine lay before him, a large basket filled with odd metal balls dangling from a thick wooden arm. Twenty Pradatha milled about in the night, waiting for something Krotah could not fathom. The twenty were too alert for him to pass unnoticed. Krotah slid his back down along the wall of the building behind him, settling himself in for the wait.

* * * * *

"They come," she whispered, her voice sharp in the stillness.

"I see them, Mithra," Roy replied, his voice husky. His eyes strained to watch the shadows shift in the distance. The waiting had chewed his ragged nerves.

"Should we launch the catapult?" she asked.

"Not yet. Wait awhile longer. When the Dark One's troops move beyond the black stone, then it will be time." Roy sucked a sharp breath between his teeth.

"It will work." Mithra's confidence only forced Roy into deeper despair.

The wide shadow crept forward, nearing the fortress base. Roy watched as the mass of Mordeth's troops wriggled like a snake, slithering closer in the night. He shivered in anticipation of the attack, fingering the smooth staff in his hand. Soon, he thought. Soon. His stomach soured at the thought.

"Now! It's time!" Mithra's voice snapped like a broken rope, releasing the tension from those around her. Activity bustled on the square below. A sharp twang echoed through the stone-walled city, reverberating so strongly they felt it in their muscles.

Small sparks of living fire danced across the sky as the catapult launched its deadly cargo upon the unsuspecting horde outside the wall. They heard the sound of the grenades bouncing around the approaching army, striking the stones at their feet. Occasionally, a metal sphere would strike flesh with the sound of crunching bones. The tiny fuses sparkled, then faded behind the silhouettes of a dozen soldiers. Suddenly light flared and thunder roared across the barren plain as the explosives ignited, blasting metal shards into the bewildered men. Shouts of anger and fear erupted from Mordeth's ranks as many of his soldiers tried to flee the deadly fire.

The catapult launched a second fiery cargo, and again the grenades exploded like an unexpected storm. Flames danced savagely through Mordeth's ranks as the powder ignited clothing and weapons. The sounds of shrapnel rattling against the stones echoed like clattering bones. Roy watched as a third volley rocketed overhead, landing in the midst of the slowly approaching army. Halfheartedly he raised his staff and let its light filter through the night, casting sharp shadows behind the advancing men. Bowmen sent arrows racing like hunting falcons toward the foremost troops. Most broke against their raised shields but some smacked into flesh, ripping through the soldiers' bodies, crumpling them to the ground.

Although the catapult inflicted a fearsome toll upon Mordeth's troops, the first wave soon advanced inside its range, the fiery bombs bursting harmlessly behind them. A cheer arose from the rear guard of Mordeth's army as they witnessed the bulk of the wave reach the wall, clattering arrows ricocheting from their protective shields. Siege ladders were lifted to the walls as rapidly as the Pradatha could hurl them back again.

A sudden noise erupted from the seaward wall, a sound like the crash of waves. Mordeth's troops had staged a simultaneous attack upon the far wall, hoping to catch the Pradatha unaware. As they stalked along the packed beach, the Roshah mages had banded together, consolidating their power as they huddled together in a small group. The line of attackers had nearly reached the eastern wall when the sea began to churn. Shouts escaped the startled army as the ocean swelled toward them, rushing with a fierce tide that crushed the unsuspecting soldiers against the hard stone walls of Hagsface. As the remnant of the attacking force retreated, the Roshah mages released their spell and the sea subsided to tranquility, the dead bodies of the assailants reduced to flotsam in the pale seafoam.

Mithra nodded to the awaiting Pradatha standing upon the western wall. The bags they held were opened, and men and women reached within, removing the small orbs. One after another they lit the cloth fuses, waiting until the glowing ember had nearly disappeared from sight, then lobbing the bombs over the walls into the clustered troops below. Lightning ripped through Mordeth's men, splattering sundered body fragments against the outer walls of Hagsface. As the frightened soldiers tried to run from the hissing grenades, the Pradatha fired volley after volley of arrows into them, dropping them like heavy stones.

The attackers quickly became disorganized, disheartened. The ground beneath Hagsface's northern wall was littered with the dead or dying. Inside the walls, not a single casualty had been reported. As the army retreated, the catapult launched a final cargo of deadly fire into their ranks. Roy watched as the bombs rattled like hail against ripened wheat. His stomach turned even as joyful murmurs rippled along the walls.

Roy steadied himself on his staff and continued looking out across the plain before him. Shadows flickered as flames licked the dead bodies strewn across the battleground. The smell of blood and burning flesh mingled with the salt air, and he felt the awful weight of guilt constrict his chest. So many dead, so needlessly. Perhaps, he thought, it would still be best to meet Mordeth alone.

The sounds of men moving toward the walled city awakened Roy from his thoughts. It seemed as though Mordeth had managed to instill enough fear into his men to overcome their distaste for fiery death. Metal clanged as the mailed soldiers stalked their prey, their uniforms melting into the darkness. Again the catapult launched a volley of grenades, inflicting some damage, but the line advanced more quickly this time and was soon inside the range of the war machine. The surge washed in upon the walled city on three sides, with only the seaward wall left unscathed. The Pradatha hurled more of the fire bombs down upon the army, the explosions sending jagged metal whining across the starless night. Heedlessly Mordeth's troops advanced upon the wall, leaning their wooden ladders against the stone rampart and lifting them again when the Pradatha cast them back.

The soldiers who had worked the catapult left the device and climbed the walls to aid the defenders. Bowstrings hummed like a dirge, repeating their song of death. Several Pradatha began to fall from the heights as Mordeth's archers closed and fired. Roy slipped down behind a merlon and pressed his head into his knees, quietly struggling with his own battle as the war raged about him.

Krotah watched from the shadows until the catapult crew left their lelthal machine. Then, deserting his hiding place, he skirted the plaza, hugging the walls of buildings. Men and women raced to replenish supplies of arrows and broken bows, to add their support when it was needed. On the ramparts, the Pradatha were busy with the war that raged outside the walls. No one took notice of the single dark figure that moved stealthily toward the main gate.

The sound of rusty metal scraping in the night snapped Roy from his reverie. Beneath him, Krotah had managed to reach the wide double doors of the western wall and remove the heavy wooden bolt that barred access from outside. As the battle clattered beyond the walls, Krotah began to swing open the gates to the fortified city. In the dim light, Roy saw a cruel smile curving Krotah's thin lips.

Roy stumbled down the steps, racing toward the gates in an effort to block the oncoming army. Krotah still stood framed in the arching gateway, beckoning the troops to enter. Without thinking, Roy lifted his staff and white fire spat from it, striking the captain of the Elite Guard between the shoulders, crushing the man like a straw doll. Sparks skittered across the stone street as Krotah imploded in a brilliant fireball.

"Rahlah!" Roy shouted, and an easterly wind began to blow. He shouted the word again, and the wind became a gale, pressing against the half-open gates. A group of Mordeth's soldiers grabbed one swinging gate and pushed the door farther open against the wind. Roy raised his staff, and they were instantly obliterated by the white-hot flames. But more soldiers appeared and continued to press toward the opening. Roy felt nausea fill his throat as the smell of burned flesh washed over him. Hands reached out to subdue him, and he swung wildly with his staff, feeling it connect against someone's skull. Then, with a great shout, he thrust the staff high, and a blue light shot into the crowd, knocking the determined soldiers back from the wobbling gate.

Suddenly a terrible darkness snapped across the night, subduing the magical blue flame. On the walls, Mithra watched helplessly as the thick darkness poured over Roy's form. She gasped as she recognized what she had seen before, at the foot of Shymney. Within the veil, Roy felt a cold grip seize him, as if Mordeth's fingers were clutching at him.

Roy grasped at thoughts of sunlight, warm and comforting, and Mithra lying in its heat. The night lurched backward toward its origin. With a supreme effort, he kept his mind focused, and the darkness hovered uselessly outside the walls.

But his concentration was needed to keep fighting off Mordeth's attack, and the Dark One's soldiers, relieved of the battle against wind and fire, once more started through the gate.

Stentor saw the swarm advancing through the western gate and, calling to the Pradatha stationed nearby, charged to the Archmage's defense. The burly barkeep cracked his cudgel against an unhelmed head, sending the soldier sprawling across the square. Two more of Mordeth's men dropped as arrows leapt from Pradathan bows. Soon a small group of men and women had formed a protective circle about the battling Archmage, repelling the enemy onslaught.

The Pradatha gained the advantage, pushing the soldiers back through the narrow gateway. Swords and spears clanged and clattered as the two armies met in close personal combat, the archers useless in the tight fighting.

Several of Mordeth's men tried to pry the door from its hinges to keep the passage open for further attacks, but Stentor and his men clubbed their way through their ranks and pulled the doors closed with a resounding clap.

The sound broke Roy's concentration for a moment, as he looked up to see Stentor and two other men ramming the crossbar into its sleeve. The moment was enough for Mordeth. A second wave of blackness crushed down upon Roy and dropped him to his knees. He wondered if he had fallen into a pit, if he could catch himself against the walls, but if he was moving, he couldn't tell.

All sense of time and motion eluded him, except for the smooth touch of death that caressed him. He fought to brush it away, summoning his own potent heat. For an instant, he sensed the darkness being repelled. He opened his eyes and caught a glimpse of the world around him. Bodies lay strewn across the square, but the gateway was still closed. He began to despair, thinking that he hadn't enough power to undo Mordeth's spell. Night swept into him again, and his eyes ached as he stared into nothingness.

He tried to picture Gwen's face but failed. But even as he tried, Mithra's visage rose unbidden before him, blue-eyed and beautiful, her hair a frame of seafoam highlighting her smile.

He felt the unmistakable touch of the western breeze, the pungent smell of brine that swept across the fortress, bringing morning. Light ignited the eastern sky as the sun burst forth from its sleepy quarters. He sensed Mordeth flinch as the crimson tip of sunrise, steeped with Mithra's words and Roy's own power, plunged into the Dark One's defenses.

He thought he heard a muffled cheer about him, but his mind was too intent on casting Mordeth back into the desert. Again he raised his staff and concentrated on Quintah, flailing against the last remnants of night. Then all was silent.

He opened his eyes and looked about him. Blood oozed from the bodies at his feet and before him, but the gate remained closed, secured by the great beam. The daylight caused him to blink, and he felt the warmth of morning penetrate his aching, cold body. He savored the splendid sensation, glad to be alive and to have finished with the ordeal. Thoughts of the war faded in the growing light, cleansing him with pure catharsis. Around him, sounds of relief and victory played like carillons.

Then the shadow came. At first Roy thought that it was Mordeth crushing against him again, but there was no chill in this shadow. The Archmage sensed a different being. It sped across the square, circling and growing wider. Roy looked toward the sun and beheld the black silhouette of Kreosoath. Higher in the sky, a dozen more black dragons hovered like awaiting death. Kreosoath tilted and circled the fortress, its great wings beating as it swept toward Roy.

The archers on the walls watched helplessly as the great dragon sped toward the Archmage, their arrows ineffective weapons against the leathery hide of the sinister beast. Despair instantly replaced the joy of moments before. Roy looked up at the circling dragon, too exhausted to resist.

The stillness that runs the jagged edge of uncertainty swelled the silence as Kreosoath landed in the square before Roy. The Archmage weakly lifted his staff in anticipation of the creature's attack, then suddenly lowered it, letting its tip rest upon the ground. A cheer erupted from the walls as Kreosoath, the great black dragon, dipped its giant head in willful submission to the Archmage.

❖ CHAPTER EIGHTEEN ❖

The Falcon Rises

"No!" The Translating Stone rattled with Mordeth's anger, but his command went unheeded. From his vantage atop the rocky knoll outside Hagsface, Mordeth could see the Lord of Dragons prostrate himself in front of the imposter. "I forbid that you do this!" he shouted, but the twelve smaller dragons circled above the fortress, unaffected by his rage. Beneath them, in the distant courtyard, Roy stood beside Kreosoath, laying a gentle hand upon the dragon's ridged neck.

"Can you understand me, Kreosoath?" The dragon's eyes whirled like ebony tops as Kreosoath replied with a low rumble, alarming the Pradatha surrounding the Archmage and the black beast. Several ran to Roy's aid.

Roy shook off his protectors, but never took his eyes off the beast lying before him. "Good. We've much to discuss."

"Much to discuss?" Mithra's voice rose in disbelief as she pushed her way through the crowd surrounding Roy and the prostrate dragon.

"Kreosoath has come to a new understanding." Roy

patted the neck of the black beast. "We have a new ally. Come, we must speak together." He looked over his shoulder at the curious faces. "Alone."

With one look, Mithra scattered the Pradatha and sent them murmuring back to their posts or to tend the wounded. The dragon followed Roy toward the city's center, Mithra keeping a distrustful distance from the great beast. Finally Roy settled down on the stones surrounding the fountain, the cool water burbling behind him. Kreosoath stamped uncomfortably.

"Does the water bother you, Kreosoath?" Roy asked.

The dragon's low rumble set loose sand dancing upon the flagstones of the square.

"I see. We can move, then."

Again the dragon rumbled a response.

"Very well, Kreosoath. I do prefer it here. Water makes the day seem cooler."

"You—you mean to say you understand that growling?" Mithra remained several paces away from the huge creature, her bow nocked and ready.

"Certainly. Kreosoath's words are quite intelligible. She speaks to me in verse."

"Verse? You mean, as in your poetry?" Mithra seemed amused, but her face suddenly contorted as the implication of Roy's last statement sunk in. "She?"

"Yes. It seems that Kreosoath is not the Lord of Dragons, but rather mistress of them. More precisely, she is the mother of them. The twelve that circle Hagsface are her children." He pointed up at the dozen black creatures hovering in the sky. Mithra seemed about to speak when the dragon interrupted with a short growl.

"Yes, she is," Roy replied, then turned to Mithra. "She knows you're pregnant."

"How? Did Mordeth tell her?"

Roy shrugged. "She just knows. It's the way of dragons, I guess. Anyway, she understands. It seems that she's pregnant, too."

"Pregnant? When is she . . .?"

Roy shrugged. "Soon. Any day now."

"Will she fight, then?" Mithra asked.

"No, she won't fight." Roy cast a stern look at the dragon. "I can't ask her to do that. Mordeth's power is too strong. But I think her presence will keep the Dark One's soldiers from attacking. Certainly thirteen black dragons flying about an enemy's hold would keep most sane people away."

"Sane ones, yes," Mithra replied. "But let's not count on sanity from the Dark Lord. We can't rely upon the walls of Hagsface to stand against a long siege. This war must end."

"True. But the dragon promises time, and each hour I gain will be well spent. Kreosoath has already told me something I didn't know about my own powers, a great deal that even Moratha didn't know." Roy grimaced as he said the name of his murdered friend. "She has come to me because of my verse, not my magic. If this is true, then perhaps her insight will tell us something about Mordeth's weaknesses, something that will turn the tide in our favor." The dragon looked up at him, her eyes gentle.

Mithra stared at the black dragon, refusing to veil her distrust. "As you will, Archmage," she said. "But you won't mind if I continue making my own plans, will you?" Without waiting for Roy's response, Mithra turned and walked away.

"Don't mind her, Kreosoath. She hasn't been feeling

well." Roy stroked the leathery hide of the dragon. "I suppose you haven't felt so well yourself. Well, let's begin. Mordeth will browbeat his troops back into submission before too long, and I've much to learn." Roy settled himself into a relatively comfortable position as the dragon's rumblings echoed through the keep.

* * * * *

"She says that dragonkind are trielemental creatures: Quintah, Keshia, and Rahlah. No mage has ever controlled dragonkind because no mage had ever mastered all three powers sufficiently—that is, until Ratha came along. When word spread that an Archmage had the power of all three, Kreosoath became duly alarmed that her children would be in danger. She is the last female of her kind. The eggs she now carries are the next generation. If they do not survive, neither will dragonkind. She allied with Mordeth in order to save her own kind." Roy tapped his staff against the red flagstones of the plaza as if trying to drive home his point.

"So why has she changed now, Archmage?" Mithra had eventually returned to the square with a number of other Pradatha, including Stentor and Tralaina, but she had not lost her wariness of the great black beast in the hours since the dragon had bowed before Roy. Years of fear and superstition were not easily washed away, and the memory of the dragon's presence at her husband's destruction kept her distrust intact.

"She heard my poetry. You've said it yourself, Mithra. The verse I've recited holds power for you—and for her. All these years, Mordeth has thought that she could only communicate through the Translating Stone, but

Kreosoath is able to understand our human speech. She understood me as I spoke to Moratha at Shymney and as I talked to myself on the beach. She understood—and she was persuaded!

"Verse is the method by which a dragon speaks. At least, when she speaks to me, I hear it as if it were verse. She communicates with me directly. We probably have a sympathetic connection due to our abilities with the three powers. Perhaps it's something more. I don't know. But when she speaks to me, I hear it as verse. When she overheard me quoting my home world's poetry, she decided I'm not the threat she once thought I was. It seems my verse came to her as if I spoke to her in her own tongue. Now she sees that the true threat is Mordeth."

"Can you control her?" Stentor asked. He, too, was uncomfortable with the presence of the dragon.

"No. I can call her to me, as I did on the beach last week." Mithra gave him a surprised look but said nothing. "I can communicate with her," he continued, "but I have no command over her. Neither did Ratha. But she's no longer a threat to us, if indeed she ever was. We need to trust her." The two Pradatha, though not entirely convinced, relented reluctantly to Roy's arguments.

"Good. Now, Mithra, do you recall how Kreosoath became agitated when she was near the fountain?" Mithra nodded. "Well, you don't know what an act of trust that was for her to follow me there. Dragons are trielemental: Earth, Air, Fire. This is their strength as well as their weakness, for when they possess the three, they must fear the fourth: water. Water's a corrosive to them. When it rains, they must fly above the clouds, or else when the drops hit them, their bodies blister. When

I first landed on Keshia, Kreosoath sought me but couldn't get to me, since I had hidden in a pile of driftwood beyond the high-tide mark. She couldn't risk getting wet.

"But Kreosoath isn't afraid of water only. There's a fifth power she fears, and that is Eth, the power of darkness. Like all creatures on Keshia, the power that the Dark One wields terrifies her. That is why I believe we can trust her. She is afraid for her children's sake, and it's Mordeth she fears."

"It's all very interesting, Archmage, but how does it help us in the battle with Morelua?" Tralaina's voice was filled with respect for the Archmage, but her eyes showed doubt.

"Don't you see the implications? If Kreosoath can't abide the fourth power, then perhaps Mordeth suffers a similar affliction. Maybe there is something that he can't control, something he cannot stand against. We know it's not the combined powers of Keshia, Rahlah, and Quintah. He's defeated all of them before, even in combination. Perhaps if they were combined with the fourth—with Roshah, the Sea—perhaps then it would be his undoing. He has sold himself to Eth, forsaking the Powers that Bind.

"We've assumed that Quintah is his bane, because it's both rare and spectacular, but we've been unable to destroy him. What if he fears Quintah only because he has the same superstition that all people have? What if Mordeth's destruction can come from something simpler? Before Ratha began to teach at Lorlita, only one person each generation was allowed to master Quintah. What if he dreads fire only because it is rare? If that's the case, then all four powers are potent forces against him, just as the foreign power of Roshah is anathema to Kreosoath.

"Perhaps there is a simple way to undo him. When Ratha, then I, fought Mordeth, we used Quintah, resorting to the other powers only when we felt the uselessness of fire. When I combined Keshia and Quintah at Shymney, I was able to knock him down. When I used Rahlah with Quintah, I could force the gate closed, even against his will. If I could somehow use all four powers, perhaps I could undo Mordeth for good."

"Perhaps, perhaps," Stentor interjected sourly. "But it seems too simple. And who can master all four? Not even Ratha could do that."

"I don't think it's necessary. I think I'll only need to use the three together equally."

"And you miss another possible explanation," Mithra said. "What if Morelua is impervious to all four powers? What if his bargain with Eth bought him protection from all of them?"

"Mithra, we cannot stand against siege forever. You said that yourself. Neither can we fight Mordeth's troops directly, even if the dragons agree to fight with us. Our only hope to end this war with no more bloodshed is for me to face Mordeth in a duel of power, and I'm prepared to do just that."

"No!" Mithra snapped, slamming her palm against her side. "I will not lose you again!" Her face flushed with anger.

"You never lost me, Mithra." Roy's voice was cool, his face nearly expressionless. "I can't sit idly by and watch more of your countrymen die. There's nothing noble in a holy war, let alone a senseless slaughter. We've been fortunate so far that so few have died. But their blood is on my hands; some were no more than children. Jerriod was only fourteen. Mazenka was sixteen. Shall all of our children die because I was afraid?"

"Shall all our children die because you were foolish?" she retorted.

Roy shrugged, passing off the possibility. "It isn't just the Pradatha, Mithra. Mordeth's troops live in fear, just as Kreosoath has. She chooses to oppose his power now, but there are many who are still deceived, many who live in constant fear. Shall we watch them die, too?"

In the desolate quiet of the plaza, Mithra continued to stare at the Archmage she had helped create, visions of a sheet of blackness covering him, even as it had covered Ratha years before. The memory was painful and thick, constricting her throat. Then a vision of Jerriod came to her, the lively boy still sweating from exertion as he raced down from Shymney with the message that Mordeth's troops were on the move. The vision blurred until it became the cell where she had found him, his throat crushed by Krotah's blow. Silently she turned and looked at the others gathered in the plaza, begging for support. The Pradatha leaders all cast their eyes upon the ground, refusing their aid. Wordlessly she turned and ran, her steps echoing on the stones of the square.

Roy licked his cracked lips. "Gather the mages and prepare them. If I should fail . . ."

* * * * *

On the hill overlooking Hagsface, the cheers of Mordeth's men quickly subsided when the great black dragon bowed before the Archmage. Ratha had been a formidable opponent, but the soldiers had been confident of victory with the aid of Mordeth and his fierce ally. Now the scales were tipped in favor of the Pradatha, and the troops were tentative, seeking the relative safety offered behind their master.

Mordeth's anger intensified with his troops' cowardice. He had railed against Kreosoath, the shrinking, sniveling lizard, always too easily frightened, but when his own troops shrank from battle, his anger turned to deadly fury. Each unit's sergeant was ordered before him as the soldiers watched intently. Fifty men stood before the black-robed Regent as he lifted his left hand into the air. The smell of tar and marrow singed the air, and the fifty disappeared.

"If any dare to fear battle again, I will send the coward piecemeal into Eth!" Mordeth shouted at his trembling troops. "You," he said, pointing at the soldier nearest him. "You are now a sergeant. Find me fifty more." Mordeth's angry eyes blistered the walls of Hagsface. "We will give the Pradatha traitors until sunset tomorrow to surrender. Then we overwhelm their walls and slaughter every traitor we find—except for Mithra Roshanna. Her I want unharmed. And remember, there are far worse things than death." Mordeth glowered at the men around him, then spun on his heel and stormed to his tent.

*   *   *   *   *

By the time night dropped upon the battlefield, the desert city and its surroundings had succumbed to an ominous quiet. Faint stars scintillated in the ebony sky. The dragons slept, perched upon the walls at irregular intervals, like gargoyles guarding the fortressed city.

Within the walls, Kreosoath and Roy continued conferring, the professor translating the dragon's growls.

> *"Through stormy night and tempest black,*
> *With cold stars shining on our back,*
> *The isle emerged, of slate and scree,*
> *A bastion amidst the sea.*
> *Born are they on Dragon's Isle,*
> *Earth-born children of wind and fire.*
> *One mother bears, one dragon sings,*
> *One generation the dragon brings.*

"I hope I've gotten the words right, Kreosoath. It seems so simple when I hear you sing them, but when I translate the Dragon Song into human speech, it loses a great deal. I understand your concern. Without you, your race would die out. The story of dragonkind is a sad one." Roy reached up and scratched the dragon's leathery neck. "I hope we can change it together."

The dragon's gravelly voice rattled a reply.

"Yes, we must defeat Mordeth first. Tomorrow morning I will issue my challenge. If dragons ever pray, then now's the time." Roy scratched the ridges above the dragon's eyes.

Kreosoath nuzzled her great face into Roy's chest, the soft rumbling vibrating throughout his body.

"Don't ever think it. You'll survive this war. And so will your children. What I do tomorrow is to guarantee that. But now we need to rest. Tomorrow requires our full capabilities." Roy nestled against the bulky dragon, and soon the two were sound asleep.

Hours later, Stentor gently shook the sleeping Archmage and nearly tasted a fiery death as Roy struck out with his staff. The professor had been deep in a dark dream of Mordeth. Roy looked about him, startled to see himself in the courtyard of Hagsface, the sound of water burbling beside him. The shadows were long, stretching across the gray flagstones.

"It's time, Archmage." Stentor's voice and face were grave; his eyes were puffy and dark-rimmed.

"You didn't sleep?" Roy asked.

"I had many plans to arrange. In case . . ."

"Yes. That was wise. But I feel strong today. And hopeful. I'll take it as a good omen." Roy stood and stretched, suddenly realizing that Kreosoath was nowhere to be seen.

"Where's the dragon?" he asked worriedly.

"She flew off several hours ago. I don't know where. Her brood is still here, though."

Roy heaved a sigh. He did not intend that Kreosoath should fight, but he had hoped, perhaps childishly, for her presence. She had been invaluable in instructing him about the subtleties of the three powers, using them not as separate tools but weaving their energies together into a single, greater force, a force Roy hoped would undo the Dark Lord forever.

"I suppose I'd best get this over with, then," he said. "Has Mithra gotten over her anger? I'd like to speak with her a moment."

"I haven't seen her, Lord Archmage—not since last night's meeting. But you know her. She should have been given Quintah as her word, rather than the soothing Roshah!" Stentor's smile was meant to be reassuring, but his white teeth, sparkling and moist in the sunlight, made Roy think of bones stripped of their flesh.

"Perhaps she'll show up soon. Have Mordeth's troops advanced?"

"No. They've regrouped upon the outlying hills. Our mages have been alerted. Everything is prepared."

"Then let it begin." Roy said.

"No. Let it end," Stentor corrected, and Roy nodded. The two men began to walk toward the western wall.

The Pradatha had gathered to watch the challenge. Word of what the Archmage intended had spread quickly through the walled city, and hopes were high. Anticipation gripped the fortress. Many of the Pradatha offered Roy their blessings as he climbed the western wall, the sun rising before him.

"Morelua! I'm waiting!" Roy shouted as he reached the top, his staff in one hand.

Roy waited for a reply, beginning to think that perhaps the Dark One had not heard him. Then a rustling movement in the line of troops signaled the Regent's approach.

"Imposter? I'm surprised to see you. How may I help you this morning?"

"I'm no imposter, Morelua. I am the Archmage of Keshia, Quintah, and Rahlah, Dragontamer and Bane of Nothingness. Today I challenge you. Today I will banish you to the darkness forever."

"Brave words, imposter. But I accept your challenge nonetheless. So come, meet me outside your walls and we will settle this."

"As you will, Morelua. I'm eager to see you gone from this world." Roy climbed down from the wall and walked toward the gate. Stentor was waiting for him when he arrived.

"Mithra's still nowhere to be found. She must be an-

gry indeed, or perhaps she cannot bear to see the battle.
But I have faith in you, Archmage. May the four bless
you!"

"May they indeed!" Roy replied quietly, then slipped
through the unbolted gate into the desert.

The sun pounded upon the sands fiercely. A slight
breeze wafting off the sea provided only minor relief.
Sand, sun, and wind, Roy thought. Good omens all.
Ahead of him, Mordeth's troops stood like pickets in a
fence, their spears and blades glinting in the morning
sun. Between them, an ebon-cloaked figure approached, and Roy watched as the Regent climbed upon
a black outcropping of basalt. Roy noticed that he would
have to climb to reach the Regent, and his mind raced
back to the thirty-nine steps he once ascended to see another Regent. Fear pushed him then, but now things
seemed different. The world was a dream, he thought to
himself, and plodded toward his waiting opponent.

"I have waited long for this," Mordeth hissed as Roy
reached the base of the basalt porch.

"It builds character," Roy replied. "You should know
by now that you cannot destroy the Pradatha or the
Archmage. We keep returning to torment you. Relinquish your false claim to the kingdom and flee—now,
while you may."

"Fool! I have no fears. I *am* fear. Your power is insig-
nificant next to mine. So let us begin." As Mordeth
raised his hand, darkness obliterated the sun, but Roy
was prepared. His staff retaliated with a burst of light,
sweeping the cold blankness away.

"Listen to me, Morelua. I have no taste for killing. I
would rather you repent."

"Is it fear that sparks your flame, imposter?" Night

leapt again from the Regent's hand, burying Roy in a blanket of black.

The staff flamed like a beacon through the night, shattering the blackness into pieces that crumbled around them. Mordeth pressed the attack, his cold death creeping again toward Roy, only to be repulsed once again by the power of the staff. The air tightened with the brewing storm, and night lashed about the glowing staff. Then the world relit and flashed in brilliance.

"You have learned, imposter. Again I've underestimated your power. But I enjoy the game."

"It's no game, Morelua. That's what you'll never understand." Roy stared hard at the dark-clad figure above him, watching the flickering black eyes of his enemy. Mordeth returned the glare, the two men locked in a battle of wills. It was Mordeth who broke the trance, his startled expression causing Roy to turn and look behind him.

Kreosoath swept from the sky with a frightening scream, her sharp talons outstretched for the attack, her massive wings blasting the air with powerful strokes. Roy instinctively ducked as the beast passed over him and headed for Mordeth. The Regent dove, barely escaping the deadly grasp of the dragon. Kreosoath turned sharply and pressed the attack, her gravelly voice filling the afternoon with terror.

But Mordeth was prepared for Kreosoath's second attack. With an angry wave, the black tar of death sped from his hand and shrouded the dragon. For a tortured moment, Roy thought his friend had managed to evade the deadly spell, but when the blackness evaporated, there was only empty sky. Roy was overcome by grief and rage. He had witnessed the end of a species, the murder of a friend. Anger swelled into the void, increased by the painful memory of Moratha. In fury, he raised his staff and struck.

Blue lightning erupted through the pause, smacking into Mordeth with a loud report. The ground shook as Roy stomped upon the ground, sending wave after wave through the living stone beneath him, knocking Mordeth off balance. The wind swelled to a gale, the sand it carried pounding into Mordeth like a million tiny missiles, scouring his flesh.

Roy redoubled his efforts, the lightning issuing from his staff in a brilliant display. The ground loosened about the Regent, and he struggled to stand against the force of the quake, only to be knocked down once more by the fierce winds. Roy pressed his attack until fatigue weighted his arms and his legs shook. Finally his rage relented, and he stood in the late afternoon. Hours had passed unnoticed. Time had lost all meaning as he poured his total power into the destruction of Mordeth. Before him, a mound of stone and sand marked the grave of the Regent.

Exhaustion replaced the rage, his bones aching and muscles flaccid from the exertion. Behind him and in the distance, he could hear the glad shouts of the Pradatha. They had witnessed the fall of Mordeth at the hands of the Archmage, signaling the flight of Mordeth's troops. To them, it was a time of celebration. But then the quiet came, like a thief stealing their joy.

Roy turned and looked. Atop the mound stood Mordeth, apparently unscathed. His evil smile froze Roy's heart. Mordeth had withstood his full onslaught, the sum of his accumulated power. He had been so sure that the combined power of the three would somehow undo the Dark Lord. Now Roy stood helplessly before him, too fatigued to defend himself.

"A valiant effort, imposter. But the Three alone cannot destroy me, although I'll grant you they came nearer than I like." His smile was a perfect parody of joy. "All the more reason to see you die quickly."

Roy sucked in the dry desert air. "My death won't avail you, Morelua," he said, grasping at his final hope. "Another will come. Another must."

"Enough! Say your farewells." Mordeth raised his hand to deliver the crushing blow, and Roy closed his eyes and wondered if this death would send him to yet another world. He heard Mordeth begin a quiet muttering, then jerked as the Regent's voice rose to a piercing scream. Then all was silent.

Roy opened his eyes. Mordeth no longer stood before him; the Regent's body lay draped across the stone, blood coloring the ground beneath him. Through his throat was an arrow, fletched with the feathers of the hawk. Roy turned and looked around him. Standing behind a nearby stone was the blue-clad figure of Mithra Roshanna, her longbow still quivering in her hand.

❖ CHAPTER NINETEEN ❖

The Bell Tolls

The winter winds blew softly through the streets of Lorlita, bringing rain and mist but little snow. Roy looked out his window at the streets below, watching people scurrying through the town on their many errands, unaware of the steady gaze of the Archmage of Keshia, Roy Arthre, Master of the Three, Dragontamer, and Loremaster. Roy had accustomed himself to the new titles and the honor they afforded him, or nearly so: He still mistrusted the deception that he was Ratha returned. The name of Mithra's dead husband was one thing he hadn't easily accepted, even now, six months since first hearing the name "Ratha."

Roy reflected on those months: his summoning from his own world and the arrival on the Western Beach, where even now the crafters were busy building a town in his honor; the flight to Shymney and his meeting with Moratha, the gentle falcon who had been cruelly slain by the Dark Lord; his flight through the Keshian mountains, through the Pass of Tears, Torvathain, with the fragrant blue wild flowers that Keshians called *cian-*

dith; to the arrival at Hagsface, and the battle that ensued. Hot tears welled in his blue eyes, sparkling in the winter afternoon, as he thought of Moratha's death and the death of the great dragon, Kreosoath. Both creatures had become Roy's friends, the only creatures of Kesh who had accepted him for himself, and not as Ratha returned.

Roy closed his eyes to his tears, his face heavy with sadness. At least the deaths had been few, a blessing dearly bought. Guilt edged the sorrow with the memory of his own destructive outburst, his unleashing of the awful power he came to possess in a spasm of anger and hatred. And it had not availed him, for when he finally relented, Mordeth still stood. Pure luck and Mithra's stubbornness were all that had felled Mordeth. Mithra had run to him afterward, hugging him, and he had been unable to respond to her joy, too stunned to understand.

With the death of the Dark Lord, Mordeth's troops were quick to submit, laying their weapons at the feet of the Pradathan leaders. A few of the commanders—Deluth of Bain, Bletha, and the cruel members of the disbanded Elite Guard—were still at large, but the Pradatha were more than likely to uncover them and bring them to trial at Lorlita. Mithra had become a folk hero almost instantly, her determination the subject of song and story. But Roy could not join in the celebration. His spirit dragged through the dust on the long march back to Lorlita, buoyed only by the secret he carried, screamed by Kreosoath as she was sent by Mordeth forever into darkness. He whispered the secret to the dragon's brood, and one by one they had launched themselves into the sky and vanished beyond the horizon.

The City of Light encouraged him as he entered it for the first time at the head of a victorious army. The people had been prepared by advance runners who had brought with them the news of Mordeth's defeat. The walls of Morlidra, Mordeth's private keep, were torn down and the stones hauled from the city. Feasts and celebrations and entertainments abounded those first days, and Roy nearly lost himself in the sweet taste of keyth, which he called qomrah, and the hard fruit cider that was the specialty of Stentor's tavern.

The festive mood dissipated with the discovery that Prince Porthera, the heir to the Keshian throne, had long ago died in the bowels of Morlidra, a prisoner in his own castle. The Keshians mourned the death of their true king as strongly as they had celebrated Roy's victory. The people had such strong emotions, so different from the austere world that Roy had once called home. Because of this, Roy sensed a growing bond between himself and the people of this strange new world.

The mages met soon afterward, as they had in the days before Keshia had a king, to decide who among them they would elevate to become their new ruler. It was no surprise when the council came and asked Roy to be their new king, but he astonished the people by declining. Power, he had said, should be given to those best able to use it; his power was in the art of teaching, and he would have no time to govern. It was Mithra who should be crowned, if anybody, and to that suggestion the mage council agreed, declaring Mithra Roshanna the rightful heir to the throne. The coronation was a spectacular affair, and even Roy managed to leave his melancholy behind long enough to celebrate with the people and their new queen.

To the people of Keshia, Roy was the queen's consort, father of the child she carried. Only through a royal proclamation that the Archmage would be forever known by his "new" name, Roy, did he manage to maintain a semblance of his old identity. Teaching became a necessity, a life preserver linking him to the truth. Word spread throughout the land that the Archmage would begin instruction again in the capital, and students flocked to Lorlita to listen to the words spoken by the greatest mage in Keshian history.

The school at Lorlita grew so rapidly that Roy sent invitations to the mages to begin schools in the various provinces, and soon institutes of learning were established in Hagsface, Bain, Silth, and Yelu. The stories of Keshia, the meaning of the true use of power, and even some of Roy's poetry were taught, along with many practical uses for some of the scientific inventions that Roy could remember and devise. The blacksmiths busily pounded and forged the prototype of a water-wheel generator to provide electricity. No one knew how the electricity would be used, but since the Archmage suggested it, there was no argument and a great deal of excitement. And the glass crafters were more than a little curious about why the Archmage had asked that they create as many small glass orbs as possible.

Like the grinding and pounding of the crafters, Roy's relationship with Mithra continued, taking on new dimension and form. As Roy gained in power, so her love for him increased in the days following the final battle. The memory of Ratha had nearly proved too much for her to overcome before Mordeth's defeat, but after witnessing the ferocious attack that Roy had launched on the Dark One, Mithra had finally accepted him as some-

one other than her lost love. Yet the respect he gained
from her altered the misplaced love to better fit their
relationship. She no longer fawned over him but treated
him as an equal, a friend and confidante in a world rapidly changing.

Poetry edged their world like a flowery border, bringing joy into their lives. In their quiet moments of solitude, he shared with her all his remembered verse, plus
many stories that had meant so much to him in his
youth. Mithra, in turn, memorized many of those passages and frequently recited them to him beneath the
starlight or in the soft glow of their candlelit chamber.
And when she finished, Roy would tell her of the world
he left behind: the university, the cities of steel and
glass, and the forlorn bell swaying gently in the winds of
Earth.

In those first weeks, Roy sent word throughout the
realm that any books of wizardry that had survived Mordeth's reign should be copied and sent to him at Lorlita.
Although he could no longer remember a single face
from his former world, something inside him ached to
return. In the library he created, he sought the spell that
Ratha had used to summon him, but to no avail. Nowhere could he find a record of the power used to
send—or bring—one person into another plane. But
Roy couldn't succumb to despair. Instead, his energies
turned toward building—the schools, the new government, the inventions—and the hope for a new world in
which he would play a significant part.

Roy reflected upon these things as he looked out at
the bustling city through his upper-floor window. The
disjointed feeling that haunted him had come again,
leaving him wistful and longing for the familiar context

of his old home. A fruitless desire, he told himself.

The study door opened, and Mithra came in. Roy turned to watch her, noticing her light step, in spite of her pregnancy. Her buoyancy belied the roundness of her belly. But that was all a part of this new world. Prejudices and superstition died hard, even here. It was Mithra's grasp of that that had saved Roy's life. Mordeth had only seemed immortal. His weakness was nothing more than their own. What courage it must have taken her, he thought, to put that theory to the test. As Roy looked at her tenderly, Mithra's eyes, sapphire blue sparks in her glowing face, caught the Archmage's attention.

"Roy, we have prepared a surprise for you," she said, excitement bursting in her voice.

"Not another banquet, I hope."

"No, a real surprise! I've had Malek busy on it for months, and the silversmith Rontha. They've finally finished, and it awaits your dedication."

"What are you talking about?"

"No, I won't say. Just follow me. And quickly, before I burst!"

Roy followed the woman down the three flights of stairs, counting each one as he tried to keep pace with her. Thirty-nine steps, he thought to himself. He walked beside her as they left the keep, but once outside, she raced ahead into the street toward the center of the city and the new university that Roy had requested be built. The Archmage was aware of the humored expressions on the faces of the people they passed as Mithra dragged him through the churning streets.

The sounds of construction penetrated through the normal noise of the city as they neared the university.

The great stones had been quarried from the Keshian mountains and hauled many miles to Lorlita at Mithra's request. She wanted the school to be a lasting monument to the efforts of the Pradatha. Before him now, the buildings rose like granite statues, a collection of buttresses and spires that reflected the tremendous creativity of the people of Keshia. Mithra wove her way through the half-completed buildings until she finally stopped in front of a tall, pinnacled tower, higher than anything around it. The upper section was shrouded with a great gray cloth, hiding the top ten feet of the tower from view.

"Here it is," Mithra said, pride swelling her voice. She waved her hand, and the shroud dropped to the ground, catching the wind like a feather and dancing around the tower. Roy looked up at the revelation, smiling broadly as he caught a glimpse of the bell hanging in the belfry.

"Malek's work?" he asked, and Mithra nodded excitedly.

"It's to signal the beginning of your classes, Professor."

"Well, let's go up." This time it was Roy who raced ahead of Mithra, anxious to see the crafted bell. He entered the belfry and stopped, astonished at what he saw. The bell was pure brass, shimmering orange in the sun. The brilliant metal was decorated with etchings that symbolized Roy's life on Keshia. He saw a replica of Shymney, and Moratha sweeping along in the sky. Kreosoath soared above the fortress city of Hagsface as breakers swelled along the shore of the Tranquil Sea. Circumscribing the bell was a quotation, written in the script of Keshia but familiar to Roy from his own world:

Come, my friends,
'Tis not too late to seek a newer world.
Push off, and sitting well in order, smite
The sounding furrows, for my purpose holds
To sail beyond the sunset and the baths
Of all the western stars until I die.

Roy read through misty eyes the words he had spoken once to Mithra in what seemed now like another age. Then, taking the hand of the Keshian queen, they turned and watched through the stone-framed windows until the sun disappeared beneath the western horizon.

Epilogue

"May we hear another story?" The child's brown eyes were wide with hope, like a furrow awaiting the seed.

Tralaina laughed. "Tomorrow, child. Tomorrow. Your old nurse is tired now." She smiled warmly at the small girl's enthusiasm and wondered if this child would one day grow up to be a storyteller. There were surely more than enough stories for all.

"But how can I sleep, Tralaina? How can I sleep now, not knowing about the dragons or about Mithra's baby?"

"Tell us that story, Tralaina, please! Tell us that story!" The other children shouted encouragement.

The old woman sighed. "Tomorrow I'll tell it to you. I promise. But I'm tired now. Now, off to bed with the lot of you. Go, and be sure to give this old lady a kiss as you do." Her voice was firm, and not even the brown-eyed child raised another complaint.

One by one the children filed past Tralaina and placed a moist kiss on her wrinkled cheek. In turn, the old nurse patted each one on the top of the head and sent him down the hall to his bed. When all the children were gone, she leaned back in her rocking chair and stared into the dying embers on the hearth, until the only sound in the room was her steady breathing, and the only stories unhappy dreams of dragons and of war.

❖ GLOSSARY ❖

-a, -ah   the
Berenta   the chief healer of the Pradatha
Bezwak   a spy of Mordeth's
Billah   a spy of Mordeth's
Chiath   Mithra's father
chontha   a tree similar to a cottonwood
Ciandith   a light blue mountain flower
cocantha   a tree similar to a maple
Deathstone   a black stone deposited in the center of
   the Great Desert, probably a meteor
Deluta   the captain of the Bain militia, under Mor-
   deth's command
Dethlidra   literally, "The City of Darkness"; Hell;
   Hades; the Underworld
Drandor   a guard who was entranced by Mithra
Drogan   a cousin of Drandor's, executed by Mordeth
Elvathain   literally, "Mountain of Tears"; a peak in the
   western Keshian range
Eth   darkness, night
Fenfeder   a major river of Keshia that flows eastward

into the Great Fen

Flanx   a Pradatha spy who infiltrated Mordeth's army

Gondsped   the king of Keshia, poisoned by Morlin (Mordeth)

Hagsface   a fortress and university city on the Tranquil Sea

Jerriod   a 14-year-old member of the Pradatha

Keshia   the Land

Keyth   a yellow fruit the size of a cherry; tastes like honey and cloves

Kreosoath   the black dragon

Krotah   the toad, also a man's name; chief of security for Mordeth

Litera   a volume; any collection

Lo   light, day, enlightenment

Lorlita   the Lighted City

Manetha   female mage of Yelu, wife of Protetha, mother of Ratha

marelock   a thick, waxy-leaved bush

Mithra   the Spirit, breath, wind, breeze, smoke; a woman's name

Mithra Roshanna   Spirit Sea-born, the name of the leader of the Pradatha

Mordeth   the Lord of Darkness, the Regent of Keshia, whose true name is Morlin, "the Mage of Governing," but whom many call Morelua, "Lord of Nothing"

Morlidra   the lord's hold

Morlin   a mage brought to Lorlita by Gondsped (see Mordeth)

-ne   born

Norshal   the northeastern forested region of Keshia

Oasis   a city in the Great Desert

Pedretha   literally, "the stranger"; the name given to the fire mage of Keshia who befriended the boy Ratha

Porthera   the prince of Keshia, son of Gondsped

Pradatha   the truth; also an underground society opposed to Mordeth

Protetha   Ratha's father, the hawk master of Yelu

Quintah   the Fire

Qomrah   "the Food of Life"; also the name Roy gives to keyth

Rachala   the queen of Keshia, wife of Gondsped and mother of Porthera

Rahlah   the Air

TM

novels

✧ The Cloakmaster Cycle ✧

Follow one unlucky farmer as he enters fantasy space
for the first time and gets caught up in a race for his
life, from the DRAGONLANCE® Saga setting to the
FORGOTTEN REALMS® world and beyond.

Book One
Beyond the Moons
David Cook

Little did Teldin Moore know there was life
beyond Krynn's moons until a spelljamming
ship crashed into his home and changed his
life. Teldin suddenly discovers himself the
target of killers and cutthroats. Armed with a
dying alien's magical cloak and cryptic
words, he races off to Astinus of Palanthas
and the gnomes of Mt. Nevermind to try to
discover why . . . before the monstrous neogi
can find him. On sale in July, 1991.

Book Two
Into the Void
Nigel Findley

Plunged into a sea of alien faces, Teldin
Moore isn't sure whom to trust. His gnomish
sidewheeler ship is attacked by space
pirates, and Teldin is saved by a hideous
mind flayer who offers to help the human
use his magical cloak—but for whose gain?
Teldin learns the basics of spelljamming on
his way to Toril, where he seeks an ancient
arcane, one who might tell him more. But
even information has a high price. On sale in
October, 1991.

One step into the mists, and a world of horror engulfs you. Welcome to Ravenloft, a dark domain of fantasy-horror populated by bloodthirsty vampires and other unspeakable creatures of the undead.

Vampire of the Mists
Christie Golden

Jander Sunstar, an elven vampire from the Forgotten Realms, is pulled into the newly formed dark domain of Barovia and forges an alliance with the land's most powerful inhabitant, Count Strahd Von Zarovich, himself a newly risen vampire. But as Jander teaches the count the finer points of being undead, he learns that his student may also be his greatest enemy. On sale in September, 1991.

Knight of the Black Rose
James Lowder

The fate of the villainous Lord Soth was left untold at the conclusion of the popular DRAGONLANCE® Legends Trilogy. Now it can be revealed that the cruel death knight found his way into the dark domain and discovered that it is far easier to get into Ravenloft than to get out—even with the aid of the powerful vampire lord, Strahd Von Zarovich. On sale in December, 1991.

FANTASY ADVENTURE

▪ THE HARPERS ▪

A Force for Good in the Realms!

This open-ended series of stand-alone novels chronicles the Harpers' heroic battles against forces of evil, all for the peace of the Realms.

The Parched Sea
Troy Denning

The Zhentarim have sent an army to enslave the fierce nomads of the Great Desert. Only one woman, the outcast witch Ruha, sees the true danger—and only the Harpers can counter the evil plot. Available July 1991.

Elfshadow
Elaine Cunningham

Harpers are being murdered, and the trail leads to Arilyn Moonblade. Is she guilty or is she the next target? Arilyn must uncover the ancient secret of her sword's power in order to find and face the assassin.
Available October 1991.

Red Magic
Jean Rabe

One of the powerful and evil Red Wizards wants to control more than his share of Thay. While the mage builds a net of treachery, the Harpers put their own agents into action to foil his plans for conquest.
Available November 1991.

Elven Nations Trilogy

firstborn
Paul B. Thompson and Tonya R. Carter

Sithel, the leader of the Silvanesti elves, struggles to maintain a united elven nation, while his twin sons' ambitions threaten to tear it apart. Kith-Kanan leads the Wildrunners, a group of elves that stirs tension by forging contacts and trade with the humans of Ergoth; Sithas strongly allies himself with the elven court. When their father mysteriously dies, Kith-Kanan is implicated and Sithas, the firstborn twin, is enthroned. On Sale February 1991.

---

the Kinslayer Wars
Douglas Niles

Kith-Kanan commits the ultimate heresy for an elven prince and falls in love with a human. Soon after, his twin brother, the firstborn ruler of all Silvanesti elves, Sithas, declares war on the humans of Ergoth, and Kith-Kanan finds himself caught between two mighty forces. On Sale August 1991.

---

the Qualinesti
Paul B. Thompson and Tonya R. Carter

One of the most fabled of all of Krynn's legends—untold before now—is the founding of Qualinost and the creation of the magnificent society of the renegade elves, the Qualinesti. Kith-Kanan becomes the first Speaker of the Suns, but he is haunted by his failures: the unfaithfulness of his wife, and the mysterious behavior of his son and successor. On Sale November 1991.

THE ALL NEW

ALL NEW FORMAT, FEATURES, AND FICTION!

AMAZING STORIES

Robert Silverberg
John Brunner
Kristine Kathryn Rusch
Arthur C. Clarke

The world's oldest science
fiction magazine …

BEGINS IN MAY 1991